ENDLESS IS THE NIGHT

a Black Sun Novel

Shawn Brooks

Ninja Nomad Press

Edited by Grigory Lukin.

Cover art by Abdullah's team at Book Cover Hub.

GET A FREE BOOK

I

January 1967

Wakayama, Japan

When confronted with the sum of all our fears, some fight, some take flight, and some play dead. Kenji Matsushima drove along a mountain road that night in the lightly falling snow, wishing he had the luxury of such choices.

He looked at his fuel gauge; the needle sputtered and twitched just above empty.

The hulk of frozen metal he piloted into the dark shook with feverish frailty, threatening to fall apart at any moment.

He barely had time to think when he left the city that morning on this spur-of-the-moment trip. *You're so boring and predictable*, Ayumi had told him two days ago as she slipped out of bed to smoke in the kitchen. Her puffs of cancer shot up into the stove's fan almost as quickly as her love for him had vanished. *I think we should see other people.* And with that, she was out the door and out of his life. At least she left the wedding ring on the coffee table.

The tires slipped on a right-hand turn, but he kept the car from crashing into the side rail. Of course, he had forgotten to put chains on.

Just keep your eyes focused on the road and everything will be okay.

He hit an incline, his wheels sloshed and nearly lost their grip as he snail-crawled his way up. Somehow, he abused the engine enough to lurch up and over the hill. In any other situation, the view would have been stunning. Great cedars and pines stood tall in the snowfall, their evergreen tops still visible though the road itself was a white haze. Even in his concentrated state of panic, Kenji absorbed these details.

Why didn't I think this through?

He slammed his hand against the steering wheel. The car responded by fishtailing. He spun the wheel with sweaty palms. The back of the car swished left and right, and then it straightened out. Having crested the hill, Kenji put the car in park. It wasn't smart to stop in the middle of the road in a snowstorm; this he knew. He also knew that it wasn't likely that any vehicle would come screaming down the road to hit him; he had seen no one for the past four hours. The static whiteness of the snow was his only companion.

All I wanted was to do something spontaneous for once. Never again.

An hour after Ayumi had fled the stale air of the apartment, Kenji stared at a wall of magazines in the bookstore down the street like a zombie. He felt the judgmental glances of other customers as they passed him, disgusted at his unshaven face and the smell of his unwashed shirt, but he couldn't bring himself to move. Coming to his senses, his eyes focused on one of the prints, not the nudie mags he always bought on the way home from the office and tried to hide under his mattress as if he were still thirteen.

No, this one was a camping magazine. The smiling, bearded man on the cover was squatting next to a hole in the ice with some large fish in his left hand. The smile, the adventure, the raw power, and the self-satisfaction on that man's face pierced Kenji's mind like a bullet. That's when the idea hit him: let's do something spontaneous, to the mountains!

And to the mountains he had come. At least the car was warm. He couldn't imagine what it would be like to crash and have to survive out there in the freezing night. Looking out his window, he saw the magnificent trees in the snow. And above them, a single star burned through the clouds and the storm. A red star. Possibly the planet Mars or a passing plane?

Kenji had the sudden feeling of being observed, of being alone beneath a featureless sky, a tiny speck on the great mountainside. Yet instead of loneliness, he felt *known*, seen, and watched. He also had the sudden realization that his life might very well be in danger. He did not know where he was, his car had no gas, and he likely was going to fly right through the side railing and into those trees. His grave would be forever under that red star, that watchful sentry in the dead winter sky.

No, no, no, stop it. Eyes on the road, everything will be okay.

Exactly eighty-three minutes later, his beat-up Kei car died of lack of gas and became stranded right in the middle of a dark tunnel. Though it wasn't snowing inside, it was somehow colder than Kenji could have imagined. His emergency lights were blinking in the recess of that icy abyss, refracting their orange glow throughout the empty cavern.

The lights splashed unruly shadows onto the curved walls, giving the impression that something was jumping out of the tunnel's far end, running straight at the car. He had noticed a sign right before entering the tunnel, that the road led to the town of Inunaki, only five kilometers ahead.

Kenji had never heard the name of the town before. Shit, he didn't even know the name of the mountain range he was in or even what prefecture it might be. Weird name for a town, *Inunaki*—"cry of the dog." *Sounds like the title for a cheesy werewolf movie,* he thought. The black shapes on the tunnel walls leaped out in cadence with the flashing lights as he thought this. They took on the shape of wolves in his mind.

How far was that town? Five kilometers? He could manage that. Or at least that's what he thought before he left the incubation of the car. He slipped on the ice as he got out, nearly cracking his head on the hood, yet narrowly escaped by grabbing the door for support.

What now? Stay and wait for help or walk towards the town?

The road was desolate. The wind howled through the tunnel.

"Cry of the dog," Kenji said aloud and chuckled to himself. He started walking towards Inunaki.

The snow wrapped its ghostly cloak around Kenji as he trudged along the narrow road. Numbness greeted his face, his fingers, and his toes. *How long have I been walking? Seems like an hour.*

He looked back and saw the faint outline of the tunnel across the gorge that forced the road to wrap and bend around the mountain like a crooked snake.

Lights.

Flashes of yellow lit up the white walls of snow that separated him from the oncoming car. They reflected so strongly off the snow that Kenji was blinded and had to cover his eyes.

Shit, a car.

Kenji was in the middle of the road. He ran to the side and pressed himself up against what he thought could be a tree. The searing headlights rushed by. Kenji waved his hands at the car but held little hope that the driver could see him.

The snow stopped falling, and the sky cleared up. Crystal stars emerged in the sky, illuminating the fresh snow in a cold, unearthly tone. The car passed him, pulled over, and switched on its emergency lights. The sudden change in both the atmosphere and his fortunes almost took his breath away.

Look at that, Kenji, told you things would be okay.

He ran as fast as his frozen muscles allowed towards the stopped vehicle. A woman leaned her head out of the passenger side. Her smile lit up the winter night. Kenji thought about removing his wedding ring but resisted the urge. He was here to prove something to Ayumi after all. In any other situation, the ring would have immediately gone into his pocket. Kenji drew nearer the woman. Something about her eyes seemed off. They blended too well with the darkness of the forest behind her.

"Need some help?" the woman asked.

"Thank you so much. My car ran out of gas back there." He stiffly pointed back towards the tunnel. He twisted too quickly on the ice and knocked himself on his ass.

The woman laughed. He got back on his feet and dusted off the snow.

"We saw it. That's why we kept an eye out for you. Poor thing, you must be freezing," she said.

Kenji felt immediate relief warm his veins. He kept walking towards the truck, but before he reached it, the woman hopped out with something in her hand. It was a bright orange container with a large black X shape made out of duct tape on its side. She was very small, up to Kenji's chest at most, and he was no physical specimen. As she walked towards him, he could see what was off about her eyes: she was wearing sunglasses.

"Umm, a little dark for those, isn't it?"

"Oh, these? Eye infection. Makes me sensitive to light." She laughed. Kenji's face went red and warm. He thought of a corny pickup line akin to "Don't look at my bright smile" but, again, resisted the urge. No need to die of both hypothermia and embarrassment at the same time.

The driver's door opened, and a man lumbered out. He was much taller than Kenji, thick at the shoulders and chest. His long gray hair spilled out from under his ski cap. He too, was wearing sunglasses.

The relief that warmed his heart now turned to suspicion colder than the air that was atrophying his skin. Both the woman and the man were wearing black ski caps, black jackets, and black jeans. The woman clutched the orange canister to her chest and hesitantly approached, almost as if unsure of herself and what she planned to do.

"You know what? I think I'm okay, actually," Kenji said and started back toward his car. He shuffled his feet quickly, careful not to outright start running, not yet at least.

The crunch of snow behind him came in quicker than he had time to comprehend. Before he even picked up his pace to a run, his vision burst into white as he felt a great force against the back of his head.

Then all was black.

Kenji woke and fixed his gaze on the woman holding the orange canister of what he now could see clearly labeled as gasoline. The world around him was muted; all sounds came at him as if through a thick wall. He took notice of nothing else save the woman cradling the gasoline close to her chest like an infant, peering at him through sunglasses set above a distinctive mole on her left cheek.

The large man from the truck was pinning Kenji to a curved cement wall next to a car with flashing emergency lights.

The tunnel, why am I back here?

The man was saying something, but it sounded to Kenji like it was being spoken underwater. The woman was smiling with her row of perfectly bleached white teeth like a mother watching her son making friends at the local playground. The man's face was so close to Kenji's that he could smell the sausage he had eaten for lunch. Sweat poured down Kenji's face, and urine soaked his pants, freezing the material to his skin. He couldn't stop the pathetic whimper that now squeaked out of his mouth.

"Please, just take it. I don't want any trouble." Kenji reached into his pocket and handed his wallet over to the man. The man let go of Kenji. He looked inside, took out a wad of cash, and threw it into the wind rushing through the tunnel. The bills scattered into the void. The woman took the wallet and looked through his cards and ID.

"I don't understand. What do you want then?" Kenji asked, stifling the sobs seeking to escape his throat.

The woman spoke up. "Kenji Matsushima, is it?" She flicked his driver's license to the ground. "You're about to be a part of something special. Something that hasn't happened in a very long time. You should be glad of the opportunity we're about to give you." Her voice was eager, slightly nervous, yet chilling in its lack of empathy.

The large man took off his sunglasses. At first, Kenji couldn't understand what he was seeing. A faint silver glow emanated from the hollows of his eyes. It could have been a reflection of the emergency lights, or even contact lenses. The woman took off her pair as well. She too had a cold silver gleam in her eyes. At the sight of this, Kenji felt his stomach retract into itself.

A strike to his face knocked him to the ground. He struggled to find his breath. Blood streamed down from the top of his head. His glasses smashed into bits that stuck to his cheeks.

"Please stop, please," Kenji said through tearful gasps.

The man held a tire iron. He looked back at his accomplice with a knowing smile. Kenji, normally a man of little action, took advantage of the momentary lack of attention and found himself springing to his feet. His legs carried him out of the tunnel, off the road, and into the forest, almost as if he had no control over what his body was doing. The snow was knee-high, yet he threw his body at it with all that he had. For a moment, he thought he might get away until he tripped over an unseen tree root and smashed his face into the powder.

As he rolled over, he saw stars shining out all over the black expanse of night. There were so many of them, all spectators to his plight. They were ardent with heavenly fire, the intensity of which gave Kenji the weighty impression they were beholding his position, watching him. He let out a silent prayer, hoping whoever might be out there was listening. He felt that someone was, and with that realization, there was no comfort. The blood in his body ran colder than the winter air.

So many stars. So many... red stars?

Before Kenji could ponder the meaning of this, his assailants had caught up with him. He tried to fight off the man, but a second crack to his skull with the tire iron silenced that nonsense. He lay there limply on the ground as the man dragged him back up the hill to the road. The man held onto Kenji's legs, pulling him along back into the tunnel, now resembling a monstrous open maw. Kenji clawed at the concrete. As the man dragged him, Kenji's nails wore down.

The man hit Kenji's right hand with his weapon. A crunching sound and blinding pain told him it had been broken. The man lifted Kenji like a toddler and shoved him back into his own car's backseat. Kenji tried to kick open the doors on the opposite side just as the tire iron cracked him across the jaw once again. Lying there on the seat, he realized he was going to die. This car would be his tomb. Looking around, he saw the back of the driver's headrest. Stuffing bled out of the fake leather in patches.

Sudden memories of losing his virginity to Ayumi, staring at that same headrest, back when there were no stuffing wounds, came to him. Funny, the details that rush into the mind in its last moments of life. The sound of rain trickled over the roof of the vehicle. It was almost soothing to Kenji.

Maybe it's not a bad idea to just go to sleep until this is over. Just let it pass. Keep looking at the headrest, a memory of a better time.

The sound now invaded the inside of the car, and something splashed over Kenji's face. The overbearing smell of gasoline forced him out of his stupor. The liquid drenched him, stinging his eyes, and the fumes began choking him. A flicker of orange and red caught his eye. The woman was holding a lit match, and her eyes, with their cool glow, stared deep into Kenji's soul. A cruel smirk crept up her lips. All the world receded from Kenji's perception, all sounds and smells and touch. He remained hypnotized by that smile.

In his mind, he saw Ayumi walking out that door with her typical puff of air out her nostrils, a sign she was annoyed. It was one of the many little things that he had loved, no, that he does love, about her. He came here for her, to prove himself a better man, and now he would never leave, and she would never know how he tried and failed to change himself for her. That hurt more than his broken jaw.

The woman tossed the match into the car.

Everything erupted in flames, and they soon engulfed Kenji. He screamed out in agony, both primal in ferocity and childlike in its desperation. The pain gave him strength enough, and he kicked open the backseat door, his flaming body spilling out onto the road as he crawled to the entrance of the tunnel.

As he lay there on that cold road, burning, his eyes did not rest on the storm of flame consuming his body. His mind did not focus on the crackling pain searing his flesh or even on the memories of Ayumi that were receding behind the wall of pain.

Instead, something above it all captured his attention. The last thing Kenji Matsushima ever saw in this world was a bright red light welcoming him as he screamed into the winter night.

2

June 2017

San Francisco

Cody Baker drove with his left hand on the wheel, the other texting feverishly. His focus shifted from screen to windshield and back again as the rain beat against the vehicle. It came in rapid machine-gun tempo as it assaulted the glass. The *ratatatat* of the drops was like nails pounding into his head, screaming at him to move. He had to hurry; he knew being late was not an option. She might be serious this time.

A chime rang out from his phone. He slowed the car to take a corner while reading it in full: *I KNEW YOU DIDN'T CARE.*

His breath steamed up his glasses and the windshield; the AC didn't work, just like everything else in this shitty Honda Civic, just like everything else in his shitty life. With his right thumb, covered in a clammy sweat, he typed out a response: *Thts not tru i care, just wat till i get there.*

The car hydroplaned at the end of the bend and swerved into the opposite lane. There was no oncoming traffic, a rarity for the city, but it was two in the morning after all. He dropped the phone and took hold of the wheel with both hands. He steadied the car and wrestled it back into its proper place. The phone pinged again from somewhere in the dark, near his feet. He reasoned it would be better to arrive alive than to respond and wrap himself around the next telephone pole, so he kept on driving.

This makes what, three times this month?

Cody was losing count of how many times his ex threatened to take her own life. He promised he was done, that the next time she texted him he would just leave it on "read." Every time he had raced over to her duplex, he had found Rachel asleep in bed, safe and sound. He would let himself get roped in again and again. Maybe it was the sex, maybe it was just having someone by his side in the long, cold hours of the morning. Whatever the reason, he kept on coming back. Like a mosquito knowing it would get smacked, yet still drawn to that warm pulse.

The light ahead turned red with three cars already stopped in front of it. There were no cars in the oncoming lane. Cody swerved into the left lane on purpose this time, and skirted around the other cars, cutting in front of them. The sound of horns blaring and middle fingers out of windows rushed by him in a blur.

Only a few more blocks.

There was something different this time. Cody didn't kid himself; he would have gone to see her, regardless. But this time she seemed serious. All previous cries for help were dramatic and loud. This time, she was much more muted than usual. That scared the shit out of him.

He arrived at Rachel's place and parked on the sidewalk in front, one tire on top of the curb with the other on the road. She lived on top of a hill near Golden Gate Park. The lights of the city formed a floor of golden brilliance below the duplex, a view fit for royalty. The fog rolling in from the bay enveloped everything, even up to the upper floor of her building, where he could see Rachel had left a light on. In the mist and the dark, the rain and the cold, the apartment took on a sinister face, one glowing eye out the bedroom window, a gaping black pit of a mouth below. The door was wide open.

Cody left the phone in the car and ran into the building, shouting, "Rachel, you okay?"

No response except the sound of running water from upstairs.

Was that the rain or the shower? Was she seriously taking one right now, after all those messages?

These thoughts soon left him. It was dark downstairs. The small living room he was standing in was barely visible. The door was open when he arrived. Something wasn't right. His heart beat weakly as he padded through the living room. A light crunching sound. He looked down and saw the shards of the lamp that had been the room's sole source of light. Rachel was never one to splurge on any expense.

He moved the beaded hallway curtain out of the way and entered. The beads clattered gently behind him, like the laughter of some small creature scampering in the living room.

The hall ended in a spiral staircase that led to Rachel's bedroom. He saw something on the steps. Tiny white things, like candy. He came near and picked one up.

Pills.

Cody ran up the stairs calling her name. His voice sounded ten years younger than he was, strained and squeaky. He turned the corner into the hall and stopped. The bathroom was in front of him, to the right. The door was open. In front of it lay a handful more pills scattered about. Steam from the shower blew into the hallway and met him with its warm embrace. He had to take off his glasses and wipe them with his shirt before he could see anything. There was something red in the hall, spilling out from the bathroom. Not a pill. Something wet, something spreading out like thick water.

His knees shook, and his mouth ran dry.

"Rachel?" he said, the word sounding like sandpaper against a chalkboard.

No response, only the hiss of the shower.

He moved forward, the unbearable weight of dread expectation crushing him.

He came to the doorway and looked into the bathroom. Crimson splotches decorated the floor. A young woman with black hair lay face down on the floor. Blood was streaming from her wrists. It painted the shower curtain and the walls. It was as if she went into a frenzied state of artistic inspiration and let her passion loose against the entire room with the paint of her body. He couldn't comprehend the scene. Pills, blood, shower, open door. He couldn't tie the sequence of events together. Had someone killed her? Had she done it herself, could she not settle on one method?

Cody bent down, his knees almost toppling him over. Before he could touch her, he stood back up. She was breathing. Slightly. Faint expansions of her back, almost imperceptible. She was alive. She tried to say something, but her words got lost in the blood and flowed downstream with it.

Cody backed up. He went out into the hall. For a moment he stared and considered. He closed the door.

The cigarette smoke shrouded Cody's view of the first responders coming out of the apartment. He looked at them from across the street, sitting on the curb next to his tire, forested park behind him. The rain had ceased, and the sky was clear. The stars shone above in crisp clarity. The red and blue lights from the cop cars reflected intensely off the wet streets. The neighbors were looking out of their windows. He even saw a few taking videos with their phones.

He took another drag and tossed the butt onto the street. One paramedic, a man in his late twenties with deep bags under his eyes, his uniform hanging limply off his skeletal frame, came over.

"You know, there was nothing you could've done. She was already beyond that sort of help. I know it probably doesn't help, but, thought I should say that."

"Yeah, thanks." Cody made no eye contact. Instead, he stared up at the sky.

"Okay, well, take care. I'm sorry." With that, the paramedic left him, got into the ambulance, and drove away.

The cops had already questioned Cody several times over the past hour, and he was sure many more were to come. For now, they were in the apartment wrapping up their collection of any evidence of Rachel Forrester's last moments in this world.

Cody remained on that street corner, looking up into the depths of space above. Tears clouded his view of the sky. The light of a few stars cut through the wetness and the glow of city lights. They cut through his thoughts.

He thought, *I hope someone up there is watching over me. Over her.*

That thought brings people comfort, at least in the movies. There on that curb, under the dark face of that eternal black night, it only served to raise the hairs on the back of his neck. That feeling that comes when someone stares into a dark forest, seeing nothing but hearing a low growl of some toothy animal—that feeling when all the evolutionary triggers for survival go off at once.

That's what Cody felt that night as he looked up at the stars.

3

Three months later

Wakayama, Japan

Cody stared out the window of the tour bus, tears on the verge of falling from his eyes. Nothing shutting them tight couldn't get rid of. However, there was no quick fix for the other symptoms. His hands shook and his breath became a gasping wheezing sound as it tried to escape his throat.

He tried to take in breath slowly with his head down. After a few minutes, he composed himself, wiped his eyes, and went back to staring out the window.

Outside, white trees wrapped in white mist flew by, like ghosts rising from the ground and being passed by, forgotten by the living. His earlier self-medication did no good, the hyperventilation came back in force. He kept on reminding himself of what his favorite dead philosopher wrote: "If it's out of your control, let it go." Or something to that effect.

Philosophy to him was mainly a vehicle for getting laid in college. What it actually gave him was a nicotine addiction coupled with an over-inflated vocabulary. Neither got him laid very much.

No matter how hard he tried, the dead man's words couldn't shut out his thoughts of the dead. Of that bathroom floor, covered in pills, blood spreading out into the hallway. He could see it now, somewhere out there in the fog. A door in a cloud opened up and revealed a red ocean. He walked through that door and saw Rachel lying there, still breathing. And did nothing.

"Earth to Cody, you alive?"

Cody shook his head as if someone had just poured ice water over it.

"Sorry, what were you saying?" Cody replied, regaining his senses, the tremor in his hands dissipating, his breath coming under control.

"Dude, you can't be spacing out all the time. I was saying, are you ready to go?" said the man with a playful smile. That smile never left his face, at least as far back as Cody could remember. It was a permanent fixture on the face of Rick Davis. That smile was etched into a face of straight lines and a sharp jaw. His hair, the color of the sun, was a wave of light. His eyes were the deep blue sky. He was so handsome Cody sometimes felt like hitting him.

He could do with a little imperfection, he thought.

The bus had stopped, and Cody hadn't even noticed. Everyone had already gotten off, and these two were the last to leave.

"Yeah, sorry about that." Cody grabbed his pack from the overhead storage and headed off the bus with Rick.

"I thought you guys were going to leave me here," said the smiling woman. She twirled her single pink-and-black braid and flung it behind her shoulders. She wore neon-pink yoga pants and a lime-green tank top shrouded in an explosively orange poncho.

Everything about her was electric.

"Oh yeah, we were going to leave you here," Rick said and planted a kiss on her cheek. She lightly slapped his face and laughed. Rick continued, "Cody wasn't going to, though, he was getting all white knight on me, saying no way could we leave such a fine young lady all by herself here."

Cody's face went hot as he smiled with his teeth, not his eyes.

Rick put him in a headlock and ruffled his shaggy brown hair. Cody pushed him off while Rick laughed maniacally. He slapped Cody's shoulder and went over to the girl's side.

"Come on, Mia, let's go check out the scene," Rick said as he grabbed her hand and tugged her towards the waiting group of other tourists. Ten people, mostly old European couples in hiking clothes too tight for them, and a single Chinese man in spandex doing hip thrust stretches, made up the crew that stood in restless attention before a middle-aged Japanese woman holding a megaphone so closely to her face, her purple rimmed glasses fogged up.

"Okay, everyone, we start hike in fifteen minutes. Go use the restroom or buy some water and meet back at ten o'clock exactly. The hike will be long, get ready. We finish three in the afternoon."

Nobody listened to the woman as she fought to make her voice heard, something even the device in her hands seemed incapable of doing. Her flustered face was now pink and wet with megaphone fog.

Cody looked around and saw hastily set up stalls selling items ranging from water bottles to good-luck charms. Somewhere in the maze of vendors, Cody detected a wafting aroma of grilled meat. On the other side of the parking lot from the stalls was an entrance to a hiking trail, with a stone toori gate over the path. Two stone lions sat on either side, with frozen snarls cut into their faces. Cody knew little about Japanese culture, but he had seen these gates at almost every temple the three friends had seen so far.

The faces of the lions unnerved him. Dead and motionless, yet frenzied and aggressive. If one were so brave as to walk past the inanimate objects, they would find a path that shot straight up the forested mountainside.

Shit, this is going to be tough right away?

Up the trail, the trees reached into the sky and blotted out the sun. Thick clouds hung near the top of the canopy, with shreds of mist threaded between the trunks below. Everything was wet as if it had just rained, or maybe the constant fog soaked the landscape just by being present. He could feel wetness in the air, cold and invasive, seeping down into his bones. His poncho offered little barrier between himself and the dampness. Everything smelled of moss and wet dogs.

It reminded him of home in San Francisco, notorious for its cold fog, yet this was more intrusive than what he had ever experienced, more intimate and violating.

Thank God this is only for one or two days.

He imagined finishing the hike early, getting back to the hotel, and drinking himself into oblivion in his room. His warm and dry room.

Cody wandered over to one of the stalls. A woman with countless wrinkles and an arched back stood behind a table full of wares. She was bent over, leaning on her cane. On the table, there were miniature owls made of wood, and farmers made of knitted wool, but by far the most numerous items were necklaces. The ones that caught his eye were made of black beads, with a large shell hanging at the bottom. One had an image of the sun painted on the shell.

"What are these?" He asked the woman.

She smiled thinly and bowed her head. "*Mimamori.*" She pointed at a sign taped to the table that read: TARISMAN. Cody smiled. He handed over a few coins, hoping that they were enough—he had never learned the money system since he arrived last week—and placed the necklace around his scrawny neck.

The woman pointed up at the sky and said, "San."

Cody smiled and held up the talisman for inspection.

Protection from the sun? Or, the sun protects me?

Rick and Mia came over, holding a few paper cups with the steam rising to their faces. Mia handed one to Cody and flashed her nuclear smile. "Coffee."

"Thank you." Cody wanted to add that he drank only tea but forced himself to smile instead. It was grainy and tasted like smoked chocolate swirled in an ashtray. They finished their drinks with a grimace and tossed the cups into an impromptu wire trash can nearby.

"Alright, man, I know you've been down, like, a lot lately. But this is exactly what you need. Some time outside, some time with a toxic optimist like myself. You'll feel better in no time," Rick said, the white of his teeth gleaming.

Cody smiled faintly. "Thanks, but I don't think being stuck with these people will make me feel any better." A pudgy German man's voice rose as he yelled something at his wife. She was trying to pull his hiking pants up past his protruding stomach and was failing at the task, slipping in the mud.

"That was never the plan, my guy." He wrapped his arm over Cody's shoulders. "We just needed to be in the group to get here. Let's start now, get ahead of everyone, and go do our own thing," Rick said, flashing his smile like a used-car salesman. An ethical one, Cody was sure of that, but a salesman nonetheless. The memory of the time Rick convinced him to shave his mom's cat when they were eleven resurfaced in Cody's mind. His mom was furious at them and took Cody's computer privileges away for a month. Rick's parents never punished him.

I knew he'd get me in trouble, *and I let him do it*, anyway.

Cody had the same feeling now but said nothing.

"You sure, babe?" Mia asked. "I don't mind waiting and heading out as a group."

"Don't be lame, Mia." He moaned and exaggerated the word "lame" and stretched it out for an indecent amount of time. "If we walk with all of these… fine people… we're going to be moving like snails. Let's get ahead and have the forest to ourselves."

Mia gave Cody a defeated look and said, "Well, the king has spoken."

"Damn right he has," Rick said. Mia fake-punched him in the gut, and the two blew up into laughter.

Buying trinkets and preparing for the elements with their new North Face jackets and Montbell hiking shoes distracted the group. Some were just now taking them out of their plastic wrappings. The trio started for the stone archway and were halfway through it when the pink-faced tour leader spotted them and froze them in place with the high-pitched squeal of the megaphone.

"Excuse me, please excuse. You can't go now; please wait."

Rick's bleached teeth sparkled in the foggy air as he ran his hands through his sandy hair. "Ms.," he looked down at her name tag, "Ms. Tanaka, lovely name, by the way," (Mia rolled her eyes at this) "my friends and I are already ready, we're much younger than everyone here, and I promise you we'll back down the mountain here at this spot before most of the other members even reach the top."

Cody knew that was a lie; the friends were planning on spending the night out in the woods.

Ms. Tanaka held a sour expression and was about to speak when a flurry of expletives blew up behind her. The German man's wife had finally fallen into the mud, taking half her husband's pants with her. Most of what the woman screamed was beyond their understanding except for the multiple *scheissas* that came pouring out of her mouth.

Ms. Tanaka drew her hand across her face, failing to wipe off the moist residue from the megaphone. She protested, but Rick kept on smiling, not once breaking eye contact.

She took out a smoke, lit it, and inhaled furiously.

Ms. Tanaka exhaled rapidly. "Okay, I guess okay. Be careful." She turned to go. Cody was glad to escape the chaotic scene of mud-covered tourists.

The trio took off up the mountain with their packs and rain gear on. Cody and Rick's ponchos were black, which made them stand out against the garishness of Mia's. The chirping of birds soon overpowered the shouting of German body-shaming. The rolling bodies of the tourists below were by now shrouded in clouds.

"See, what did I tell you? Much better already, yeah?" Rick said.

"Sure, yeah, I guess so," Cody said quietly while he stared at his feet. Rick smacked his shoulder, flashed that perma-smile of his, and led the way.

Mia came up next to Cody and whispered, "How are you really doing?"

Cody held her eyes for a moment. "Why do you care?"

Mia held her hands up in the air. "Whoa, calm down, buddy, just being nice."

"Sorry, that came out wrong. I'm just not really in the best frame of mind, you know?"

"Yeah, I do. We all get stuck sometimes. From now on, though, don't be a dick about it."

"For sure, sorry for the dickishness."

She smiled, winked, and rejoined Rick up the trail.

Cody breathed deeply and loosened his body now that he was walking alone. The birds sang above him. He stopped, closed his eyes, and threw his head back, taking in the moment. Though the mist was prevalent, there were sharp blue patches of sky above. Some sunlight poured through and warmed him before being overtaken once again by the mist.

The path wound around the mountain at an even incline. It wasn't the most arduous of hikes he had been on, but enough to remind him he hadn't gone to the gym in months. The trees were tall, thick, and ancient. At every turn, he saw small statues of Buddha with red cloth tied over their heads. Moss covered most of their bodies, and the ravages of time had worn their features down. Their dead eyes stared off into the infinite nothingness.

"Rick, what were these called? *Jizo*?" He shouted this up the trail at the couple, who were encased in their private bubble of love.

Rick smiled and shrugged his shoulders. Mia tossed her hair aside as she looked back. "Yeah, I think that's what they were called." They both stopped and walked over to Cody.

Cody stopped to take a picture with his phone.

"Yeah, *jizo*, like guardian angels. I remember reading that they watch out for travelers and children."

This nugget of knowledge came courtesy of a water-worn pamphlet about the trail they were on. He had it somewhere in his pack, or was it in the trash can at the hotel? Cody flipped his bag around and rummaged through a side pocket. It was there, crumpled and wet, with some of the ink running down the pages, but still legible.

He was right; the little statues were like guardian angels.

The pamphlet also had a map of the mountain. Areas of interest, such as temples or viewpoints, were drawn in a colorful, cartoonish fashion. At the top of the page, it was titled *Welcome to the Kumano Kodo in Wakayama.* The area on the map was vast, probably covering several hundred miles of terrain.

The particular trail they were on was on the edge of a vast, unmarked mountain range, an outpost of touristy fun and games right at the border of an unknown wilderness.

"Good for you, since you're a traveling child and all," Rick said with a laugh.

Cody once again imagined slapping the smile off Rick's face. He'd never do that, of course, yet he often enjoyed the fantasy. It was the same with the bullies back in high school, his boss at the insurance company, and even here with his best friend. Yet instead of striking that handsome face, what Cody actually did was give a puff of a laugh.

"You're an ass," Mia said.

Rick responded by picking her up and threatening to throw her off the side of the trail. She squealed and waved her limbs about like a toddler.

Cody winced. *I don't know how long I can handle all this sugar-coated lubby-dubby shit,* he thought.

Although Cody wasn't against romance, he really didn't want to think about it at that moment. Whenever he thought of love, instead of romantic getaways or even unrequited angst, what came flooding into his mind was the closed bathroom door.

Where he wanted to be at this moment was back at his mother's house in Oregon, doing nothing at all. Maybe getting lost in a book. Maybe picking up some old dead guy's philosophy. God knows he could have used some right now. More than being wet, outside, and stuck with Romeo and Juliet here.

Instead, the moment he found himself in was at the mercy of Rick's buoyant adventurism. The tide known as Richard Davis also swept Mia along. No one could resist that pull. At least, Cody had never seen someone successfully do so. He knew his friend meant well, but sometimes well-meaning intentions weren't enough to cover for idiocy.

They hiked for an hour along the switchbacks, climbing higher and higher. At one point, they could see the parking lot. Cody saw nobody, so he figured the tourists were already on their way, though he doubted they'd gone far. There were other hikers on the trail. Mostly elderly Japanese with hiking poles, dressed in stylish yet functional outdoor gear.

Jizo popped up every now and again. Covered in moss, displaying a detached smile and closed eyes. They seemed at peace with the world. Cody envied them. They came across a waterfall, spilling out its life onto the rocks far below. They passed by a few small shrines. Each one had a water basin with a metal or stone dragon watching over it. Someone had set several wooden ladles on the basin.

Cody watched and saw an older Japanese man wash his hands and mouth with the water before proceeding to the center of the shrine, bowing, and clapping twice before bowing a final time. When the man had gone, Cody tried to emulate the ritual but fell short of putting the water into his mouth. National Geographic documentaries about malaria popped up in his mind and, while he was sure this water was fine, he would not risk it.

They moved up the trail and came to a larger temple complex called the "Temple of Peace." A sign in English told them it was built over a thousand years ago by Tendai Buddhists, who were also skilled warriors. Cody skipped the mass of text involving dates and names and found one line that stood out to him. The monks of this temple caused controversy because they prayed for the salvation of the Shinto gods. He knew Shinto was the native religion of Japan but always thought that it and Buddhism were sort of mixed now, official BFFs.

What sort of God would need salvation? He wondered.

They went in, took some pictures, and rang the bell in front of the altar. Rick jumped on the bell's rope like Tarzan and yelled out monkey sounds. Mia echoed the sounds and filmed it. They uploaded all that peaceful Zen to Instagram. Cody would have died of embarrassment had anyone else been around to witness the episode. They moved on from the temple and went further up the path.

Every time another hiker passed them going down the trail, Rick went for a high-five. All the hikers looked Japanese and responded with limp hands and plastic smiles. Mia filmed it all. Cody tried to blend in with the jizo and disavow all connection with his friends, just fade into the moss and the impermanence of the world.

One hiker, a child of about eight with his mom and dad, dropped something on the trail as he passed by. Cody noticed this and went back to pick it up. It was some kind of comic book (in Japanese, of course) with a giant blue cat thing on the cover. Cody smiled, remembering his obsession with Spider-Man back in middle school. He loved the character but always felt more at home with pre-spider bite Peter Parker going to school, failing with girls, and getting bullied than he did with the super strong spandex hero.

He ran down the trail to catch up with the boy. He surprised them, but the family quickly returned his smile, and the boy took his comic.

They said some words Cody didn't understand until the boy, through puffy cheeks and a gap-filled smile, said, "Sank you."

Cody replied, "Arigatou."

There was a slight, awkward bowing of heads. Cody left them and ran back to his friends, who hadn't even noticed he had left.

Maybe they wouldn't notice if I stayed on the bus?

After rejoining them, they soon came across a wooden sign written in Japanese, English, and Korean. It read: THIS IS THE END OF THE TRAIL. DO NOT GO BEYOND THIS POINT, TRAIL IS NOT STABLE. FOLLOW THE PATH TO THE LEFT AND HEAD BACK DOWN TO THE PARKING AREA.

Someone nailed the sign to a tree. Beyond it, a trail climbed the mountain, but someone had blocked it off with fat logs and dead branches, forming a wall to keep people out. The trees past the wall were dead and gnarled, their branches curving down like claws ready to snatch up anyone stupid enough to walk under them.

"That's it? This is the hike everyone was raving about? The one we just had to see? And it's over like that?" Rick's face turned a purple-red hue and he swore under his breath. He threw down his backpack with a thud. It was stuffed with a sleeping bag, as were Cody's and Mia's. Rick also held the tent.

"You okay?" Cody asked.

"Babe, chill, it's no big deal," Mia added.

"No, no, I'm not, and no, I won't chill. This was supposed to be something we could do just to, I don't know, get away from it all. It was supposed to be better than this."

"Why are you acting like this? I didn't think this would be so important to you," Mia said. "And if it was, why didn't you check to see if the hike was longer? That's what you told us when we left, a*n overnight hike in the mountains.*"

Rick inhaled so deeply his chest unbuttoned a part of his raincoat. "People said that this was an overnight wilderness adventure, okay?"

"People? Okay, so what was the name of that hike, then? Mia's normally lively face had become stony and expressionless.

"I'll show you." Rick flipped through his phone and brought up the picture he had taken off the Reddit thread about hiking the Kumano Kodo.

"Are you fucking joking? Reddit?" Mia thumbed her way through the pictures. "Rick, they spell the name of the trail differently each time someone talks about it." She pointed this out to him while he remained silent. Cody went through his bag and took out the weather-worn map.

"Hey guys, the name of this trail is Kami Korin. What name did you think this was, Rick?"

Rick's face was a mix of purple fury and embarrassment. He took his phone back from Mia and enlarged the photo. "Kami Koya."

Mia snorted an angry breath through her nose. "Not even close to the same name."

"What do you want from me? I don't speak Japanese."

"But it's written in English, dumb-dumb."

Cody raised his hands between them and said, "Guys, calm down. I mean, it's all of our fault, isn't it? None of us double-checked what..." He paused and went quiet.

Rick shot in, "What 'what'? None of us double-checked to see if Rick had fucked up again?"

"But that's exactly what happened," Mia said.

Cody tried once more to calm down the primal forces that were unleashed before him. "It would've been much worse if we'd thought it was a day hike, and it had turned out we'd gotten lost overnight, right? Let's just enjoy the walk down and get some drinks back at the hotel."

Mia's stony expression softened, but her arms remained crossed.

"Fuck that. I didn't come to a new country just to get drunk at some lame-ass hotel. No offense," Rick said.

"None taken" would have been the polite reply. Instead, Cody remained silent.

Rick went on, "Life is short, guys. This may be our only time we get to travel and really live. Do you really want to spend it doing the same boring shit some fat tourists could do? No, not me. I can't live that way."

Cody chuckled. Rick raised his eyebrows at this. "I've never heard you be so serious before," Cody said.

"Same. I don't like it," Mia put in.

This broke the tension, and the friends laughed together.

Rick continued, "Nah, I didn't come halfway across the world to do basic shit like that. Come on, guys, do you want to say that you turned back on an adventure when it was staring you right in the face?" His voice was rising, and he stood tall, like a general rousing his troops. His face showed no emotion.

Mia said, "All good in theory, but where is this adventure you're talking about?"

Rick chewed his lip, paced, and looked around. He pointed somewhere off the trail and said, "What if we check that out over there?" Cody followed his friend's finger and looked out at the path beyond the sign and the wall of wooden debris.

There was another, smaller sign posted on a tree. It was written in red Japanese letters spray-painted onto the board. He couldn't read what it said, but the intent was clear: DANGER, DO NOT ENTER.

Rick wasn't pointing at the path itself but at something else—Cody could see if he squinted hard enough—a shrine, barely visible through the thick foliage. The path seemed somehow darker and colder than where they were currently standing. This was stupid, of course: the same amount of sunlight poured out on both sides of the dividing wall of branches. Though it looked the same as their current trail, it felt different, down in the guts, down in the soul.

The feeling someone has when they walk through a park at night. They don't see anyone or hear anyone, but the spine still chills and the hair on the neck still rises.

"I don't think that we should do that. Looks closed off for a reason. There are probably ticks and snakes in the grass," Cody said. "It could also be unstable; it's closed off for a reason."

But those weren't the genuine concerns. What disturbed Cody the most was the feeling in his bones, a cold surge of energy that made him want to run in the opposite direction. He couldn't label why he felt that way, just that he did.

"I'm with him, babe," Mia threw in.

"Just for twenty minutes. I want to see what's over there." Rick picked up his commander's charisma once again. "We've got to make up for this lame-ass hike. And who knows, if we get lucky, we can do some off-grid camping; we've got all the gear for it. Then we could just hitchhike back to the hotel tomorrow morning. Japan is safe, nothing to worry about," Rick said as he headed over to the path without looking at the other two.

We really shouldn't be doing this.

Mia pouted at Cody, threw her hands up in the air, and called after Rick, "Only twenty minutes, okay?"

Rick fist-pumped the air in reply.

Cody said no more and followed them to the wall of sticks and logs.

Rick leaped up and pulled himself over, and then he helped Mia up, leaving Cody to climb up by himself. The wall was shaky but held their weight. They all jumped off and landed on the overgrown and out-of-bounds trail.

4

Rick led the way, stomping through the tall grass, whistling as he went. Mia skipped along his side. Cody hung back and trudged along. It really was colder and darker on this side of the makeshift barrier. He pulled his poncho tighter across his chest. He couldn't hear the birds anymore.

It was as if they refused to enter this part of the forest. The gnarled branches of the dead trees hung above his head, ready to strike.

Mia suddenly appeared at his side. He nearly yelled out but kept his mouth shut. She slapped his back and said, "So, what do you think of Japan so far? Everything you thought it would be?"

"Yeah, it's something."

The sound of silence rang for an eternity. The squish of the leaves under their feet filled in the conversation for them.

"So, what kind of music do you like?" Mia's face went red. Cody liked the immediate embarrassment for asking a middle-school-appropriate question. He laughed.

"Did I ask something weird?"

"No." Silence lingered, and Cody's muscles tightened.

"I know I'm awkward and all. But we only met two weeks ago," Mia flashed a very Rick-esque smile in that moment. "If we're going to be spending more time together, we should get to know each other."

Cody looked straight ahead and sighed. "Umm, you don't have to pretend to be interested in me just because I'm Rick's friend."

"Not doing that. Ass." She pulled away.

"I'm sorry; I didn't mean for it to come out like that." This phrase was becoming his theme for the day.

"How did you mean for it to come out then?"

Their feet squashed more leaves, causing many to lose their lives beneath the weight of the awkward silence. He cleared his throat. "I just don't open up to people right away, unless I know that they're going to be around for a while."

He glanced at Mia's face. Her eyes were wide, like a vengeful Greek fury.

"Got it. You don't think I'm going to last with Rick, so why bother, right?"

"I'm so-," Cody began, but she walked faster ahead and caught up to Rick just as he bent back some extended branches, only to have them snap back with force at Mia, who was directly behind him. She didn't need to duck to avoid them as she stood only five feet tall.

"Be careful, dick."

"Whoa. Sorry," Rick answered. He stopped for a moment to check Mia's face. Probably to see if he had accidentally scratched her with the branches. She batted his hand away and walked past him, taking the lead up the path.

Rick looked back at Cody and mouthed, "What the hell?"

Cody shook his head and waved his hand as if to ward off the embarrassment. Rick hung back until Cody caught up.

"You're having fun at least, right?" Rick asked.

"Oh yeah, loads."

Rick chewed his bottom lip. God, how Cody hated that habit. His whole body tensed every time he saw it. Then Rick let out a sigh and said, "Hey, if you're not having fun, we can turn back. I know I can get carried away sometimes, but all I want is for us to have a good time. Make some good memories out here."

Cody's body let go of its tension. "No, it's alright. Let's just see what's up here quickly and head back, okay? I'm not feeling like an overnighter anymore. I don't think I'm down for camping even if we find something."

"Deal. And...what do you think about Mia? I think she might be the one."

Cody smiled and said, "Oh yeah, she's a keeper."

Rick's smile widened until he resembled the Cheshire Cat, the glint of mischievousness also present.

"Yeah, she is. Tough as nails, too. Needs to be to keep up with these." He kissed his biceps and flexed.

"Why need a girlfriend when you can just make out with yourself?"

"Nah, tried it. I'm too much for even me to handle. Gotta spread the joy," Rick motioned with his hands like he was doing the wax on, wax off from the Karate Kid, laughed, and punched Cody on the shoulder. His body was receiving far too many of these blows today. Rick raced ahead to catch up with Mia.

Cody didn't mean what he said. It wasn't all right. But he hated to see sincerity on Rick's face; it didn't suit him. He also couldn't bear the thought of having to speak his mind. All he wanted was to be left alone with his thoughts. As suffocating as they might be, he got some sort of sick pleasure out of it.

On the trail, there weren't any snakes, ticks, giant man-eating bugs, or pitfalls as he had feared, just a few mosquitoes buzzing by his ears. He swatted them away, but they kept up their assault unbothered. The path was stable and not falling apart. None of this assuaged Cody's mind of the constant thought they shouldn't be here. It not only seemed colder here, it was foggier, and somehow less welcome.

After twenty minutes of venturing down the path, they could see it. Just above them, lurching over a ridge, was a corner of the roof of some kind of shrine. It looked just like the ones they had already seen on the trail so far: shingled roof, with a curved arch, like a wave. They made their way around the switchback and came to the shrine's entrance. Dead branches formed another makeshift barrier, though smaller than the one they had already cleared. Rick rammed ahead, throwing branches aside and crushing others underfoot.

Mia helped him. Cody watched. In a few minutes, they moved enough of the debris to get through. Before them stood the entrance to the grounds.

The toori gate of the entrance looked similar to the one at the beginning of the hike, except for the fact that it was split down the middle like some giant had cleaved it in two, leaving the support beams leaning to their sides. Instead of two lions on either side, there was something else, the details too obscure to see from a distance. As Cody approached, he could see them in more detail.

The statue on the right was headless and lay in pieces. The one on the left was intact. It looked like a frog with razor-sharp teeth, hunched over as if it was about to pounce. It looked scorched, as if someone had set fire to it. Spray-painted graffiti in Japanese covered it. Cody imagined some teenagers coming out here to get wasted and fool around.

What a horrifying place to do that.

Spotting empty beer cans, soda bottles, noodle cups, and heaps of trash strewn about the place confirmed his suspicions. The garbage had deteriorated and bleached after many days out in the sun. They walked through the devastated gate. Chest-high grass filled the courtyard, and little else was there.

Vines, some dead, some alive, covered the shrine. There was a rope inside the shrine, the kind Cody had seen at other places of worship where people would ring it and pray. It was barely hanging on by its thread. The rest of the shrine was like the frog statue, blackened by fire and falling apart.

The wind blew through the bamboo trees that surrounded the complex, their collective music sounding like the hiss of a thousand snakes.

The place didn't just look disused; it looked purposefully destroyed.

"Okay, we came, we saw, we conquered. Let's go back," Cody said.

Mia looked distracted, chasing after a dragonfly, trying to catch it in her hands.

Rick, with his hands on his hips, chewed his lip some more and looked around. He walked over the edge of the grounds near a wall of foxtail grass. He swept the plants aside and shouted something at them. Mia went in after him. Cody stood where he was, glancing back at the path they had just entered through. The hissing of the trees rose in pitch, and the wind raised the hairs on his arms. Then, without a word, he followed.

"Now this is more like it," Rick said.

As Cody walked through the sticky grass, he came upon a clearing with a ledge at its far end. Rick ran over to it and shouted for him to come over and check it out. He took a selfie by the ledge with Mia, once again lifting her and dangling her over the ledge.

Cody followed but kept glancing back at the way out, and at the sun, not quite close to setting but near enough to keep him on edge. The shadows of the trees were reaching across the clearing, painting the grass black with the anticipation of the coming night. He moved over to the edge of the clearing, also filled with the trash of teenage debauchery, and saw what Rick was now beaming his smile at.

A valley stretched out, surrounded by mountains. Mist hung low over the forest below. It moved like ocean waves crashing through the few visible trees, dark green rocks jutting out of the sea. The valley looked like a different world, a thick layer of cloud separating it from the world of the sun. The dense gray matter obscured most of the forest.

Cody didn't like what he saw. There was no reason for it, just the same feeling he had not to enter the closed-off trail. He felt cold down to his blood, down to his atoms. He felt like the mist below was gazing back at him. Looking down, Cody froze in place. The ledge he was standing on was mostly a sheer ninety-degree drop of at least fifty feet. The fog obscured the bottom.

Rick moved closer. "Hey, do you see that?"

Cody strained his eyes against the glare of light reflecting off the mist, but he could make out something dark in the middle of a large patch of yellow, not too far away. Wisps of black rose from it, surrounded by what looked like large stones. It was just a momentary glimpse as clouds rolled over the spot as quickly as they had left it.

"I have no idea," Cody said.

Rick squatted and began climbing down the ledge.

"What the fuck are you doing?" Mia said, her dark skin lighting up with shades of red.

Her hands were on her hips. With Rick below her, it almost looked like a mother scolding a child. *"That sounds about right,"* Cody thought. Rick dropped to another ledge just below where he had been standing. It was a space large enough for maybe four people to stand on. There were some earthen steps leading down to it as if it had at one point belonged to an actual trail. Weathered and dull yellow tape lined the edge.

A small statue stood atop a wooden pedestal in the middle of the shelf. It looked like a man (without many features, more of a skillfully crafted stick figure) with its arms raised out to the sky. It was on its knees. Burnt-out incense sticks were lying in its hands. One of them was still sending up a faint puff towards the sky.

Rick bent down and took a selfie with the statue, sticking out his tongue and making a devil sign with his fist.

Mia crossed her arms and shouted, "Babe, come back. This is real dumb."

He looked up at her, smiled, and before a word could pour out from his beaming grin, a loud cracking sound erupted from beneath them. It shook the ground and Cody's spine. It was the sound of thunder from deep within the earth. The ledge collapsed.

People build good, meaningful things over years of hard work, but it takes mere seconds to destroy them. Rick was standing, and then he wasn't. He was smiling, and now terror painted his face. He grabbed onto what remained of the ledge and hung there, suspended above the drop.

Both Cody and Mia yelled a flurry of expletives as they scrambled down to the part of the shelf left intact, not big enough for either of them to stand on fully. They each grabbed one of Rick's arms and began pulling. Cody yanked his arm with all his strength. Sweat stung his eyes. He felt his joints being pulled out. Despite the chaos, he remained keenly aware of one fact: the ground beneath him was slipping, spilling out over the ledge like water.

The dam burst.

He fell into the rocky current and flew off the edge. The world spun around him as his face smacked against the cliff wall and his body somersaulted its way through roots and rock. In what took approximately five seconds from start to finish, he experienced a lifetime. He saw their bodies falling through the air as if they were sinking in the water of a pool. He viewed the scene as if detached, observing the crisis like a ghost floating in the air.

As the ground came up to kiss him, Cody wasn't thinking about his own death.

All he saw was the red bathroom floor.

All he saw was her chest inhaling air.

All he saw was the door he closed as he ran.

Then he saw the ground.

Close up.

5

Ringing pierced Cody's ears, his vision blurred, and his body ached. Just below the high-pitched whine, he could hear something crying, the sound a hurt dog would make. As reality came back into focus, he realized Rick was that dog. He was whimpering and clutching his left leg, rocking back and forth.

Cody remained lying on the dirt, staring at Rick. Mia was nowhere to be seen. Cody still wore his pack. Rick's had spilled its contents out on the ground like a frat boy on a Saturday night.

"Fuck. My leg, Cody, help me."

Cody didn't move until Rick shouted at him a second time. Then he sprang up and ran over to him and said, "What do I do?"

"Is it bleeding?"

Cody rolled up Rick's pant leg and saw nothing. No blood. Some bruising around the ankle, but nothing that required first aid (for now). The adrenaline subsided, and Cody's heart calmed down. He noticed the dozens of cuts across his own body now. But after a quick check, he determined that he was fine.

"Wait. Mia," Cody said, looking back at the cliff. She was above them, having landed on a higher ledge.

She wasn't moving.

"Shit, shit, shit." Cody scrambled up to the ledge by scaling a large boulder and jumping up. She was lying there with her eyes closed. Her body was spotted with cuts and bruises. Her bright pink hair was now dyed brown and red. He shook her. She woke up and lifted herself into a sitting position.

"Where..." she started and then ended with a sputtering of coughs.

"You guys okay?" Rick asked.

"Yeah, she's banged up some, but I don't see anything major," Cody shouted and then turned to Mia. "You okay?"

Her eyes slowly opened all the way. "Yeah, I think so."

He helped her up and offered her his arm to get down to the ground, but she jumped off herself. Mia saw Rick's leg and ran over. He said he was okay and refused to be pitied. She ignored this, helped him to his feet, and propped him up against the cliff wall.

"Shit," Rick said, staring up at the spot they had fallen from.

Cody followed his eyes and saw the cliff face. It had no roots or ledges or anything protruding out that somebody could grab onto. It was a clean, nearly smooth rock wall. Even if Rick weren't injured, they wouldn't be able to scale it. The wall offered no gentle slopes, trails, or anything that could be of use.

It's a miracle we even survived the fall.

Mist shrouded the top of the cliff where they had been standing moments before. The area they had landed in was a wide patch of dirt with no trees or any other vegetation. In front of them the rock wall; behind them was a sea of trees. Tall cedars, growing close together, guarded the forest entrance. Mist kept the tops of the trees from view; darkness filled in the spaces between the trunks. It was a quiet, stolid, unknowable land.

"It's okay, it's okay," Rick inhaled deeply with obvious pain on his face. "We know the trail is on the other side of the cliff. So, all we need to do is keep that spot up there in our sights. You can see those grooves going down its side, yeah? That's from us falling down. Keep that in our sight so we don't get lost, and let's move around the base of this hill. There's got to be another way up, or maybe the other hikers can hear us if we yell."

Rick started yelling out into the gray sky above. Cody and Mia joined him. No response.

"Phones," Rick yelled and told everyone to get theirs out, international roaming be damned. Each one checked their phones. None of them would even turn on. Rick kept smashing the power button, but nothing happened.

"Mine was at least at half power," Mia said.

"Mine was almost full," Cody put in.

"Alright, fuck the phones for now, we should start walking," Rick said.

They took a few gulps of water from their thermoses and put them away. The men gave Mia a few minutes to overcome the dizziness that came from the fall. When they all seemed good to go—all things considered—they got moving.

Mia and Cody helped gather Rick's gear that had spilled out of his pack and helped him put it on his back. They stood on either side of him and supported him as he walked. Rick grit his teeth so hard, Cody could almost hear them crack. They began moving along the rock face like Rick said to, with Rick hopping on his right leg. After ten minutes, they met a sight that killed the light in their eyes. After rounding a bend, they saw the entire mountain range on their side of the valley. Every wall of rock shot straight up into the sky.

No paths, no climbing holds, and no hills they could walk up. Rick leaned against a tree and pushed his supporters away. His face was beet-purple, and humidity and sweat wet his bare arms.

"Okay, I've got the tent, and we all have water and some food, yeah? The food and stuff are just for a day but shouldn't be a problem. Water is dripping from all the trees." Rick laughed, yet somehow it gave off a discomforting vibe. "Good thing we prepped for an overnighter, am I right?"

Cody clenched his fist, hit the rock wall (he immediately regretted that part), and said, "This is all your fault, Rick. We wouldn't be in this situation if you would've just listened and not fucked around. I wouldn't even be here if you hadn't dragged me on this fucking ridiculous 'find yourself' bullshit of a trip." Cody stopped to take a lungful of air. He surprised himself with this sudden—but was it really so sudden?—outburst.

"Hey, don't blame me. You went along with it. And when did I ever force you to do anything? You're a big boy. Stop being such a pussy. We have other things to worry about right now."

"I'm not being a—never mind."

Mia cut in, "Guys, stop it. We have a more serious problem here that we have to solve first. No one knows we're out here, Rick's hurt, and I don't know about you two, but fuck camping out here. Even if we have supplies, I do not want to spend the fucking night out here. Nobody knows where we are and... I just feel *off* being here." Her face went pale, and her eyes flitted around her surroundings.

Cody's eyes stung with salt, but he held his breath and his tongue. Images of his fist breaking Rick's nose crossed his mind not for the first time that day.

He shook his head and said, "Well, we still have our stuff. It looks like it just rained, and water is literally everywhere. Rick, you have the tent as well. So, worst-case scenario, we can spend one or two nights out here and we're okay."

Mia scoffed and walked off by herself.

Cody tried to explain himself again, but Rick called after her, "He's right, we're in bad shape, but it's not that bad. We'll be fine."

Mia kept on walking away from the men, towards a large tree outside the forest area. It had fallen and propped itself up against another, larger tree, making a slanted bridge. Mia hopped on it and squirreled her way up towards the canopy.

"See anything?" Rick asked.

She was silent for a moment. "Yeah! There's smoke over there." She pointed into the forest they had yet to enter.

Rick beamed. "Smoke? That means people. We need to check that out. How far away?"

"I don't know, five miles, ten miles, I have no fucking clue."

"I'll go check," Cody said.

He pulled himself up the log, climbed up, and came to where Mia was pointing. Thin black spirals twisted towards the sky, mixing with the low-hanging fog, a winding display of darkness and light. The smoke rose slightly above the tree line before dissipating. It looked like it was coming from a singular source, not a widespread forest fire, and that most likely meant it was people who had set it, and people meant salvation. Cody and Mia slid down the tree-bridge.

"So what's the verdict?" Rick asked.

"I'm guessing it would take us two hours to reach it if there were no trees in the way and if you could walk. As it is, it could take us an entire day. And it will get dark before we reach it."

"Alright, let's do it; let's move our asses to the smoke," Rick said.

"I think we should stay where we are. When you get lost, I think if you stay put, it's easier for people to find you," Cody said.

"Fuck that. Do you not see my leg swelling? And even if people come looking for us, it could take days. If we get to the smoke by tomorrow, that could still be faster than just waiting here. And if there's smoke, there's most likely people around."

"I saw something else," Mia said. "Across the valley, there was another set of mountains, but there was a road, maybe a highway. It was clear as day, and I saw it coming down onto the forest level. Even if there are no people by the smoke, there's got to be somebody by the road."

Cody started to speak but stopped.

"You have something to say?" Mia more demanded than asked.

"Like I said, we could get more lost if we move, and the tour guide lady will notice that we're gone soon, right? I say we stay put."

"That could take days. The group doesn't even know where to look, assuming they notice that we're gone." As soon as Rick said this, it started raining. "My leg hurts and could get worse. It's going to get cold here, and with all the humidity, that's really going to suck. We need to get out of this now, so let's go."

Cody said nothing but refused to move.

"Dude, don't just stand there. We have to get moving, alright?" Mia said with a deep sigh as she gave Rick her right shoulder to lean on. A response bubbled in Cody's throat, but he gave in, went over to them, and helped support his friend.

They entered the forest, Rick wedged between Cody and Mia. There was no path to follow, only wide berths between some trees that would have to substitute as one. Dead, wet leaves covered the floor. Yet no over-grown vegetation blocked their path. The mist bled down even under the canopy, making it impossible for them to see the roof of the forest. The trunks of the white trees, wide and thick, grew into the fog to unknown heights, while the far-off distances on ground level were a mystery of white haze.

The oppressive ceiling of cloud weighed above them, making the forest seem smaller and more mysterious than it would have otherwise. The smoke was nowhere to be seen, obscured by the giant trees. They were blind at sea without a lighthouse to guide them, adrift and at the mercy of the uneven forest floor, with no way of knowing what lay in front of them.

"Anyone know where we're going?" Cody asked.

Mia pointed back the way they had entered. "If that is where we fell, then we just have to keep going straight, and we'll hit the smoke."

They hit a hill. In the rain, their feet slipped on the leaves as they hiked upwards. Despite their ponchos, rain seeped in through all openings. Rick's weight—220 pounds of solid muscle—was dragging Cody down. He looked over at Mia; her face was covered in sweat he could see even in the rain, and she was silently panting. She didn't complain despite her obvious pain. Rick just stared off into the distance, his mind lost somewhere in the mist.

Cody slipped on a patch of loose leaves, and all three of them fell forward.

Rick yelled and threw a fistful of forest debris at Cody. "Fuck you, man, you did that on purpose!"

Cody, with dead foliage and dirt in his hair, stood and wiped the mud off of his glasses with his shirt.

"I didn't do it on purpose; I slipped."

Rick scowled and struggled to his feet with Mia's help.

A wall of cloud passed through the forest, engulfing them. Anything beyond a few feet in front of their eyes was obscured. Cody could see the outlines of his friends, but the passing white wisps obscured their features. In a moment, they were all transported to a world without details, without form, without direction. The rain turned to freezing sleet as it lashed out against them. It poured so hard, they could no longer hear what the others had to say. They were all drenched, but Rick shivered the most violently.

Cody swallowed the earlier accusation and gave Rick his own poncho. He tried to refuse it but, under Mia's stern glance, accepted it. Cody gave Rick his shoulder, and they started up the hill once more in silence.

After a short while, they reached the top. The mist was thicker here. They moved slowly to avoid running into a tree or veering off a sudden drop. Being so close to each other gave Cody the extra warmth he needed now that his white T-shirt was soaked. Rick had stopped shaking, yet he still gritted his teeth and pursed his lips.

The mist lifted until they could make out the shapes of the surrounding trees. Cody hadn't noticed it before, but there was a shimmer about them, a slight reflection of light that danced across the trees, like the light from a swimming pool at night, casting its glow in bouncing waves. Cody neither knew nor much cared to know where the light came from.

They came upon a large stone and set Rick on it, taking a moment to catch their breath. Surrounding the rock were small pools of water created by the rain. They took out their water bottles and filled them to the brim. The water was murky, and Cody nearly retched at the thought of what diseases lay inside the bottles. The torture of the humidity and of carrying Rick pushed his body past the revulsion, and he drank.

The rain lessened to a light kiss. Some of the mist lifted even more, and now Cody could see most of the hilltop. He left the other two on the rock to have a look around.

Maybe I can see more of the valley from up here?

He walked twenty feet away, maintaining sight of his friends, and came to what he thought was the edge of the hill. He could see nothing of the valley. Just more vague, dark shapes hiding in the eternal grey expanse. He turned to walk back when something caught his eye.

It was a large shadow under some vegetation. Something appeared to be hiding under it, just as a child might hide under blankets, thinking they've fooled their parents, even with their feet sticking out.

Cody moved over to it and pulled away some vines.

"Guys. I found a car."

They gave him an amused and unbelieving stare.

"No way," Rick said.

Mia ran over, leaving Rick on the stone.

"Holy shit," she said.

It was the burned remains of some kind of Jeep. The tires were gone, as was any glass. Dark brown rust and black charred flakes had replaced whatever color it once was. Something had peeled back the roof, leaving only a few jagged edges. Some lines—ten of them, to be exact—were etched onto the dashboard and ran across to the side of the car. Cody put his trembling hands over the marks, a near-perfect match.

"Well, what is it?" Rick called out.

Mia described to him what she saw . The wavering in her voice caused Cody unease.

"I don't like this," she said.

"People toss their shit out all the time," Rick answered.

"Not in the middle of the woods like this," Cody said. "Look around. Where is the road that brought it here? And why burn it unless you're trying to get rid of something? Like erase something. Maybe that's what that smoke is. We could be walking in on someone getting rid of evidence."

"Guys, that's dumb. We're in Japan; there's no drug ring gang shit like that here. It might just be someone getting rid of their trash. You know, not wanting to pay a fee or whatever for it."

Mia and Cody said nothing. They returned to the stone, resumed their positions under Rick's armpits, and continued on. They passed by the ruined shell of the Jeep. Cody's eyes lingered on it as they walked on, pondering the meaning of the ten lines. The mist lifted even more and revealed a set of jizo now and then, scattered about the forest floor as if some child had thrown their toys around the house with no care to where they landed. Cracks marred their faces, splitting their serene smiles into awful screams of terror.

Some had strange symbols carved on their foreheads. They were circles, like crude eyes or even the sun. Someone had vandalized them in the same way as the shrine back by the ledge had fallen from.

Thinking about these little shattered stone men haunted Cody's mind. But not as much as the ten lines that marked the inside of the car.

Not marked, scratched.

The marks lined up perfectly with the shape of two human hands.

6

T he rain stopped.

Some rays of light stole their way through the clouds and landed on Cody's face. He closed his eyes and let the warmth sink in. Two seconds later the sensation was gone, replaced by the touch of the cold.

The light was a tease. They were all still soaked, walking along a ridge at the top of the hill where they discovered the car. Cody reflected on the implications of the ten lines, yet said nothing. Who would listen to him anyway?

They carried on in silence, the only sound the squelch of their feet against the leaves and the drops of water falling from gigantic branches overhead.

"My dad is going to kill me," Rick said, his grimaced face sandwiched between Cody and Mia. Cody glanced at him sideways but said nothing. Mia also remained quiet.

"I'm always screwing things up. He paid for this trip, did you know that?" Cody shrugged—Rick did give him his ticket. He had assumed it came from Rick's wallet, not dear old dad's. "Not directly. I was supposed to use the money to go back to school. 'Go and make something of yourself,' he said. 'Grow up and do something with your life,' he said. Well, he was right about that. I'm always fucking everything up."

"That's not true," Mia said.

"No, it is. Look at where we are now. It's my fault. Everything I touch turns to shit."

His voice quaked and then cracked as he spoke.

Cody fought the urge to say, "I told you so." The only words he could manage to let out were, "It's okay." The words were limp and lacked power. Rick's falling face showed that he also felt nothing in them. Cody had never heard Rick apologize before, and while he knew he had issues with his father, Rick had never once talked so plainly about it. The emotional nakedness put Cody ill at ease. Rick had a rare moment of opening up and was left with no one to answer him. He might never get this chance again.

The wet stamping of leaves beneath their feet became a tapping sound against concrete. They couldn't see the road—the grass had grown too thick — but they could feel the solidness of it.

"This leads somewhere. We are getting out of here, baby," Rick said. His former optimism returned to him in force.

"Maybe. It looks old and out of use, though," Cody said in a decibel barely above a whisper. Whenever this road had last seen traffic, gas was probably $1 a gallon. Now, it seemed disgustingly out of place here in the deep woods.

Rick pointed out a short bamboo tree that had been broken in half and now lay on the ground.

"You guys take a break. I think I'll try this out for a while." He picked it up and leaned against it like a staff. "This will work. Thanks for all your hard work, men," Rick saluted and bowed.

Nobody laughed. But at least they wouldn't have to break their backs holding him up anymore. The relief that came over Cody was instant. It had gotten warmer; it wasn't raining, and now he didn't have to support the dick that got them lost in the first place. In his mind, Cody cursed Rick. It was his fault that they were there, lost in a foreign country, out in uncharted territory. It was also Cody's fault too, if he was being honest. He had known the smart thing to do at that moment, as in "don't fucking jump on unstable ledges," but he, typically, said and did nothing. At least Mia had tried.

If it weren't for the feel of the road on his shoes, Cody would never have guessed a road existed at all. A signpost came into view. It was probably bright green at one point but had now turned a sour yellow and a sickly orange with rust, decay, and fungus. Beyond the sign, the trees receded, and soon a town came into view. It was below them, down the sloping road. Beyond the settlement, in the woods that continued on the other side of it, they could see smoke in the air.

They were on the right path after all. Red shaded the scene below. The sun was setting and turned into a fiery crimson orb through the filter of the hazy sky.

The town was a small place, a hamlet of about ten one-story buildings. No one was on the streets. From a distance, it didn't even really look like a town; it looked more like Angkor Wat, a ruin swallowed by the jungle long ago. The buildings were modern, though. Some power lines stood diagonally above the ground, leaning against the buildings. The few visible lines were hung, detached from their posts, like impotent tentacles. Massive spiderwebs wrapped around them, almost as if they kept them from falling to the ground.

They walked down the road and entered the village.

Dead vines wrapped around the buildings, embracing them tightly in their tendrils. The shards of former windows littered the streets. Iron bars were slotted in their place like jagged teeth, each one bent out and away from the windows. The front doors were boarded up. The planks were shattered and scattered about as if they were forcibly torn off, with only a few remaining in place.

Life-size dolls made of straw lay in the fields nearby. Whatever grew there once was now wild grass. The dolls were green with mold and had smiles stitched onto their faces. Cody walked by one and stepped closer to see it. The eyes were black beads, and the dress was a tattered blue material. It was torn and shredded and even had burn marks on it. Yet it smiled. An eternal smile born on a dead face that had never known life.

Deep purple splashes were streaked across the main road, where the tall grass thinned out enough to see the concrete. The color was both vivid and faded at the same time. It ran along the entire street and led away from the town, into the fields, toward where the smoke was still rising. Most of the homes were covered in several feet of grass, but one of them had a clear front yard. Cody could see the purple-rust color spilling out of the front door to join the stream in the street. The door of that house lay in pieces on the dead lawn. One of its walls had collapsed in on itself.

"Creepy place," Mia muttered.

"And nobody home, great," Rick replied.

"It looks like something happened here." Cody felt the familiar weightlessness of another hyperventilation episode about to hit. "That's blood on the street. It's old, but it's blood. And those doors and windows look broken into."

Rick raised his eyebrows and smiled with only his upper teeth showing. "Sure, maybe." He kept on walking.

Mia looked back at Cody. "Yeah. But it looks like it happened a long time ago."

A deep shadow stretched over the town. The woods in front of them were now shrouded in darkness. The sun had set beneath the mountains behind them.

Rick stopped his pace and rested on his staff. Even though he was only thirty-four, he looked aged and shriveled as he held himself up. He said, "We have to stop for now. Too dark to keep going. We'll get more lost or hurt. Let's set up camp."

Cody wanted to protest. The town creeped him out. But he agreed. It would be stupid to keep on moving at night in the woods, and he was done with making mistakes.

They unpacked the tent and pitched it next to a looming house, the only one that wasn't sagging and drooping like a bent-over hag. Hung up their wet clothes inside their tent and changed into drier ones, which were made damp even from inside their packs—the humidity was inescapable. They ate the trail mix and protein bars they had brought along. They also had some instant ramen, but their hunger refused to let them wait until they got some water boiling. They ate it raw. After gorging themselves on snacks, all they needed was a fire. It was fucking freezing.

"Everything is wet; we have nothing to start a fire with," Mia said. "Unless this shitty portable stove is enough to warm us up."

She looked despondently over the object she had just taken out of her pack before putting it back. Cody glanced through the open door of the house next to their tent. The darkness of the entrance was impenetrable and uninviting. "There might be something dry inside," he said.

"Well then, go get some," Rick said. He was lying down inside the tent, his leg propped up on his pack.

Cody hesitated and didn't move. Mia sighed and stood up. "I'll go."

She went inside the house with her flashlight. The two men could hear her rummaging around. Some objects fell to the ground, and she cried in pain as she probably smacked her head against something. A few minutes later, some pieces of what was once a dresser came flying out of the dark doorway.

"There, done and done." She came out of the house, bouncing and smiling like a cheerleader.

Cody helped gather the pieces, finding some old cloth wrapped around one of the boards. Mia took the stove from her pack, turned it on, and used the open flame to ignite the material. Soon after, they had a fire going.

Cody tried not to look Mia in the eye. To her credit, she did not call him a pussy. To Rick's credit, he did so quietly and only once.

They were warm, and their gear had dried some. They all slept in the one tent they had brought, flap open, so some of the heat from the fire could enter. Rick was snoring. Mia's eyes were closed, and she lay still. Cody was sitting up and staring into the dark as the fire died down to ashes.

The stars were bright. It was here that he noticed that the mist had lifted completely. The sky was clear, and the lights of heaven burned fiercely in silver hues. Cody had never seen so many stars in his life. They lit up the ground around the ghost town in their brilliance, not as bright as daylight, but nearly so.

He thought for a moment that a full moon must be out, but he couldn't locate it. The light was strange, unnatural, and far brighter than should have been possible.

The forest beyond the town, however, remained dark and inscrutable.

At first, he thought it was a final ember from the dying fire he saw in that darkness. Then he realized it was out there, in the woods, and a good deal away. It was a tiny speck of dancing orange light in the distance. It came from the direction of the smoke trail. It was firelight, of that he had no doubt, but what it implied was beyond him. Was it the source of the smoke they had seen? Was it a group of campers? A functioning town?

As Cody stared at the light, minutes passed, and it did not waver. His eyelids became heavy. Just before he fell asleep, he thought he heard something. A beat. A deep, rhythmic pounding that at first felt like his own heartbeat. But it wasn't from his body; it too was from somewhere out there, near the distant firelight. Another sound accompanied the beat.

It was like the wind.

A high-pitched whistle like the rush of wind through a tight tunnel.

But it was more... *human* than that.

His eyelids shut. Sleep took him.

Cody backed out of the bathroom fast and turned to escape that dank and dark apartment. He was going to leave and never come back. He stopped when a gurgling, bubbling sound came from the woman. Cody looked over his shoulder and saw she was sitting upright, a smile plastered on her face. She opened her eyes, hollow and black and endless. From deep within, somewhere beyond that infinity of space, a silver light burned.

She opened her mouth, blood spilling out as if from an overflowing cup. Her face changed. Became white as snow, with lips red as fire, stained from the overflow of her mouth.

She whispered one word to him: "Soon."

7

The sunrise came filtered through another gray sky. The mist again consumed the clarity of the previous night. It lit up the valley in the same way a California fire, shrouded in smoke, would amplify the sun into a greenhouse death ray. There was no more rain. Today was going to be hot.

They woke up, ate what was left of their food, and began breaking down their camp. Rick couldn't stand without Mia lifting him off the ground. She rolled up his pant leg and saw that the skin had turned a deep purple.

He leaned against his staff and waved her away from him, refusing any more help. He swayed and gnashed his teeth in pain as he watched the other two pack up. When they finished, they walked out of the abandoned town, through the field of tall grass, and into the tree line once more.

The smoke signal was stronger than it had been yesterday. Thicker. As if whatever fire had fed it had reignited overnight.

Cody thought about telling the other two what he thought he had seen and heard during the night. But he wasn't even sure if it was part of his dreams or not. Rachel's bloody face came into his mind, and he shuddered, feeling cold despite the sweltering atmosphere.

At least I know that was a dream.

They walked through a thick patch of trees, brushing giant fern leaves out of their faces. After what felt like twenty minutes of silent marching, they came into an open field across from two mammoth trees that may have lived for hundreds or even thousands of years. They were so wide that even if the three friends linked arms and tried to encircle them, they wouldn't even get close. Their bark was smooth and white and wrapped in a single thick rope with strips of white paper hanging off it.

The wooden monsters stood on either side of a dirt path that ran between them, the first hiking trail they had seen since yesterday morning. On the trees, symbols were carved into their bright flesh. They didn't look like the Japanese symbols they had seen during the past week of their stay in the country. Those characters were more complicated, more filled out, and more nuanced. These were crude and resembled a child's attempt at drawing stick figures to represent the things they saw around them, more like prehistoric cave paintings.

There were pictures of animals, maybe a dog or a cow or some kind of quadrupedal beast. There were clouds with lines falling from them. That was easy: rain. Then came one symbol that Cody couldn't understand. He could see a stick-figure person walking up a set of stairs in one, with objects at the top that looked like fire, or the sun. The pictures were a story being told in simple images, yet they kept the stylistic flair of Japanese.

They were to Japanese what the cavemen were to modern man, predecessors of what was to come.

Mia stopped and placed her hand on the image of the fire-sun. She lingered and seemed lost in it.

"Babe, what are you doing?" Rick asked.

She shook herself out of the trance. "What? Nothing, I don't know, I just... felt like I've seen this somewhere before."

She pulled herself away from the carvings and rejoined the two men. Nobody spoke afterward. Cody didn't mention the last image he had seen before they passed the trees, one of a stick figure person dancing in the middle of the flames with what looked like a giant eye above it.

Beneath their shambling gait, the leaves and dirt of the path gave way to stone. Potholed and cracked, it was covered in the debris of the woods, but at least it was a human-made path. The trees on either side of it spread out further and further as if the forest was fleeing from its presence.

In their stead, stone figures appeared alongside the road, mostly covered in moss and broken into pieces. Cody couldn't tell what they were, save for one. It was intact, an image of what looked like a man on his knees, sword clipped to his side. It was similar to a samurai but wore a mask made of several cracked human skulls stitched together across its face. Four skeletal limbs extended from the mask, each one bent at an opposing angle from the other.

Aside from the samurai statue, the scene looked more Roman than it did Japanese. From what he understood, Cody thought most buildings in Japan were made of wood and didn't survive the centuries of aging or the disaster of World War II. Here there were stone columns and broken-down archways, clearly ancient, covered in some archaic script.

The smoke came into view once more, straight ahead, behind a set of more titanic trees that formed a wall blocking the path. Each tree had the same markings etched into its sides as the ones at the beginning of the path. There was one gap in the tree-wall big enough to squeeze through. Cody and Mia leaned Rick against a tree and pushed themselves halfway through. Rick sat down and faced away from Cody. Cody then grabbed him by the waist and pulled him in, and they spilled out on the other side.

"Fuck," Rick said, clutching his ankle.

Cody stood up, leaving Rick to rest on the ground, and looked around. Mia sat on the ground with Rick. They were in a circular clearing; tall trees rimmed the entire perimeter, with a dirt road leading in on the opposite side. Charred remnants of cars, buses, and motorcycles littered the ground. They were blackened and rusted over. There were at least a dozen vehicles, though most had been reduced to bits and pieces scattered across the meadow.

Rick looked over at Cody. "It's a junkyard, has to be."

A dozen cars, a dozen individuals, or a dozen families? This could just be a junkyard, the final resting place for some nearby village's unwanted vehicles.

"Then why are they all burned?" Cody asked no one in particular. And no one in particular decided to answer.

A junkyard? No, that wasn't it. You don't hide cars in the middle of the forest and burn them, unless you are trying to erase a trace of something. How did they even get here? There was no opening in the perimeter large enough for some of the bigger cars.

At the center of the field was the source of the smoke, though now it had been reduced to nothing more than what Cody's dad could produce whenever he tried to grill steaks on the BBQ. The smoldering was at the top of a set of stone stairs, worn down and aged. The stairs formed a four-sided pyramid, with stairs on each side, the top ending with a flat surface instead of a point. It was three stories tall. Its appearance resembled a Mayan pyramid or a Babylonian ziggurat more than it related to anything Japanese.

Cody ascended the stairs. His legs shaking with each step, he could only hear the pounding of his heart as he went up to find the source of the smoke. Mia ran up and joined him.

The smell hit him before he saw anything, and with it, he knew what would be revealed. He had been to enough outdoor cookouts with his dad's overcooked steaks to know the smell of burning meat and fat. The sweet but greasy smell of flesh that it gives off when it sizzles and fries.

As Cody reached the last step, he tripped and fell. Looked back, and saw that the step was missing a foot-sized section in the top right corner. He got up, turned around, and saw a black mass at the center of the smoke. He waved some clouds away and coughed. Bent down, under the smoke, and could see what lay beneath.

He couldn't tell if it was a man or a woman, but it was definitely an adult human. In some places, scorched flesh clung to the bone; in others it had melted away completely, revealing the skeleton underneath. The body was on its knees, hands lifted towards the sky, fingers splayed wide open. Steel chains bound its wrists and were cemented to the ground. The body was in the same position as the statue at the ledge. It was dead but frozen in place. It was almost as if the thing were pulling against the chains.

Could rigor mortis have done that? Just leave a body frozen in that position?

The jaws were opened, Cody imagined from screaming, but there was a hint of a smile, as far as a skeleton can smile. It was almost as if the horrid thing before him was happy to be where it was. A gold cross lay across its neck, fused into the black skin by the heat. Cody bent over and vomited onto his shoes. Mia's face drained itself of all color. Her knees shook so hard they actually made a knocking sound.

When he picked himself up, he noticed a ring around the body. A circle of ash and scorch marks, as if some rocket engine had landed on the platform, making it ground zero. He looked out over the valley from his new vantage point. In the ocean of gray, he could see two other pyramids rising above the mist, each one sending its own smoke signal into the sky. Behind the larger of the two, there was a looming mountain. A great smoldering mass devoid of any vegetation. From its summit, a thick ashy cloud poured out into the sky.

"What's going on? See anything?" Rick's voice snatched Cody out of his paralytic state. Without a word, he ran back down the stairs. Mia didn't move. Cody turned back and grabbed her sleeve. "Come on, we should leave."

She stared into the ashes of the body without blinking. A faint silver light reflected in her eyes. Trick of the light? Cody shook her. She snapped back to attention.

"What?" she stammered, her body trembling slightly.

Cody held her arm and lower back and guided her down the steps. He could feel her shaking the entire way down.

"Whoa, look who is getting all friendly in my absence," Rick said.

"There's a dead body up there. Burned," Cody let out a single gasp.

Rick smiled through his teeth. "Dude, stop fucking with me." Cody's face rippled with shakes; tears were on the verge of falling down his face. Rick's smile vanished.

"Are you serious? Shit. Like an accident or something?"

"It had chains on its wrists; no way it's a fucking accident," Cody said.

Off in the distance, outside the circle of trees, a deep bass reverberated. The thunder of its bellow repeated in a rhythmic, wild, and untamed beat. Birds took flight from their nests at the drumming. It was the same sound Cody had heard last night.

A horn blew. Cody remembered its sound, like a conch shell he and his sister had forced their parents to buy for them on a trip to San Diego. The last time he heard one, he was with his mother out back behind the house during one of his dad's failed BBQs. Weird how this one memory was so relatable to the present moment. They had just purchased one and sounded it off at sunset. His mom was a bit of a hippie and thought it was a good way to welcome the end of the day. The sound brought an odd joy then. Now, terror fell with the call.

The wave of sound grew closer, coming to a fever pitch of excitement. Several figures entered the clearing from the far side of the pyramid. Cody and Mia grabbed Rick and pulled him down to the ground. They crawled over to a nearby burnt-out husk of a truck and slid themselves under it.

Five people came into view on the dirt path and walked towards the pyramid. The first three leading the way were young men with toned muscles, about Rick's size. And that was saying something—Rick was stacked. They were carrying drums, smacking sticks into the leather with fury, sweat flying off their faces. Another man followed the procession and soon made his way to the front. He had shoulder-length grey hair, despite his youthful face, and held a conch shell, stopping every five feet to sound its call.

They all wore black clothes, like robes but shorter, exposing their knees, with red designs that looked like waves curling up their chests. They had wrapped red bandanas with black circles in the center on their foreheads.

Next to the man with the shell was a woman. She wore a robe of red and white, like splattered blood over fresh snow. She wore a hat, circular and wide, made of straw, stretching out past her shoulders with a thin white veil. Bells hung from her ankles and wrists, singing out a slight chime with each methodical step. The rim of the hat hid her eyes, but her lips shone forth in brilliant red.

Everyone stopped at the steps of the pyramid except for the woman and the man holding the shell. They walked up the monument, one step in front of the other, with purpose.

Cody couldn't see what happened next; the truck's underbelly cut off the view. He heard the shell blow one more time. He saw the wide straw hat re-emerge at the top of the pyramid. It bent down towards where the burning corpse would have been.

Fuck this angle, I can't *see anything.*

The hat rose once more. He glimpsed the woman's cheeks. Was that black stain there before? He couldn't tell.

The shell blew once more. The drumming stopped. The hat disappeared and came back into view a minute later at the bottom of the stairs. The procession walked back towards the trees with no more beats of the drums. The only sign they had been there was the cloud of dust kicked up by their feet as they marched.

After a few minutes of holding their breath, they exhaled. Cody helped Rick out from under the truck and leaned him up against it.

"The fuck was that?" Rick asked.

The drumming hadn't left Cody's mind. The frenzied beats were in tune with those of his heart. He struggled to hear what Rick was saying until he asked the same question again.

"I don't know, but I heard those drums last night."

Mia stared wide-eyed at him. "What? Then why didn't you tell us?"

"I just didn't know whether I actually heard them or not."

Rick's face became grave as a headstone. "The fuck, man, what is wrong with you?"

Cody could feel their eyes on him. His voice faltered in his throat, yet he continued, "I also saw a fire, I think; it would have been coming from here. And..." He trailed off. Mia yelled at him to finish the sentence while Rick stared at him unfeelingly. "And I think I heard somebody screaming. It could've been the wind, but if it wasn't, then... the body we found could've been someone who was murdered last night."

"No, don't believe it. I heard nothing last night, did you, Mia?" She shook her head. Rick went on, "This is insane! What, these people are a cult going around killing people? There has to be an explanation for what we just saw. Maybe it was some kind of funeral procession. Don't lose your minds over this, guys."

A funeral? Not out of the realm of possibility. But the red flags were mounting into an ever-growing heap. Cody would rather hike in the opposite direction and face the wilderness alone, even if he had to break every nail climbing back up the cliff face.

But he said and did nothing.

"So... where do we go now?" Mia asked.

"Let's just talk to those people. I mean, is there really any other choice?" Rick said.

There is, Cody thought. *Fucking back the way we came.*

No one spoke up. Rick led the way into the woods after the procession.

They had only been walking for a few minutes into the forest when the bright sky suddenly turned dark.

A thick, black, industrial-smoke-colored cloud passed overhead, blotting out what little sunlight there was. It happened in an instant. Everything was nearly pitch black at what could be no later than the early afternoon.

"The hell is this?" Rick shouted.

They couldn't move without risking further injury. The sound of the drums picked up again from not too far away. The drumming came close, moved near their side, and passed by them. Rick spoke up, but Cody clasped his mouth shut.

"What the hell?" Rick said in a muffled tone.

Cody pointed in the direction of the sound of the drums. Silver lights bobbed up and down like fireflies. They floated along in pairs, stopping and scanning the area around them. They were so bright that they lit up the immediate area nearest to them. Cody saw the silhouettes of legs and bodies as they walked by.

Were those eyes?

Rick stopped speaking altogether.

The lights were like the shine an animal has when a beam of light reflects off its eyes at night. These silver eyes were different in one respect: there was no obvious light source to reflect off, and the light seemed to come from within them, emanating outward. For a moment, just for the briefest of seconds, Cody felt the eyes rest on him. Whether they could see him (and Cody thought there was no way they didn't see him) they moved on and joined the rest of the eyes as they became enveloped in the shadows of midday night and the fading drumming sounds.

When all became silent, Rick spoke up, "Okay, maybe things are a little weird, I'll admit it. But let's not freak out."

"Don't freak out?" Cody's voice cracked as he spoke. "Rick, it's the middle of the day, and it's dark as night out. And those lights we saw, those were eyes. Things are not just a little weird; things are fucked up beyond saving. We need to go back the way we came and wait by the cliff face. I'm not taking another step further into this damn forest."

Rick had a genuine look of shock on his face as Cody spoke. "We don't even know where we are right now. We should stay put until we can see something at least. What do you think, Mia?"

Their eyes had adjusted just enough to make out each other's faces. Mia's eyes were miles away, focusing on some distant world neither of the two men could hope to understand. Once again, a faint reflection was cast in her eyes. A glimmer, a spark, then it faded away.

"Babe, you okay?"

She shook her head as if shocked by a taser. "What? Yeah, yeah, I'm fine. What should we do? I don't think it matters. I have a feeling, this dragging cold feeling, that we're never leaving here again."

"Bullshit, we're not." Rick held her hand. "I'm getting us out of this."

"We don't even know what 'this' is," Cody said.

They stayed where they were and met the enduring midday night in silence. The dark air was heavy with foreboding. All Cody could hear was his labored breathing and his blood pumping forcefully in his neck. Aside from that, no ensects buzzed, and no animals called to one another. It was as still as the depths of space. Cody started to fall asleep. Rick slapped his shoulder and whispered, "Something is out there."

A faint red glow was on the horizon, like a bloody sunrise. It moved steadily between the trees. It was a far way off. It was vibrant in its crimson glow. It turned away from their position and disappeared further away. For just a moment, Cody thought he saw something inside the light. A shadow of some figure was moving within the light, or was the light coming from it?

Cody's eyelids grew heavy. The weight of stress came crashing down on him.

He fell asleep.

8

M s. Tanaka, known as Hiromi-chan by the young bartenders and hosts in the city, especially by Taro-kun (oh how she loved Taro-kun with his plastic-perfect features), put her feet up on a pillow shaped like a cat in a top hat.

The gaudy purple polish on her toenails glinted under the flickering lights of the apartment.

Smoke from her cigarette engulfed her face. She liked it like that. Sooty, grimy, and bad for your health. She didn't need another doctor telling her to exercise more or to stop eating fried chicken. And if he were to dare say to stop smoking, she might just actually go to jail for murder. If she were to stop, she supposed life just wouldn't be worth living anymore.

She leaned back on the tatami floor with a groan that was worthy of an Oscar. The cloud of smoke followed her on the descent.

"Hey, *Oyaji,*" she said, shouting over the buzz of the talking heads on TV.

"What?" came the disgruntled reply from deep within the kitchen.

"Grab me another beer." No "please" needed. No "please" wanted. Her husband of forty years was beyond caring about such things, and she knew it. She was also beyond saying them. This didn't mean they didn't love each other; their love was the kind that survived countless lack of please-s and thank you-s. It even survived the death of their youngest daughter at only four years old.

A short and pudgy man waddled into the living area. He walked past the wall of cat clocks in slow motion. There were pink cats, red cats, and, above all, purple cats. Each clock was unique in its grotesque portrayal of how a feline could be twisted into a diabetic coma-inducing state of cuteness. The one thing they all had in common was that they let out a high-pitched meow exactly at noon and exactly at midnight.

"*Hai.*" The man dropped her beer next to the cat pillow. She swiveled on the ground without standing and scooped it up with her right leg. She felt proud of the accomplishment.

"It's warm," she complained.

"So what?"

"So, get me another, asshole."

The man grunted assent and went back to the kitchen. What he did there all night while she watched karaoke battle re-runs she neither knew about nor cared for. A fly landed on her knee.

Smack!

The purple swatter shot out from her side and slew the beast faster than even she could see. She was just that good.

"Ugh." The man dropped another beer on the cat pillow. This time it was cold. Ms. Tanaka grunted approval to her husband, and he grunted back. All was well with the world and was as it should be.

She turned her attention back to the singer on TV. Some man in a suit was destroying her favorite *enka* song, *Tsugaru Kaikyo Fuyugeshiki.* She smacked the TV with the swatter. Unfortunately, he didn't disappear. At least he had a perfect smile to look at. White, straight teeth— the stuff of dreams.

She did her best to forget the tribulations of the day. She barely spoke any English; she had never even been outside Japan before. Somehow, she wound up as a tour guide for fat, rich tourists, bussing them around the mountains all day.

She detested the job. It was mostly okay until disasters like today. Mud-covered foreigners flopped around the ground while she tried to herd them onto the trail. She nearly died hiking that thing herself. Took her over six hours to complete it. By the end, she was reduced to a blob of sweat and ruined makeup.

She took a bite of her chicken and a drag of her smoke. Washed it all down with her Asahi beer. The perfect combination for an imperfect day. Where was Taro-kun when she needed him?

Her imagination almost helped her forget the day. To forget the Chinese man gyrating as he stretched in neon spandex (she secretly liked the color, though), to forget the two white men and black girl who ran on ahead of everyone else like they owned the place, to forget the drunken Germans singing loudly on the ride home.

The man singing on TV failed the challenge. *Serves him right*, she thought. How dare he destroy such a national treasure on live television. *That smile, though, is beautiful.* She felt like she had seen another smile, a perfect smile on a handsome face, just recently. *Where was tha-*

"Hey," her husband bellowed from his secret kitchen lair.

"What?"

"You need to buy more pork on the way home tomorrow."

"You're home all day, why don't you?"

He didn't respond. She could hear the *chaching chaching* of a slot machine. Must be gambling away his retirement in online casinos, the bastard.

Maybe I should just quit my job and do that all day too.

"Idiot," she said.

"Ugh," he grunted.

Another fly landed nearby, on the TV, exactly on the perfect smile of the man now leaving the studio in near tears. She smacked it so hard that the machine rocked.

She turned it off, finished her fried food banquet, and passed out right there on the floor, some crumbs acting as a mini-blanket draped over her massive chest. As she dozed off, she dreamed of Taro-kun with his dazzling smile. His real smile was crooked, but she didn't mind. The man from the TV's smile was transplanted onto her favorite midnight snack's face. A perfect smile. Did I see one today? Not on TV, was it...

She sat up so fast that the crumbs flew off her spectacularly buoyant chest. Her husband dropped his casino-earning device in alarm.

"What happened?" he shouted.

It just now became clearer to her mind, the three empty seats on the bus ride home. How could she not have noticed then and there?

"I'm going to lose my job."

She almost smiled at the prospect. All thoughts of that smirk disappeared when she realized she might be held responsible for three foreigners getting lost on her private tour. She didn't even have the proper insurance to cover her ass.

She stood up with such speed, her husband let out a bewildered cry and dropped his phone for a second time.

Not on my watch, she thought.

She put on her jacket and left the apartment.

9

Cody woke with a start. His breath was wheezing, and there were tears on his cheeks. Another nightmare.

The black cloud had disappeared. What time was it? It felt like an entire day had passed when in reality it couldn't have been more than a few hours, could it? The forest lay still, save for the melancholy song of a few birds. The sounds were a welcome break from the unbearable silence of the afternoon night. Cody cracked his back with a grunt, the movement waking Rick. He had tears in his bloodshot eyes.

"You okay?" Cody asked.

Rick stared at him in stunned disquiet and said, "I had a nightmare is all."

"Me too. About Rachel." Cody surprised himself with the openness. "What was yours about?"

"My dad. He was yelling at me, as usual. Telling me I was a fuck-up this and a fuck-up that. But this time, he had these glowing eyes, like the ones we saw when it got dark last night, I mean, earlier today. Shit, this sky is messing me up. Anyway, he had these eyes, and I just felt them digging into me. And then he just leaned in and whispered, 'Soon'."

At this, Cody's eyes widened, and his heart quickened. "Rachel told me the same thing."

They stared at each other in silence.

"What does this mean? What the fuck is happening?" Rick asked as if Cody should know the answer.

Mia walked towards them from the bushes (she probably just peed) and said, "I saw my mom. She was a single mother raising me and my sisters. You know this, Rick. She was dating this asshole, an abusive drunk deadweight. He was in the dream too. He and my mom were standing over my baby sister's body, her blood all over their faces. They told me to join them. She... she also said, 'Soon.'"

Mia's voice was lifeless. She spoke as if reading a script.

They sat there, not speaking. They had no answers and no comfort to give one another.

Rick broke the silence. "Alright, let's walk. Same plan as before it got dark, let's find those people."

Cody paused. "I think we should go back the way we came. Whatever we saw earlier with the glowing eyes," Cody shuddered, "they went that way." He pointed to where they had seen the eyes disappear. "So I say we go in the opposite direction. There could be some kinds of animals out here that we don't want to mess with."

"And then what? There's no way to climb back up the mountain, genius." Rick stopped himself. "Sorry, I know we're stressed and that things look weird, but we know nothing about what's going on. I say we find those people and ask for help. They look weird and all, but that's it; they literally did nothing wrong. And of course, there are animals out here; it is the fucking forest, but nothing is going to hurt us, dude."

"If we retrace our steps back to where we fell, maybe somebody from the tour group has already let the police know, and if we just wait, I don't know, someone will find us," Cody said.

"Nobody's going to be there. Look, I know you're scared, but maybe what we saw were fireflies or some shit. And those people, maybe it was just a funeral thing, like I said. Our best bet is to keep moving to the road Mia saw across the valley or run into those people, whichever comes first."

Cody dug his nails into his palms. Rick's eyes were resolute and steady. Cody gave in. "Okay, maybe you're right. Sorry for overreacting. So where to?"

Rick thought for a moment. He pointed at something and said, "Do you see how there's an incline over there? It's a hill. We climb that and see what we can see from there. We'll be out of here in two, three hours tops, I promise."

"No, we won't make it," Mia said.

The men looked at her without a word.

"We're never getting out of here, I just know it." Her dull face began moving again, emotions flooding back into her features. "Sorry, I was just, I don't know–" she trailed off.

Rick and Cody exchanged looks. Rick spoke up, "It's okay, Mia, we're going to get out of here, I promise you. I'll do everything I can to fix this."

She nodded her head. Her eyes were glassy with tears, though none fell.

They walked towards the hill and started up the summit. It wasn't steep, and didn't look very promising in terms of how high it was. Cody didn't think they'd be able to see anything at all. Rick limped along with his stick, breathing heavily with each hop up the hill.

We really should just go back. We should never have left the spot where we fell; somebody would've come looking for us. Or maybe they wouldn't have. Maybe Rick was right.

He smiled at that thought. When had Rick ever been right about anything? But he had a way of getting them out of trouble, whether or not he was "right". Cody could trust that fact. Maybe what they had seen back at the pyramid was just some misunderstood cultural or religious thing. They were out in the middle of nowhere, in a foreign country, so these people probably just had some weird traditional way of doing things.

He wanted to believe this, but he couldn't. Some primal feeling deep within his bones told him they were in danger. Cody did all he could to silence that voice, but he couldn't shut out the white face of that woman with red lips, her cheeks smeared black. He couldn't shut out the silver eyes in the dark. The open jaw of the charred corpse.

They came to the crest of the hill. As expected, they could see nothing aside from more mist and treetops, except for one thing that stood out in the gray.

Rick hopped in excitement. "Cody, do you see that? What did I tell you?"

To their right, not too far off, sat a town. Not a derelict like the abandoned one yesterday, this one looked taken care of. They could see buildings clustered together, maybe a few hundred of them. The town was an island in the sea of clouds. They could see figures moving around— people flitting around the streets. A large mountain sat at one end of the town, vomiting smoke into the sky. It looked like it might be an active volcano. At the far end of the town, there was a paved road that disappeared into the forest, and just beyond that, a sloping hill that led into another mountain range.

"Dude, that road leads back out of here, I'm sure. And somebody down there has to have a cell phone," Rick said, joy bubbling up in each syllable he spoke.

Cody feared that the people they had seen earlier might have come from this town. Behind the town was the smoking mountain he had seen yesterday. In front of it, though he couldn't see it now, he knew there was another stone pyramid.

But even if those people came from this town, they could just be a group of crazies, assuming what they had seen was even nefarious. The town itself would have police, or phones, local schools, and all the trappings of respectable society, he told himself. They descended the hill and walked in the direction they thought would take them to the town. There was something resembling a trail. It was overgrown with grass, but it was definitely man-made. If they were lucky, it might just lead them where they wanted to go.

After an hour of hobbling through the forest, Cody wondered if they hadn't gotten lost again. All he could see was mist, and trees, and then more mist, and more trees. The mashing of wet leaves beneath his feet made him sick and uneasy. Rick refused both Cody and Mia's (though she no longer offered) help and limped on, grunting as he went, leaning on his bamboo staff.

Soon the ground became a flat dirt path. The sickening sound of the moist leaves had ended, as nearly as Cody's sanity almost did.

They came across a sign in Japanese. None of them knew what it said, but the red letters and exclamation points denoted importance. It was weather worn, most of the wood rotted, and half of the words faded. Beneath the officially painted letters, there were figures carved into the wood of the sign's post. They were identical to the ones they had seen back at the clearing. Crude stick figures of people, fire, and dancing.

Cody strained his ears for the sounds of drums and horns. But there was no sound save for the electric buzz of some unknown insect.

Rick started slowing down. His face was now a light shade of purple; sweat rained off his forehead.

"You don't look good; let's sit down for a moment," Mia suggested.

"No, I can keep going." Rick faltered in his speech, and his body swayed.

He fell face-first into the dirt.

Mia rushed to him and, with Cody's help, rolled him over. He was breathing and mumbling the word "dad" under his breath. Cody and Mia dragged him from behind and set him up against a rock. Cracked lines of blood formed Rick's lips, which made his face's purple seem even darker. Mia took out her water bottle, now mostly empty, and gave Rick its last dregs. She rolled up his pants and exposed his ankle. It inflated like a grotesque, rotten balloon.

After drinking Mia's water, Rick's eyes brightened sapphire-blue, his face returned to a semi-normal color, and he was picking himself back up, not without obvious strain.

"Alright, let's keep moving; that town can't be far away," Rick said.

Mia smiled and rubbed his back.

"Maybe you should rest some more," Cody suggested.

The couple ignored him and kept on walking.

Hours passed as they moved forward. Cody noticed out of his periphery that Rick was glaring at him.

"Do you need something?" Cody finally asked.

"You let me get away with too much, you know that?"

Cody looked away from him. "I don't know what you mean."

"Sure you do. You've always let me do stupid shit ever since we were kids. Remember how I kissed your prom date? Yeah, of course you do. And you just sat there and fucking let it happen, right in front of you."

Cody's face went hot.

"Whoa, babe, where's this coming from?" Mia said.

Cody agreed with her sentiments.

"And with Rachel," here Cody's face seethed with fire as Rick continued, "she was fucked up in the head from day one. And you just went with everything, just let her abuse you and lie to you about being pregnant. Then she goes and kills herself." Now Cody's face was volcanic. "Who just walks away from someone bleeding to death? No matter what Mia could ever do to me, I would never just leave her there, dying alone. So you fucked up by being with her in the first place and then fucked up even more by not helping her."

Mia tried to stop Rick's words from escaping his face with her hand but failed.

Cody snapped. "I know, alright. I know I'm a fucking piece of shit. But you know what? Didn't leave you back where we fell, did I? We wouldn't even be here if it weren't for you, don't forget that."

Rick laughed. "Yeah, a lot of help you've been."

Cody shoved Rick into a thorny bush.

"What the hell?" Rick yelled. Tears streamed down his face, and his lips, all chewed up, quivered. He was unraveling.

"I'm sorry. Here." Cody offered Rick his hand. Rick rejected it. Mia came over, but he pushed her hand away as well.

Rick seemed smaller now, somehow diminished. The brazen smile and the authoritative voice fell away. They were replaced by whimpers and wild eyes.

Rick got up by himself, his arms bearing fresh cuts from the thorns. He plastered on his perma-smile. He seemed delirious and lost in his faith that everything would work out if he just kept on grinning.

"Sorry, guys, I don't know what I... I'm just tired; let's forget it."

Cody wouldn't forget.

Cody's stomach rumbled and tied itself into a knot. All their food supplies were now gone. Or maybe it wasn't hunger but the onset of a vicious attack of diarrhea that would be sure to come soon. Cody thought that there could be no way of escaping the consequences of drinking out of the plentiful dirty puddles. He felt lightheaded, and his muscles moved as if through quicksand. He drooled as he thought of getting back to the hotel and grabbing a Snickers or even a carrot. He didn't think he could eat meat for a while. At least nothing grilled.

A gust of wind blew through the trees and blasted them in the face. A dark cloud filled the sky, and the hair on their arms stood tall. The forest was as dark as if it were night once again. The change came swiftly, so fast that it made Cody tense up as if he were going to get punched. This time, it wasn't pitch-black: the stars shone brightly above, through the clouds, providing light for their path.

Rick's smile, which he had been mindlessly wearing as he hiked, vanished. He bit his cracked lips so hard that they bled slightly.

"Fuck," he let out. His voice echoed in the dark air. "Fuck it, let's keep moving; the town can't be far away." Cody didn't move. Mia stepped back from where she was heading.

"Rick, this isn't normal. Nothing that is happening is normal. Look up, stars don't come out in the middle of the fucking afternoon, not like this," Mia said. "This is the second time this has happened; no way it's an eclipse or anything like that."

Rick didn't look up. "I don't know; I don't care. All I know is that the town can't be more than a mile away. Let's book it."

"No, this isn't right," Mia said. Her dark eyes reflected the starlight above; it was that bright.

"Come on, guys, don't lose the plot now; we're almost there," Rick said.

Something captured Cody's attention. An electric feeling in the air. He blocked out Rick's voice and heard, somewhere behind him, a high-pitched scream. Turning around, shushing Rick with his hand. He had heard it now, too. The screams were desperate, filled with pain and agony. From its direction, an orange light flickered softly through the trees. The smell of barbecue filled the air.

"Shit, do you think..." Mia's voice trailed off.

They knew without having to see. The screams, the light, and the images of the burned corpse from earlier flashed before Cody's mind. The smell of summer barbecues with his dad, forever ruined and tainted—if he ever got out to have it again, that is. No one moved towards the plea for help; no one dared.

It broke Cody's heart.

The sound of drums almost beat in tune with the screams, some kind of horrid melody. Beside the fire in the distance, pairs of silver lights bobbed up and down, in tune with the drums.

Is that coming from the town?

As soon as it had come crashing into their senses—the screams, the drums, and the lights — they all stopped. Nothing but the black stillness of the void. The stars seemed to glow brighter as the darkness in front of them deepened. The sky burned with a red light. Everything became filtered through that scarlet shade. It was as if someone had dipped the world in blood. The light was cold to the touch. Cody stopped.

He looked up.

There was a single red star that shone the brightest in the sky. It felt like its light was falling only in the area where they now stood, a spotlight that had sought them out and finally found them.

Something fell to the ground, far away from them, and shook the foundations of the forest like a bomb blast. They fell to the ground as it shook. The red light vanished from overhead. Yet now, off in the darkness, another red light came to life. It grew bigger, brighter, hotter.

"Is that... coming this way?" Rick let out.

They got up shakily off the ground, and each of them vomited. Cody's ribs hurt as if they were cracked. His insides felt unstable.

The red light moved closer to them.

They ran as best they could, given the shock to their systems. Even Rick ran or, rather, pole-vaulted his way after Cody and Mia. They dashed through the woods in the dark. The trees behind them crashed to the ground, the impact of their great bodies shaking the earth. Or was it something else that shook it? Another tree fell near them. Rick was lagging, yelling at them to wait.

They didn't.

The red light fell on them. It was cold to the touch, and it burned like ice. Everywhere that Cody's skin was exposed burned. He smelled the burning of hair—his hair. The flaming light lit up the path ahead, a blood-red trail through the trees. More trees came thundering down. The ground quaked in rhythm as if in tune with footsteps.

Footsteps? No fucking way.

One shake, a moment later another shake, one after the other, left foot, right foot. It came closer and closer as branches fell in front of them, on them.

Cody tried to glimpse what was behind them. He saw the trees shake and part before... something. A throbbing light, a mix of red and silver, shone through the spaces between the trees. And behind that light, inside of it, was a deep, shadowy form. It shouldn't have been possible, that combination of light and dark, yet there it was. The light walked; it moved and pushed obstacles out of the way; it was alive, and Cody caught a momentary sight of that shadow in the light, looking directly at him.

Cody and Mia came spilling out onto a road, a paved road, and fell face-first onto it. They rolled over and faced the woods they had just escaped. The thunder of pursuit ceased. They picked themselves up with knees of rubber, turned back, and came face to face with nothing. Some trees were still rocking back and forth but soon stopped. The light was gone. The stars hid themselves under the cover of mist, and the light of day burned through again.

Rick came into view, limp-running as best he could. He scowled at them and seemed ready to explode, the purple now having inflamed his face again. But he said nothing.

The darkness passed, and it was day again. It was still. A gentle, warm breeze flowed over them. They looked around. Behind them, the forest. The trees were no longer moving. Only their branches moved in the wind. If anything had actually been pursuing them, it was now gone. The sudden transition between flight and the serenity of the moment left them momentarily stunned.

In front of them was a road not overgrown with vegetation. In fact, it looked freshly constructed. At the end of the road, the clouds seemed to fold back to reveal a town. Right at the entrance of the town, there were several rice fields with a few men wading in the water, picking up the stalks. They looked up from their labor and waved and smiled, calling the trio over to them.

Rick smiled and waved back. His face was wild. Caked with blood, dirt, and a reddish hue. Anyone would be forgiven for thinking him a madman. The farmers came closer and passed a large green sign on the road. Under the Japanese symbols naming the town, there were some English letters.

They spelled out the name of the town: *Inunaki.*

IO

Rick started forward to meet the two farmers coming out to meet them. Cody put his hand out and rested it on Rick's chest.

"Stop. We don't know them. We don't even know what the fuck just happened back there."

"What happened is, I don't know, a storm? Yeah, that shit was intense, but look around, everything is back to normal."

"A storm?" Mia almost shrieked. "Then what the hell was that light? And those screams we heard right before?"

"And these guys over there could be a part of the group we saw at the pyramid," Cody said.

Rick raised his hands in front of his face as if defending himself against attackers. "Look, I don't know. Maybe it wasn't a storm, maybe it was a mass hallucination, aliens, ghosts, fuck if I know, but freaking out about that doesn't help us right now. And these guys, look at them. They look normal, this street is normal, everything is fucking normal now. This looks like a modern town connected by a road. Is there really any other option for us? Let's go ask them for a phone."

He approached the farmers, who were by now close enough to see the whites of their eyes. They were still in the field on the side of the road. Cody and Mia held back and exchanged glances. The men wore blue, loose-fitting clothes, with a white cloth draped over their heads and necks. Sweat gleamed on their skin. Water submerged their legs up to their mid-calves as they stood in the field. They held curved blades in one hand and rice stalks in the other.

"*Omae wa nani shiteiru*?" said one man, with a scruffy salt-and-pepper beard and a smile that caught the light.

"Sorry, we don't speak Japanese," Rick said. "We need a phone. Police! *PO-RI-SU*." He gestured widely, his hands mimicking talking on the phone.

The farmers exchanged glances and laughed. A hearty laugh came from deep in their stomachs.

"*Porisu?*" the bearded man said. "*Koko ni inai na. Aiko-san eh tsurete ageru. Eigo shaberu kara.*"

The bearded man dropped his tool and the rice stalk on the road and climbed out of the field. He wiped the sweat from his face and smiled so widely and so brightly, even Rick couldn't hope to match it. Rick grabbed the man's hand and shook it. The man's eyes turned sour, but he kept the mask of a smile on.

"Thank you, *arigatou*, much-o *arigatou* my man." Rick kept shaking the man's hand until the latter squirmed away. The man smiled some more and waved at the trio to follow him. Cody's heart weighed him down to where he stood, not wanting to budge an inch. Mia had left his side and rejoined Rick's. Cody looked back at the trees, still swaying gently in the wind. If he had to choose between standing there alone or going along with this strange man, he would choose the latter.

The farmer led them through a stone toori gate that arched over the entrance to the town. It was fractured down the middle, with the two posts leaning away from each other. Statues stood on either side of the gate: not a frog, lion, or fox, as they were used to seeing on their trip.

These were a medley of a creature with a snake's head, the body of a bird, a turtle's shell on its back, and it seemed to be covered in scales.

Red paint leaped up their chests like fire; gold washed down their heads like melted metal. They had proud faces, the snake eyes closed as if sleeping, the fangs bared as if ready to strike.

A bell tower stood inside the gate, to their left. The bell itself looked like it weighed at least 1,000 pounds. It was bronze and had carvings of an unknowable scene. A ladder went up the tower to a platform where the bell rested. The tower rose just slightly above the nearby trees.

Rice, potatoes, cabbage, and other assorted vegetable fields lay on either side of the road they walked on. Dragonflies hovered about, and a sweet smell of flowers, mixed with some heavy incense, danced in the air.

The farmer took them to a shrine just on the outskirts of town, inside the gate, and past the bell tower. He pointed to it and left them. The three-sided gate to the shrine was vibrant in red, black, and yellow hues. Statues of the strange snake-headed creature stood on either side of the gate. A young woman was on her knees before the altar, tending to the incense inside. She rose and faced the newcomers as they stood at the entrance.

Her face was snow, her hair the night, her lips fire. A small mole rested on her left cheek.

"Hey, whoa, hi," Rick sputtered out like a sprinkler.

The woman smiled without showing her teeth. "Welcome," she said in English, her voice coming to Cody's ears like a soft rain, washing away the filth of the world.

"We need help. We're lost, my friend is injured, and there's something out there," Cody pointed back towards the woods. "Something chased us. I don't know what it is. Can you help us?"

He stopped and had to catch his breath.

She stood still, her crimson smile floating in space. "Oh, I'm sorry to hear that. Don't worry, because from now on you'll be safe here." Her voice was singsong, but her eyes remained steady and unblinking.

She lifted her left arm and extended her hand out to them. She clothed herself simply in jeans and a black shirt and wore a pair of white running shoes. It shocked Cody to see something so modern out here in this surreal valley. She looked as if she could fit in anywhere and wouldn't stand out on a city street. Yet her movements barely registered with the eye. They were fluid and graceful, and they were courtly, regal even.

"We found a body as well. It was all burned up. We saw a woman there, too. She looked like you," Mia said, her eyes narrowed at the woman.

Cody hadn't even considered that she was the same woman he had seen at the pyramid. That woman was from an ancient and obscure time. The one in front of him was from his world, from a world he could understand.

"It's horrible to hear that you had to see that." The woman took a gliding step forward with a concerned expression on her face. "We have a tradition here where we burn our dead. You must have heard that is how we Japanese do things—cremation, I mean. We just have a different sort of way of going about it than most. Still, it must have been most unpleasant to come across that. And yes, you would have seen me there. I'm a priestess in this community. I lead all rites and ceremonies. My name is Aiko Koike."

They all introduced themselves. Aiko nodded her head slightly and held eye contact with them individually as they spoke, not blinking once. Her eyes rested on Cody and Mia the longest; they passed over Rick's in seconds.

She bowed and then turned towards the altar of the shrine, bowed, and clapped her hands three times.

Cody put his hand on Rick's right shoulder and whispered, "Rick, doesn't she seem... a little off?"

Rick paused and looked the woman up and down. "Well, no shit she does. But I mean, new culture, mountain town, who are we to judge?" he said with a laugh.

"No, no more laughing shit off. I'm serious," Cody said, not a hint of a smile on his face. Rick, for once, was at a loss for words. Cody continued, "But we might not have a choice. The road is here somewhere on the other side of the town, and if things get weird, we can probably follow it back out to civilization."

"There's something wrong here. I don't know what it is, but I can feel it," Mia said.

Aiko finished praying and walked over to them.

"We don't see many foreigners here. It would be my pleasure to offer you our hospitality, Cody, Mia, Rick." She giggled and held her hand to cover her mouth. The childish act didn't match the adult figure who stood before them. Even though Aiko was acting a part to appear cute, there was the weight of history in her voice. There was subtle authority and power.

"Sure, that would be great. But what we need is a phone to call our tour guide and get back to our hotel. We've been out here for almost two days, I think, and we need to get someone to look at Rick's leg," Cody said.

A rustling of leaves.

The friends all turned to face the sound, somewhere back towards the gate, their bodies tensed. There was nothing there except for the two farmers off in the distance harvesting their crops.

When they turned around, Cody gave a start. Even Rick jumped. Aiko had moved closer, an arm's reach away from Cody. She smiled and held his eyes for what felt like an eternity without speaking. She moved over to Mia and did the same. Lastly, she went to Rick and placed a hand on his left shoulder. She looked down at his leg and whispered something to him. He blushed, and his eyes watered. Then she turned around and walked away towards the town, beckoning them to follow with her eyes.

Rick's face was frozen.

"What did she say to you?" Mia asked.

"I... just... nothing, it's not important, let's go."

Mia looked at Cody with a wrinkled forehead and a frown.

They followed Aiko.

They soon came into the town. Rising over and behind it was a mountain, its summit shrouded in fog, as was the entire sky over the town. The homes they passed each had a sloping thatched roof and looked like they had been transported forward in time by a hundred years. A few telephone poles stood tall in contrast to the two-story buildings. All the roads had pavement, they were narrow, and a few stoplights hung still above deserted streets, yet they could see no cars.

They walked two blocks, seeing no one else. The silence and awkward tension rose as Aiko led them down the street.

The town was large enough for hundreds if not a few thousand people.

Then where is everyone?

"Aiko," *Cody began.* "Why is this place so deserted?"

"Do you see where we are?" She asked. "This town was built in the middle of the mountains. It was thriving once, but as more and more people left for bigger cities, and as families stopped having so many children, it just dwindled to almost nothing."

Cody nodded his head and looked around. Most of the homes and shops looked clean, not run-down or decrepit.

Did they take care of them even though no one uses them anymore? That's odd.

Soon, a cacophony of shouting filled the streets. They turned another corner, and in front of Aiko were six men carrying some kind of object with poles on their shoulders, moving down the street. The object was a stone the size of a large suitcase. It had some engravings and had a rope wrapped around its middle. It sat on top of a wooden tray.

The men were yelling "*rase rase rase*." Now it all made sense. Cody and his friends had been to a Japanese festival in Kyoto just two days before starting the hike. People gathered, drank their body weight in sake, and carried portable shrines like the one they were looking at now. And Aiko's ceremonial dress from earlier? Not too different from what they saw some young women at a shrine wearing.

Many people were out, all gathered around the six men throwing the shrine up into the sky. "*Rase rase rase*!" The shouting rose into the sky and washed over the crowd. This seemed like the kind of event that would bring everybody out. The one exciting thing they would do all year. Despite this, only a few dozen people were visible in a town that could house hundreds. People were laughing. A few kids were running around. Nothing could have been more wholesome at that moment.

"What are they doing?" Cody asked.

Aiko stopped next to the parade and talked to them softly, yet each of them could hear her clearly despite the shouting. "Our community's harvest festival. We thank the God who has provided for us, protects us, and has given us abundant life."

"Which god?" Mia asked.

Aiko coolly held Mia's gaze. "The only one worth having around." She turned around and began walking ahead again.

Mia looked stunned, as if something in that woman's eyes had pinned her to the spot. She recovered a moment later, and they all followed Aiko down a side street.

As they turned onto it, something caught Cody's eye. Just above the buildings to the left, a wisp of smoke rose into the sky. He could see the town square for a flash of a second before they went down the side street. A grove of trees was at its farthest end, and just above them, a stone platform came to a point, like a pyramid.

They walked down the alley. Cody thought about what he had seen for a moment. It could be fire from some burning trash. He decided he didn't know what he had seen. He said nothing.

They came to a house on the side of the main street. A two-story home with a shingled roof, and black-and-white painted wood on its outside. Aiko slid the wooden door open and motioned for them to sit down on the straw mat floor inside.

"Please take your shoes off before entering," she said.

They did so and entered the house. The room was brightly lit. There was no furniture, save for some floor pillows and shin-high trays with some dirty cups with leftover watery tea leaves in them. Everything else was clean—sterile even — with not a trace of dust in the place.

"I am sorry, but we don't have many phones left in our town. Most of us just don't see the point in paying for them when we have other priorities. There are too many distractions in the world today. This home belongs to Mr. Okayama." She waved her hand behind them, and a man came out of the recess of the home. He had deep creases around his eyes and mouth, yet was surprisingly youthful at the same time. His skin glowed, his teeth were blazingly white, and his muscles filled his shirt.

He was a kindly-looking man, the type you'd expect never to forget a birthday card. It had to be a card, handwritten. He seemed like the type to insist on that.

"I'm sorry to trouble you," Cody said.

Mr. Okayama bowed after Aiko translated the message. He waved them over towards the kitchen, where the landline was on top of a coffee table. Rick showed Mr. Okayama the number from a business card he'd kept in his wallet. Mr. Okayama made the call for him. It would be easier that way, to skip the language barrier and have someone else do it for them.

Mr. Okayama said some incomprehensible words into the phone, nodded his head in silence, replied a few more times, and hung up. He spoke to Aiko, and she gave a slight bow.

"He says that your tour guide is anxious about you and has been searching for you. Since it's getting late, they will be here tomorrow to pick you up at nine in the morning."

Rick beamed. "Great, thank you so much."

Cody chimed in, "Yeah, you've been helpful."

Aiko led them back outside after they all bowed to Mr. Okayama and put on their shoes. "You can stay at my father's house tonight. We can prepare a meal for you and help this one with his leg." She led the way down the street.

Rick beamed even brighter. "See, man, told you everything was going to work out."

Cody replied in a hushed tone, "I think something is wrong here."

Rick laughed but quickly stopped after seeing the blaze in Cody's eyes. "What makes you say that?"

"Back at that guy's house, when he was on the phone. Did you notice it?" Cody asked.

"Notice what?"

Mia answered, "It wasn't plugged into the outlet."

II

The streets of Inunaki were immaculate. Not a shred of trash, not even a smudge of dirt on the exterior walls of the homes. The buildings themselves were in top condition.

Not something that Cody would have expected from a remote mountain town that supposedly only had a few landlines out of the countless homes that were around. The houses and shops looked like something he would have imagined Japan was like back before its first contact with the West. Water wheels turned in the river that ran along the outskirts of the town, people fished with nets, and they hauled their crops in wooden carts.

It was all very idyllic, all very sweet, all very innocent. The fields just outside the town were bright green. Corn grew taller than a lanky man and thicker than a fat one. The rice was vibrant in its iridescent glow. It was almost enough to put Cody's mind at ease. This could have been heaven on earth. A welcome respite from their harrowing hike.

Save for one fact: the phone wasn't plugged into the wall.

Maybe shadows obscured the outlet on the wall, so he just couldn't see it clearly. But he could have sworn that it wasn't plugged in. Or was it? He doubted himself, but the suspicion lingered. Moreso because Mia had seen the same thing. Could they both be so wrong?

Aiko broke his thoughts by announcing, "Here is where you will stay for tonight. My father's home. He passed away some time ago, so it's just me here."

She blushed, flushing the whiteness of her face with a deep pink hue. There was something childlike and honest in the way she carried herself. "I must be boring you with all my chatter."

"Not at all," Rick said as he entered Aiko's home. Cody saw that he was no longer limping as much, and his staff no longer touched the ground. In fact, he didn't look injured at all.

The house was simple: a single story and small. As they approached, Cody looked up and saw a faint stream of smoke rising from behind the home, maybe from the backyard.

This is what I saw earlier— the smoke that could have been from a trash fire.

They took off their shoes, and Aiko opened the shutters, allowing light to fill the home. There were no light fixtures inside, no light switches, and no electric appliances of any kind. There was no dust, no disrepair: it looked like a brand-new home built recently.

A black-and-white portrait of a severe-looking man adorned the far wall. Underneath it, a bowl of incense burned. A fresh white rose in a small vase sat next to the bowl. They walked past the portrait. Its eyes were black as coal. Cody instantly disliked him. Something about his posture said, "This is my house, get the fuck out." The date beneath the frame read:

1928/1/13—1967/8/23

Must be her grandfather. Looks like he was a real dick.

Aiko moved to the wall to the right of the portrait, lowered herself to her knees, and opened a sliding paper door. Inside the room was a wide space with a straw mat floor. The center of the room had a depression with some kind of cooking pot hung over it. At the far end of the room, there was a low stand with two dolls on it. One doll was male; the other, female. They were dressed similarly to Aiko's funeral dress, in white-and-red robes. Their faces were porcelain, their eyes black as death.

A faded painting hung on the wall behind the dolls. It was done in a traditional Japanese art style: abstract but holding a certain realism in it as well. In it was a man surrounded by white light and wrapped in gold robes. He was beautiful, seductive even. He smiled, but the light in his eyes, even though it was a painting, was cold and unfeeling. He was floating down from the sky to several people on the ground, on their knees, their hands raised in worship. It reminded Cody of a Jesus painting back in Sunday school.

"You can rest here. I'll bring you some tea and some food. I assume that you all would like to bathe as well?" They nodded. "I'll have someone prepare a fire to warm up the bath; it should be ready shortly after I bring you something to eat." Aiko's voice was low, smooth, and flowed like the perfect harp melody.

"Thank you so much. How far is the nearest town, by the way? Walking distance?" Cody asked.

Aiko's face remained steady, showing no emotion except for her faint smile. However, Cody detected the slightest twitch near her right eye. Something that only lasted half a second but spoke volumes to him.

"The nearest town is much too far away to walk. And you may have already noticed, but no one here owns a vehicle of any kind. Ours is a traditional community. We are deep in the mountains, so we'll just have to wait until your tour guide comes tomorrow to get you."

"There's no bus or anything?" Mia asked.

"Then what about the traffic lights we passed?" Cody put it in.

"Like I said," Aiko said, a slight red hue passing over her face, "many people have been leaving our town. Those of us who stayed desired to live more... simply."

Aiko rose, left the room, went back down on her knees, and shut the door. They could hear her footsteps leaving the house.

"We are so lucky. I know things were shitty for the past few days, but hey, now we get a free mountain getaway," Rick said.

Mia ignored him. "Something isn't right here."

"What? Phone 'not plugged in'," Rick air-quoted.

Mia punched him on the shoulder.

She continued, "You don't think things are a little weird here?"

"Well, of course they are. It's a hick town in the middle of nowhere. But I seriously doubt old man Okayama is going to murder us in our sleep," Rick said.

"It's that woman," Mia said, her eyes glistening with half-formed tears. "I just don't feel right around her."

"I agree with you on the overall vibe here, Mia," Cody said, "but Aiko explained everything, didn't she? She's been nothing but nice to us."

Mia looked at the floor. "Yeah, I guess so. But that doesn't explain what happened with that light that knocked us on our asses."

"Well, you got me there, no fucking clue. But does that really matter anymore?" Rick asked.

They sat in silence for a few moments. Their exhaustion sapped their minds of the ability to converse.

Cody looked up at Rick and asked, "Hey man, how's your leg? I noticed you weren't limping as much anymore."

Rick's eyebrows arched. He rubbed his leg. "You know what? Completely better. How about that?" He rolled up his pant leg. His ankle was no longer swollen, and his skin was only slightly purple and bruised. It appeared as if he bumped it into a coffee table, not that he fell from a cliff.

Cody was no expert on injuries, but Rick's leg had healed far too quickly, hadn't it? Even Mia looked at it with a mix of relief and doubt splashed across her face. No one commented on it further. Some time passed with little to do. Soon, sleep took them.

Someone knocking on the sliding door awakened them. It opened, revealing Aiko with a young girl, no more than sixteen, kneeling at the threshold. They arose, picked up the trays at their feet, and came into the room.

"I hope this is enough for you. And the hot water for your baths will be ready shortly."

"Thank you, ma'am," Rick said, eyeing the contents of the trays greedily.

The others shared his gratitude, and Aiko along with the girl excused themselves.

Cody's mouth watered, and his stomach roared. All rational thought left him as he dove into the food and drink. He was sure he had rice clinging to his five o'clock shadow and crushed tomato running down his chin, but he didn't care. The sweetness of the rice, the savoriness of the fish—he had tasted nothing so good in his entire life. He actually cried.

The room seemed to grow brighter. Cody's nerves calmed down. His once-soaked body and muddy clothes seemed to dry quickly. The stress of the past few days was washing away.

Maybe things weren't that bad after all.

Whatever happened to us is over.

Tomorrow, we're getting out of here.

12

"It looks like someone fell over here," said the police officer wearing a white helmet with a golden star on its front.

The small group of men rushed over to the clearing. A woman wearing purple-rimmed glasses, who somehow walked with more authority than the cops, accompanied them. She pushed two of them out of her way as she looked at what the man out front was pointing at.

He was standing by a ledge that looked like some giant hand had gouged it out of the earth. Huge crevices were dug out of the side of the mountain.

"Someone slid down the hill here," the man said. "See? This was recent. You can see how all the undergrowth is cleared away in a line that goes all the way down. That's from a person's body sliding down."

Ms. Tanaka leaned forward and saw a pile of dirt and stones at the bottom of the high drop.

If they fell here, they'd be flattened like a fly on my swatter, she thought. She tsked and hummed.

"But there's no one down there right now? They must have gotten up and walked away. No way they could have climbed back up," she said.

The helmeted officer looked down. "Yes, but..."

"But what?"

"If they're in that valley, they're gone."

She looked around at the men. No one met her eye.

"What do you mean? You're police. It's your job to do something. Come on, let's go find them."

None of the men moved or spoke for a moment.

An older man with hair white as whipped cream spoke up. "Tanaka-san, I'll send out a search party into the hills surrounding the valley, but we will not go down into it."

"Why the hell not?"

The older man hesitated and looked around at the younger cops near him. He said, "Back in the 70s, my father was a cop here, and he and his partner got called out to investigate what happened to a couple of missing motorists. It all started with the disappearance of a young man named Kenji something; I forget his family name. They found his vehicle on the side of the road, hollowed out by fire. Never found the kid. Then it was a young couple on their way to Hawaii for a honeymoon. They left their town and planned on driving right through the valley here. There used to be an operational road down there, you see. But they never made it to the airport. See that road on the other side of the valley? It's out of use now. Landslides blocked the way years ago and have never been cleaned up. There's no in and out down there. A man my father knew on the force went out there, trying to figure out what was going on, and went missing. He never came back home, just another number on the tally of the missing."

She frowned at him. "He died? That's awful, but what does that have to do with this?"

"More officers were sent after that. Same story. Then, their families started disappearing, right out of their beds. Some even lived as far away as Tokyo. The prefectural government got involved and sent in a large task force to see what the hell was going on. They came back but found nothing. The reports all said there was nothing suspicious in the area, absolutely nothing but uninhabited forest, and after some further investigation, the case was dropped. The thing is, just a few years later, the people who led that task force also went missing. Some more teams were sent in, found nothing, rinse and repeat. We've learned a long time ago that no one messes with what goes on in the valley."

She couldn't believe what she was hearing. If she could pull herself away from the heaven that was her set-up of fried chicken, horrible karaoke battles, and fly-swatting to be out here, then surely Japan's finest could do the same.

"I don't get it. Even if all that happened in the past, why would it be so dangerous now? That was long ago; surely whatever gang was behind it is gone by now."

The officer, whose name Hiromi just now read on his badge as Ohiru, said, "Tanaka-san, I'm sorry. I will not send my men into the valley unless I can get a large team together. That may take days, and even then, we need to wait for the prefectural authorities to sign off on it."

With that, he led his men away, but not before calling out to her, "We won't stop you if you want to pursue this further, but we will not come looking for you if you disappear."

The cops left the clearing.

Even as a little girl, Hiromi found it difficult to squat down. She didn't even bother here. Instead, she leaned her frame over the edge to get a good look at the obvious site where those stupid foreigners had fallen. She didn't get it, why all this fear? There was no way she held more courage in her middle-age than all these trained cops.

She laughed.

Of course, she did.

She pulled out her phone.

"Taro-kun! So good to hear your voice, darling. I need a favor."

13

The steam inside the bamboo tub filled Cody's nostrils, every muscle relaxed, and exhaustion overtook him. He floated there in the bath for what seemed like an hour, maybe a week, possibly an eternity. The past few days of being lost in the woods seemed like a distant memory. Even the cold terror of facing the unknown lights in the woods couldn't compare with the bliss of the hot water. And yet there was one thing, one minor thing that kept hammering away at his brain.

The phone wasn't plugged in.

The lack of which could only mean one of two things: either Cody or Mia was hard of hearing. Or they were being lied to.

He got out of the tub, dried off, got dressed, and headed back to the main room, finding Rick snoring so loudly that the floor vibrated. Mia was sitting on the porch outside the front door of the house. A deep brown and purple color stained the cloudy sky. Lightning streaked across the sky in the distance, and a faint sound of thunder reverberated across the hills. Barely visible rain showers were falling over the forest off in the distance. The air was full of the sweet smell that comes from being out in nature at the end of a hard day. Only a cold beer could make it sweeter.

"So, what do you think of all of this?" Cody asked as he sat down next to Mia.

She stared out into the lightning-fractured sky and didn't answer.

"Mia?"

"Sorry, I was lost for a minute. What do I think? I think this is all bullshit. It looks nice, but we saw what we saw. We saw those trees fall. We felt that burning red light. We heard those screams. And that phone was not plugged in, trust me on that. We should just go."

"Rick thinks nothing is going on, even after all we've seen. And I think that, yeah, things are weird, but not so much that we should just jet. I think we're fine until morning, and if things still seem strange then, we can leave right away. I don't want to risk being out there at night," Cody nodded towards the forest. It wasn't the dark of the woods that scared him; it was the lights found within. Here in this town, everything seemed safe, and far removed from the horrors of the forest.

"Promise me we'll leave tomorrow morning no matter what? I know everyone has been nice to us, but something really is bugging me about Aiko, something about the way she looks at me and..."

"And what?"

Mia shook her head. "Nothing. Just promise me, okay?"

"Promise." Cody stretched out his right pinky, and Mia locked her own with it. "Everything is fine."

Mia let go of the finger lock and looked up at the sky. "Yeah, maybe." She dangled her feet off the porch and swung them. "I just have this, you know, this sinking feeling. It started when we fell off the ledge. It was small then, like an itch somewhere on your back, but you don't know exactly where it is. But now there's this something in me that feels like I'm being pulled down somewhere where no one will ever hear me again. Like I'm dangling over some dark hole that I can't see the bottom of and something is calling my name from it. I'm terrified, I'm scared shitless, but I want to go to it. I feel drawn to it."

Cody looked around, unsure of how to respond. "Well, we just have to make it one night. First thing tomorrow, we're out of here. Whether or not these people are lying."

"Yeah, just one night."

Cody had a look around before it got dark. He wanted to familiarize himself with the town's layout in case things went sour tomorrow morning. He left Mia, walked down the steps of the front porch, and went out onto the town's main street. It was a block away from Aiko's home. The festival had died down, but four men were nearby, talking with each other, leaning up against the wall of the house opposite Aiko's.

As Cody walked by, the men nodded and smiled. Cody returned the civility. Once he had passed them by and gone forward a few steps, they stopped talking. Not the awkward silence that happens as people struggle to find the next word to say; it was pure silence. Mid-sentence stoppage. Cody turned around, and they started speaking at the exact moment his eyes were on them.

He observed them. They spoke, they moved, they looked at one another and laughed. Cody stilled his breath to listen to their words. He kept hearing the same ones, or something akin to them, repeatedly. Something that sounded like *konya konya*. It could have been his ignorance of the language, but the men seemed somewhat plastic in how they spoke.

There was emotion in their voices, sure there was. But there was something off about how they spoke and how they moved, something Cody couldn't piece together, something he left for his subconscious mind to stew on for later.

Aware that he was gawking, despite the men paying him no mind, Cody turned and walked away. He noticed their conversation ended the moment he started moving, but he would not turn around again.

No one approached him or even seemed mildly interested in his presence. Earlier, when they first entered the village, everyone was all smiles and waves. Now, he may well have been invisible to them. He went over to an older woman who was drying her clothes out on a line that ran from her open door to a wooden post in her yard.

She, very much like Mr. Okayama, had the wrinkles to prove her age, but the shine of her skin and the grace of her movements would have had Cody guessing she was in her thirties at most, like himself. She had a white bandana on her head and pushed up the sleeves of her pink shirt while she stretched her linen.

Cody began, "*Konnichiwa.*"

The woman responded, "*Konnichiwa.*" Those podcast lessons on the bus ride might come in handy after all. He fumbled assorted vocabulary through his mind.

"*Genki desu ka?*" He was sure that meant 'How are you?' but the woman just smiled at him and went back to her work. The smile disappeared soon after she looked at her clothes. He said either something incredibly offensive or this woman didn't care about his existence.

She went back to work and failed to grab a piece of linen, yet her hands raised to the line all the same, as if she were miming the actions of earlier. She appeared not to notice what she had done. The next attempt succeeded, and she grabbed the cloth. She was on autopilot. Cody could relate. Many a morning coming into the office he would forget to buy a coffee but would instinctively reach for it on his desk, anyway. The difference is that he would immediately recognize his mistake; he wouldn't drink the empty air.

Cody left the woman and tried out his new linguistic courage on a few other people, but got the same result every time: an amused smile, and then total lack of interest. He was fine with that; he would have preferred to be ignored entirely until they left the next day. But he was uneasy and wanted to suss out the situation, to see if anything was off. And he was on the verge of getting those answers.

Met with walls of silence, Cody resigned himself to walking around and exploring without embarrassing himself further. He continued down the street from Aiko's home and came out into what looked like a town square. Only a few people, maybe six, milled about, cleaning up after the festival.

At the far left end of the square, to the left of where he was standing, he saw a wide road. It led out of the town, up a hill, and buried itself somewhere in the depths of the forest. That had to be the road Mia had seen, the one that went into the mountains and out of the valley.

In the center of the square, behind a wall of short white trees, he could see the top of a stone structure. It came to a point, like a pyramid but with a flat top. Black smoke rose from it, lightly, almost imperceptible but it was there all the same. A brown-and-rust-colored monster of a hill overshadowed the pyramid. It, too, was sending up ash-colored smoke into the sky. Not smoke... More like clouds? This was what he had seen as he stood atop the first pyramid when he found that burned body.

The two mammoth objects—mountain and temple—seemed to tower above him in that moment. Cody felt himself an insect by comparison, a meaningless thing standing before something that had existed for centuries, likely millennia. What is a man to do when faced with the ageless things of the world? How can he hope to control his fate when the universe is not even aware of his existence?

Cody went back to the house and could hear laughter coming from inside. The sun had dipped beneath the hills in the distance; the purple of the sky was now wine-red. He went inside. Mia was sitting in the tatami room on the floor near the doll display, dressed in one of Rick's black sweatshirts. It was at least three times her size. Rick was awake, laughing and talking with Aiko, who had donned her priestess robe once again. Anyone who could kneel in that dress deserved an award.

She turned toward Cody. "Please take a seat; we are just about to begin dinner."

"What's with the costume?" Cody asked.

"Dude, rude," Rick said.

Aiko's stolid expression didn't falter. "I wear this every year for the harvest festival. As I told you earlier, this is my job, and the day's celebrations are not yet over."

Cody sat down on the floor cushion despite every nerve in his body telling him to stay where he was. Something was off about this place, and though he could not quite pin down what that was, he no longer held any doubts. He felt like telling his friends that they should leave. Why? All he could say was that he felt something was wrong. Sure, Mia also had the same feeling. But without something obviously nefarious to show him, Rick wouldn't be on board.

"Aiko was just telling us why she can speak English so well. Go on, tell him," Rick said, leaning back against the wall.

"The radio," she said. "Things here in town were boring for me as a child. We didn't, still don't, have the internet or even television. So, I would listen to my father's radio when he was at work. Every Monday evening, there was a program called 'Let's Up English.' Ridiculous title, right? A woman who had lived in the States ran it. She would play these silly children's songs and stories. It was all very childish, but it helped me to learn."

"That's great," Cody said.

Maybe that's why her English sounded so formal and stilted. It could have been mimicked from some program that didn't know how actual people talk.

Two young women dressed in white and red kimonos came into the room holding trays of food and set them down in front of the guests. Cody recognized one of their faces: the younger girl who had brought them food earlier that day. The pattern of their dresses was flowery, with golden swans stitched into the fabric. Steam flew off the plates. Grilled fish, boiled sweet potatoes, and a variety of unknown vegetables that were white, purple, and pink. They ate the food and drank the tea that was offered.

Cody's mouth watered and his stomach jumped with joy as it filled. Yet he didn't taste a thing; his mind was preoccupied.

"I feel grateful that you three came to us today," Aiko said. "You were just in time for our harvest festival, and we were just in time to help you as well. To think that, on our most important day of the year, we could be here for you on the most challenging day of your lives. There are no coincidences."

Mia rolled her eyes.

Rick raised his teacup and said, "And thanks to you, we've had a great time so far. Makes us forget the past two days."

He raised his glass to toast Aiko. She ignored him. His face drooped down, and she continued, "I truly believe." She set her eyes on Cody and didn't speak for a long pause. "I truly believe that each of you is here for a reason."

The ticking clock on the wall sounded like thunder in the silent room.

She turned to face Mia. "Even if you don't believe that, there is always room for you here in our community. We can offer a place for anyone to feel safe, to feel loved, to feel in control of their lives."

"So what? This is some hippie cult? You guys believe in some lovey-dovey god you pray to a hundred times a day and, maybe, just maybe, he'll make all the monsters go away?" Mia said, raising her voice to a near-shout. Her hands shook as she spoke.

"Yes, yes, we do." Aiko's stare forced Mia to look away.

"Our God hears us, and we hear him. If we perform dutifully, if we give up the things that hold us to this world of pain, we can have a life full of peace. A life of no pain," she looked at Cody. "No frustration," she placed her hand on Mia's knee. "No struggle." She glanced briefly over at Rick.

"Am I not picking something up here? You guys look like you're about to screw or something," Rick said and laughed, though his eyes showed fear.

Mia softened her face. "So, who is this god? Are you guys Buddhist?"

Aiko smiled, her teeth shining in the rays of the crimson sunset spilling into the room. "He is the only God, dear Mia, dearest child." Aiko's voice was full of fireside warmth on a winter day. "The only God who gives a damn about any of us. I wouldn't be surprised if no one outside this valley knew of him, though they should, and one day will. He is the God of stars, Amatsu-mikaboshi. The God born of the blood of the fire god. The one who does not need the sun by day nor the moon to give him light by night."

Aiko waved her hand toward the faded painting on the wall, the one that reminded Cody of a vintage Jesus. Despite the brightness of the colors, the eyes remained dead and cold. Despite the warmth of the room, Cody's body went numb. Thoughts rushed in of the fires seen through the gaps between the trees, of silver eyes in the dark, of the red light that burned his skin. A god born from blood? A god of stars?

Light and flame, death and sacrifice.

These words drilled their way into Cody's mind and refused to leave. The beat of the drums came back to him. Not from outside in the real world, but from within him. The beat drowned out all thought.

Ricked laughed. "Okay, Aiko, I like ya and all, but you sound a little nutty right now. I don't want to be rude. I appreciate what you've done for us, I do, but I don't think any of us want to sign up for the Kool-Aid line."

Rick put his arm around Mia. She pushed it off, her eyes fixed on Aiko.

"How can you be so sure?" Mia asked. Not a hint of mockery in her voice.

"I wasn't at first. I grew up here in Inunaki, like almost everyone else you have met so far. I moved to Tokyo when I was fifteen to get away from," Aiko smiled a bitter smile, "to get away from my father. He wasn't a good man. Did what I had to do to survive in the city. I had to sell my soul and more. I came back a little while later when I heard that my mother had died. It was then that he showed himself to me. He spoke to me in my darkest hour and led me to Him. He showed me how I could be free. Free from both my father and from my sadness."

Mia leaned forward as Aiko spoke, and nodded at every word she said. She lost her gaze in the depths of Aiko's hazel eyes.

Aiko rose to her feet quickly; the bells on her ankles chimed softly. "I would like to show you what we can offer you here in Inunaki. There is no time to waste; the light of the sun is almost gone. When you see what Amatsu has done for us, then you can choose for yourselves."

She turned and left the room through the open door, beckoning them to follow. Rick and Cody exchanged glances.

"Are you buying this?" Rick asked.

"Rick, I need you to listen to me. I think we need to run as soon as we can."

Rick didn't argue, for once. "I think I'm picking up what you were talking about earlier. This is getting way too preachy for me. Mia?"

She had already gotten up and was following Aiko to the other side of the house.

Rick whispered, "Shit. Alright, let's go get Mia, quiet-like. And then I'll make up an excuse and we'll just go."

"How's your leg?"

"Hasn't hurt once since I took my bath." He rolled up his pants to show Cody.

There was not even a trace of a bruise left. The men followed the two women to the red door that sat next to the black-and-white portrait of the stern-looking man.

"This is the way to our family's garden. My father loved to work here often. When he wasn't drinking or making my life a living hell, he was here. It's fitting that it should be where he spends his days now."

A scowl came over Aiko's face like a storm cloud. Her steps quickened and hit the ground hard as if she were angrily approaching a misbehaving child. She gripped the door handle so hard her knuckles turned white.

Rick leaned into Cody. "Isn't her father dead?"

Aiko eyed the portrait to the side of the door with her eyes half-opened, head tilted back, and frowned. "My father. I'd like you to meet him."

So, *the picture wasn't of her grandfather. But if he died in 1967, wait... how old is Aiko? She looked not a day over twenty.*

Aiko opened the door.

Mia screamed.

14

Cody's mind went back to the clearing where he discovered the body. Back to looking into the open jaws of the blackened skeleton with hands raised in the air. It reminded him of the Jesus painting of the man in the white light, his worshippers beneath him raising their hands.

They were flesh and blood and were full of life. The skeleton's mouth was an open void into terrible unknowns. What horrors could that silent scream speak of? What unfathomable reaches of darkness had those burned-out eyes seen?

Before him now, in Aiko's garden, he was staring into that same endless pit of darkness. He heard another scream. Not silent and dreadful, but loud, ear-splitting, and frantic.

He was looking at another burned corpse, and this time Rick couldn't deny what he was seeing.

"What the fuck!" Rick yelled.

A body burned beyond recognition was kneeling in the garden, hands outstretched to the sky above. Its wrists were chained to two metal bolts that had been fastened to a cement platform. Smoke sizzled off its ruined flesh. It looked fresh. It gave off heat.

"May I introduce you to my father?" Aiko's face quaked and her hands trembled. "The man who took great joy in causing me pain. Look at him now." Aiko was smiling darkly. "The great man brought so low."

Though she spoke in even measures, every syllable conveyed a bottled-up shriek. She spun around in fury, her robe smacking the walls and knocking off a vase, shattering it. Her eyes were wide, with red lines streaked across them. They looked like fault lines in the earth preparing to expose the fire beneath.

"This is the pain the old gods of the world let into our lives. These are the monsters that they allowed in to harm the innocent." She undid the sash of her robe and showed them her chest. A deep fissure of cuts from the top of her breast to the base of her collarbone marked her skin.

Cody felt like he was on a ship out at sea, rocking back and forth. He nearly lost his balance and crashed to the ground. His world nearly drowned in the emptiness of space. He had to hold onto the wall to keep from falling.

The sun was almost gone. The air was thick with dusk. Aiko's eyes flashed. Not with emotion. A silver light shone forth, iridescent and beautiful, alluring and dangerous. It contrasted with her natural brown eyes, creating a mesmerizing color. It was faint at first but grew brighter with every moment.

"What our God, Amatsu, the Dread Star of Heaven, offers you is justice against those who have hurt you." She flashed her silver eyes at Mia. "In his world, no fathers abandon their children. He offers release from the pain of guilt." She swirled over to Cody, grabbed him by the shirt, and pulled his face near. Strangely, he could feel the sudden burn of ice on his cheeks. She pushed him away. "He offers an end to ignorance and to the needless waste of life." She sneered at Rick and spat on the ground.

"All he asks of us in return is," she paused, calming the sudden tempest of her words, "sacrifice." Her voice became low and guttural. Her eyes rested on Rick.

In the silence that followed, another sound came into focus. A scratching sound, like mice in the attic clawing their way through the floorboards, or cockroaches scurrying across the kitchen floor. Something exhaled a weary and despondent sigh.

The corpse turned its head towards Aiko. A gargled voice spilled out of its burned throat. It tried to stand, but the chains held it in place. Aiko faced the horror of the dead man and caressed his chin, smiling at his expression of pain and suffering. She slapped his face. Ash stained her palms. She turned towards the trio, who had been stunned into immobility.

Rick snapped out of it. He shoved Aiko against the wall. Her head smacked against the stone siding with a sick crunch, and she fell to the ground. Blood trickled from her head.

The dead man turned his face toward his daughter. Rick grabbed Mia's hand and ran, yelling at Cody to move. Without waiting for him, they ran through the house to the locked front door. The only pack they could grab as they ran was Cody's: he had set it outside the straw-floored room, near the front door, just in case. They put their shoes back on with shaking hands, Mia dropping one before getting it on, losing precious seconds.

Rick kicked the flimsy frame twice and broke it down. He shoved Cody's pack through the door first, and then he and Mia made their way through the splintered exit hole. Cody was still in the garden, beholding the terror of the scene.

"Cody, move your ass," Rick yelled.

Finally, he moved with legs of water, grabbed his shoes, and caught up with the other two.

They leaped off the porch and onto the road. They stopped.

A dozen people surrounded the property. Mr. Okayama was among them in his kindly glasses and sweater vest. He no longer looked like the sweet old man who would send you money on birthdays. Now, there was murder in his eyes.

No, it wasn't just that. Everyone's eyes glowed with a dim silver light, just like Aiko's had. The people of the town stood still in front of the house as if awaiting orders. No lights were coming from the homes or the streets. The eyes of the people were little stars populating the growing darkness of the coming night.

Aiko's voice came from behind. "The choice is yours, Cody and Mia. To choose a life beyond the reach of pain. Or to be offered unto Him. You will see what will happen should you deny Him. Rick, I'm sorry, but we have no need for you beyond what you can give us tonight."

"How the hell did she get up so fast?" Rick asked.

She gracefully glided across from the garden and headed towards them. Blood stained her neck and the left side of her face, yet she moved effortlessly.

Is the blood retreating up her neck?!

The townsfolk surrounded them, not completely encircling them, not yet. Rick took Mia's hand and caressed it. He kissed her. Then he looked Cody in the eyes and said, "I'm sorry, both of you. This is my fault, and I have to fix it. Stay on my ass and run."

With that, he let go of Mia's hand and bolted to the right, plowing over a shorter man in a straw hat. Cody and Mia stuck right behind him. Cody wasn't sure if he stepped on the fallen man's face as he ran, but he heard a crunch that could have been a nose—he didn't care. If he tried hard enough, he could imagine he was running over frozen grass or seashells. They ran along the street until Mr. Okayama suddenly jumped down from a nearby roof and veered in front of their path.

The fuck? He was just behind us.

He was far too athletic for an elderly man. Fuck, he was far too athletic for any man, the way he just leaped up and then down from the roof without so much as groaning. By now, the sun had completely set. The eyes of the villagers were now no longer dim and faint, but were burning bright. Cody nearly had to shield his eyes against them. Mr. Okayama's eyes were a sharp silver; his mouth opened in a predatory grin with spittle running down his chin. His once vibrant skin was now gaunt and shriveled, mummified even, stretched far too thinly across his skull.

Rick sprinted ahead, yelling out "sorry" to the elderly man as he wound his right arm back and lunged at him. His fist sailed right into Mr. Okayama's jaw. There was a sickening snap. Rick's fist flew back–he cradled it and shouted in agony. A tooth fell out of Mr. Okayama's devilish grin, and he took a step back, yet did not otherwise seem affected by the blow. Mr. Okayama grabbed Rick's shattered hand and pulled it towards his face, holding it like a toy.

Rick fell to his knees, stunned.

Mr. Okayama ripped Rick's entire right arm off. The muscle and bone made a shredding sound as Mr. Okayama eviscerated them. Shock painted Rick's face. The hole that was once his arm spouted blood like a sprinkler. Shredded bone and meat surrounded it. He collapsed onto the ground. Mia's voice shot out into the night like a squealing tire. Cody's knees nearly gave way and sent him to the ground as well. But he didn't fall. Some force from deep in his bones sprang to life and forced him to move. He pushed Mia forward, and she ran. More people were filling the street and walking towards them.

They sprinted past Rick. Cody didn't check long enough to see if he was still moving. He saw Mr. Okayama standing still, not running after them. Instead, he held the detached arm in front of himself, holding it in both hands. He was about to bite into it, mouth open and drooling. Aiko's voice rang out from somewhere behind them, and he dropped the arm.

Cody's heart beat in his ears. He could feel the blood pumping through him like acid. He outran Mia and kept on going. She followed closely behind him, sobbing through her gasping breath. The townsfolk did not run after them, but that would not stop him from running.

Fuck fuck fuck. Rick. We have to go back for him.

That thought would have to be put on hold for now. Getting out of the valley was the top priority.

The stars came out. They shone so brightly, unusually so, that Cody could see the road that led out of the town and back towards the cliff face. Thank God it was such a small settlement. They ran towards the broken entry gate and came to a halt, slipping on the dirt as they stopped so suddenly some gravel shot up in the air.

Under the cracked stone toori gate was an impossibly tall man. His head grazed the bottom of the archway, a height of at least fifteen feet. He was thin, and his fingers were long, longer than Cody's legs, yet his gray mane of hair was even longer, reaching to the ground. The fingers curled up as if the man was in constant agony. His silver eyes rested on them like a terrible searchlight, illuminating their bodies in the darkness. It burned their skin. He walked towards them, each stride so long that he wouldn't need to run to catch them.

For a moment, Cody couldn't move. His blood had turned to ice and froze him in place. It wasn't until Mia tugged hard at his arm and screamed into his ear that the iceberg in his veins broke up.

The tall man strode towards them with his massive strides. He grinned, drool splashed onto the ground in buckets, and his eyes glowed hot and bright.

They ran into a home on the right and shut the door. The tall man's steps shook the walls, and picture frames fell and shattered to the ground. Cody grabbed a desk from the corner and propped it up against the entrance. He looked to his right into the living area and noticed the entire wall was one sliding paper door with no locks.

Shit.

Mia rushed into a nearby closet and tossed a broom at Cody. He caught it and wedged it in the space between the wall and the sliding door's edge. It was probably not more than a toothpick to the giant, but it was something. Just then, a voice erupted from outside the house. Like the footsteps, the voice also shook the home and Cody's bowels.

The walls rattled.

They ran deeper into the house.

There was a small closet in the room they ran into. It was hardly big enough to hide even Mia by herself. They went inside, and Mia tripped over something on the floor, falling into an open crawl space. No way Cody was fitting inside, so he ripped off some clothing from the hangers and covered her. She tried to say something. He shut the closet behind her. No time to argue when a giant man is knocking at your door. The door! He heard it slide open and stop with a soft thud. Saved by the broom.

He heard it snap. Shit. There was a dresser in the room with a space between it and the wall. Cody slipped into that space.

The giant growled and spoke. The language that boomed out of that throat did not sound like Japanese, the little that Cody understood. It sounded harsher, more ancient. Cody could feel the vibration of that Paleolithic voice in his ribcage. From his vantage point, Cody could see some of the main living area as something dark entered it.

Long fingers came slithering in like the tentacles of some forgotten sea monster. Each finger moved on its own. They somehow moved independently of a fixed point, such as a wrist or hand. Writhing like eels and feeling along the walls, one entered the bedroom. The finger hovered above the floor and scratched at the walls, removing the wallpaper in wide strips. It wriggled around as it tried to come further into the room, but wasn't long enough. It gave up and retracted. A crash came from the next room. The wall shook and splintered.

This guy can tear apart this entire house; *he doesn't need* to *fit inside.*
Another crash from just outside the bedroom.

A face filled the doorway. Cody quickly ducked his head behind the dresser. The light in the giant's eyes lit up every object in the room and then vanished. Peering out, Cody could see that the man had turned away and was moving to another room across the hall. The giant couldn't stand up straight and went about on his hands and knees. His massive bulk squeezed through where it could. He broke the doorway of the room on the opposite side.

His shoulders bent and shattered the wood as he forced himself inside.

The door to the closet opened. Mia crept out, low to the ground. She motioned with her thumb towards the room's only window. It was high up, with the bottom part of it matching Cody's eye level. Cody shook his head. Fear gripped him to the point of paralysis. He knew he couldn't stay there; the thing would eventually find him. Mia stood and tried to open the window. It was stuck. A hollow voice of thunder echoed from the living area. Great footsteps shook the house as the giant charged into a wall.

Cody ran over to the window, both of them now trying to lift it. The window budged only slightly. They struck the glass with their fists and shattered it. They heard the crashing of furniture being tossed around and the splitting of more wood. The tall man must have been turning around and trying to get out of a room. The noise stopped. Mia started punching out the broken shards of glass as Cody looked back at the door. He nearly screamed.

An open mouth filled the entire doorway like the smile of a dog with its saliva splashing onto the floor.

The tall man spilled into the room like a beached whale. He entered headfirst, arms pinned to his sides. Despite not being able to use his arms, his mouth was proving more than capable of causing damage. The jaw unhinged and widened. A deep tunnel of dark death, lined with serrated teeth, moistened with spit. It ate its way through the dresser, the bed, the walls, anything and everything that it came across.

Cody helped Mia knock out the rest of the larger broken pieces of glass. The great mouth was devouring the floorboards behind them. Was it growing in size? He could feel the heat of its breath. It moved his shirt about as if it were a gust of wind. Cody put his hands out in front of Mia.

She used them to lift herself up and out through the window. She shot out with little effort, though she cut her hands in the process. Cody jumped up and grabbed the sides of the windowsill, broken glass making incisions into his palms. He was never one to excel in gym class. He still carried memories of classmates mocking him for not being able to climb the rope in the arena. Cody could only make it up by one, sometimes two reaches of his hands before falling.

Whatever athletic capability that lay dormant in him then came to explosive life now. He lifted himself out through the window and fell hard onto the ground outside.

He gasped for breath. Mia took his hands (he winced at that) and pulled him to his feet. Before he could offer gratitude, the wall behind them split. A crack fissured it in half. Through the hole that was once paned with glass, they saw the giant rise, staring at them with the cool light of the moon in his eyes. He punched a hole through the outer wall and began to force his way outside.

Cody and Mia skirted the house as the giant broke it apart. They ran towards the stone archway at the entrance to the town. Behind them, the giant rose through the wreckage of the home. His silhouette filled the sky. The white light of the stars rimmed the dark shadow of his mass. They ducked behind a large oak on the side of the road. Just behind them was a dirt path that led into the forest. In front of them was the paved road that entered town.

The giant swiveled his head, his silver eyes revealing what lay hidden in the dark, like a lighthouse seeking the lost on the dark waves of an unruly sea. Except this was one light that was sure to bring anything but rescue.

The light passed over the tree that had become their sole hope. It lit up the ground on either side of the tree and rested there. Cody held his breath, expecting to feel the barrage of the giant's steps moving towards them. Instead, the light passed over to the road leading back into town. Then came the shaking of the ground as the tall man moved away. Cody peeked out from the edge of the tree and saw him move in the opposite direction from where they were hiding. Silver eyes lit up in the distance. As the sound of his footsteps became a distant rumbling, they looked out at the path ahead and ran into the forest.

The stumps of fallen trees blocked the way. Cody jumped up and climbed over one, extended his bloody hand to Mia's, and helped her up as well. They jumped off on the other side. They fell over, panting desperately.

They had been running for fifteen minutes. Since their escape from the house, they had not heard the giant, or anyone else, come after them.

"We have to get out of here and go get help. Maybe get back to where we fell from the first day," Cody said.

"What about the road? Rick said--" Her voice cut out in between sobs.

"That brings us too close to the town."

"But it's closer than the cliff, right?"

Cody sighed. "We could do that. But we'd have to skirt around the town and be real fucking quiet."

Mia fell to her knees and cradled them. "We can't leave him. He's still alive."

"Do you know that for sure?"

"Yes, I saw him moving. Oh God!" Mia stood up and walked around in circles, breathing heavily. "What was that? He just... just ripped his..." She fell apart in a torrent of tears.

"I don't know. But they're not human. Maybe they were once, but now," Cody's mind went back to that painting in Aiko's house. "Now they're something else. And we can't help Rick."

Mia's eyes went wild. She picked up a stick and raised it above her head, threatening to bring it crashing down on Cody's face. She didn't hit him but thrashed the stick about as if she would.

"You fucking coward. I knew it. Rick told me you were like this. I thought maybe you were just shy at first. But with your ex-girlfriend. What sort of man sees someone dying in front of them and just walks outside to wait for the ambulance? If it were me," she smacked the stick against the trunk of a tree, shattering it, "if it were me, I'd do CPR or at least attempt it. You? You just fucking ran away. I see it now; this is who you are—a coward."

"That's not how it happened. And wait a minute, Rick told you this?"

"Does that even matter right now? Look, fuck it, I don't care. I'm going back to help Rick, with or without you."

She threw the stick down and started climbing back over the log.

"You can't go back, Mia."

Before she answered, chanting from the darkness filled the air.

"Gisei gisei gisei."

The ravenous beat of the drums came next, followed by the blowing of the conch shell.

Cody ran in the opposite direction. Hopefully, it would lead them back the way they came. Mia wasn't very far behind him. The chanting kept pace and didn't let up—it was right on their tail. They rounded a large tree and stopped. A girl, no more than sixteen, was standing in front of them. The girl who had served them their meals. She was short, shorter than even Mia was, and that was saying something. She smiled a toothless grin that looked stapled on either side with a tightly strung lip. Silver eyes lit up her pasty face with an eerie glow. The chanting was close.

"Gisei gisei gisei."

The rhythm of the drums drove Cody's heart wild.

Mia bent down and grasped along the forest floor. She picked up a metal pole pointed at one end. Cody found a fist-sized rock. The girl took a gentle step forward. She cocked her head to her side as if she were a dog trying to comprehend a new trick.

"Back the fuck off," Mia said, pole brandished like a sword.

The words that had come from that tiny girl's mouth were the same that had come from the tall man. Deep and ancient words gripped Cody's heart. Mia lowered the weapon and stared at the girl, her eyes glazed over as if she were high. Cody, too, lowered the rock as if in a trance. The girl went on speaking, no longer sounding like a girl, more like a man, a man who chain-smoked and drank moonshine.

The girl lunged forward. Cody dropped his rock as he flinched. The girl jumped on him, clinging to his neck like a child. He fell to the ground. Her smile widened as her saliva drenched his face. He tried and failed to lift her off himself. She was half his size, yet held him down with the weight of a mountain.

She leaned in close to his face. The light in her eyes washed out his peripheral vision. In the shiny depths of those eyes, he could almost hear a voice, something calling to him, something ancient, something evil.

A pointed end appeared in front of Cody's face. The lights dimmed. Mia had rammed her weapon through the back of the girl's neck. Heavy and thick blood rained down on Cody's face. It felt solid rather than liquid. She hung limp. Cody pushed her body off himself.

"I didn't... I didn't mean to." Mia was on the verge of collapse; her arms were shaking so hard.

"It's okay, you had to," Cody said, shame filling his chest as he got to his feet.

As they turned away from the girl's body, they stopped in their tracks. A rustling sound from behind had caught their attention. They turned and saw the girl rising to her feet. The metal pole was poking through her throat like a toothpick on a piece of cheese as she gripped it and pulled it out of her. She threw it into the forest. She smiled her thin smile again. Sinewy threads stretched across the gaps until they fully sealed the wound, and then the hole closed. The girl's body changed. Grew larger with various bone-like spikes bursting out of her back and wrapping around her front.

They didn't stay long enough to see what she would turn into. Mia shouted at Cody to run, even though his legs were already on autopilot. He rocketed through the woods and soon outran Mia.

There was no reason behind the direction they chose; they were running on pure adrenaline and instinct, with no sense of direction to guide them. They ran through bushes and thick overgrowth. Rain fell hard, but the canopy shielded them from most of the deluge. Looking back, Cody could no longer see the silver eyes or hear the chants of the villagers under the roar of the rain. Even the beat of the drums had faded. After five minutes of sprinting, they slowed down to a walk. Mia turned into the thickest part of the woods and started heading back toward the town.

Cody followed her, wanting to explain himself and apologize. He knew that going back for Rick right now was useless. Both of them would be taken instantly. Rick punched that man—that thing — right in the face, and his hand shattered. The shriveled thing that was once Mr. Okayama tore Rick's arm off with ease. How was that even possible? No, there was no way they could save him. Not if the strongest among them was helpless in the monster's grasp.

Their best bet was to get back to the cliff and hope a search party was out looking for them. Then they could go back for him if… if he was still alive to go back for. Mia would understand once he explained himself.

"Hey," he started.

Mia either ignored him or couldn't hear him.

Cody ran up to her side and grabbed her arm. "Hey, I know you're pissed at me right now. And yes, maybe I'm a coward. But if we go back now, we both die. We need to get somewhere where we can get help."

Mia bit her lip. A habit she probably picked up from months with Rick's infectious personality.

"I know, but..." She sat down in the mud and held back tears, though with the rain one couldn't tell if she was successful. "I know, but... we have to do something."

"We are. We have to go back to the cliff, get help somehow, and come back for him. If—" Cody choked up. "If he's still alive."

She nodded and stood up. They moved through the dark, the hideously bright light of the stars no longer providing a way forward.

God of the stars.

These words rested in his mind. They were ridiculous, of course. But given what they saw, something abnormal and beyond their comprehension was happening, and of that, there could be no doubt. Looking up at the night sky, full of rain clouds, Cody was glad there were no stars. If what Aiko said was true, the black sky was almost a welcome sight.

"What was that thing chained up at Aiko's? It moved," Mia said.

"I don't know, but she said it was her father."

"It was dead, Cody; it was dead, and it moved and it spoke, or at least it sounded like it did."

"Yeah, it was dead. And it was her dad. It looked like she was torturing him; you saw the chains, right? And that portrait of him in the house, it said he died in 1967."

"Are you serious?"

"That means he's been there, chained up and dead for," Cody did mental calculations, "dead for fifty-five years. So, how old is Aiko? She doesn't look a day over twenty."

"Cody, you suck at math. It's been fifty years."

They laughed. In the icy rain, this warmed them.

"Maybe, whatever this star god thing is, keeps her young?" Mia asked.

"And makes people into zombified monsters with bright eyes?" The thought could almost make Cody laugh. If it weren't for the image of his best friend's arm being shredded away from his torso, then yeah, it would be hilarious.

The rain stopped. With the end of the torrent, the smothering clouds receded, and the stars shone, hot-white in the sky. Screams ripped through the forest. They were like the scream they had heard right before they found Inunaki. On second thought, they weren't similar; they were the exact same tone of despair and pain. Cody and Mia exchanged hesitant glances.

The sound came from their left. There was no way to tell if that meant it was from the town or not. Everything had become confused in their flight.

Cody felt a physical weakness and a heavy sleepiness keeping him from moving forward toward the sound. He remembered dropping the rock not twenty minutes ago; he remembered running away as Rick was attacked, and he remembered the closed bathroom door.

What if that's Rick?

He took a deep breath and forced his legs to move towards the sound.

The horrid orange glow pierced through the spaces between the trees. The screams mixed with the crackle of fire. They moved closer to it, not enough to be seen by anyone, but close enough to see what was happening. Cody brushed a branch heavy with dense leaves to the side.

A clearing opened up before him. They could see a few people in red robes, beating their drums, walking back into the forest on the opposite side. In the center of the field, a stone pyramid behind some short trees. At its highest point, they could see a flicker of flames. It had to be a person up there, a human torch. Someone was on fire, burning at that very moment. They screamed and roared in agony. The voice was deep and male.

Mia clasped her throat. "Is it?"

"It's not him. Listen. I know that's not his voice."

Cody had a momentary lapse of heroism, thinking about putting the poor soul out of its misery. But how? With what? Mia turned away and buried her face in Cody's soaked shirt.

"Let's go," he said.

Just as they were turning back, Mia pulled his arm back and stopped him.

"Cody... he's not dying."

"What?"

"Just wait and shut up for a minute."

They stood there in silence as the moments passed. Cody looked once more at the pyramid. It was true. Even after waiting five more minutes just to see what would happen. The man continued to burn.

The man did not die.

15

Mia stood there in the burning man's glow. The light of his pyre reflected in her dark eyes, iridescent and beautiful.

"I want to do something for him," she said.

From his vantage point in the bushes, Cody looked around the clearing and saw no one else. He didn't quite believe it to be safe; the people could come back at any moment.

"It's awful, but I think we should leave him."

Mia didn't respond. She walked into the clearing.

"Shit." Cody followed.

There were large, shadowy objects in the clearing that he couldn't make out. Rocks or small trees, perhaps. The two of them exited the treeline and walked tentatively toward the pyramid. As they approached, the light of the fire fully washed over them. The rain fell again. The downpour fell on the fire. Steam sizzled off it, but it wasn't strong enough to put out the blaze.

Cody shook his head to rid himself of what the strength of that fire implied. When they walked closer to the shadowy objects, the light of the fire revealed them to be the husks of cars. Very similar—too similar — to a place they had already been.

Was this the same pyramid, the first one we found? But that wouldn't make sense; *we're at least hours away from* there, *and we're walking in the opposite direction.*

They ascended the steps, looking over their shoulders as they went. Reached the summit. They came face to face with a pitiful sight. The screams made Cody wince and nearly paralyzed him. Mia extended her arm as if to touch the man.

"Whoa, Mia, stop." Cody grabbed her hand. "What are you doing?"

She made no response. She stood there with a blank stare, the one Cody had become accustomed to seeing on her face since they first entered the valley.

She stopped short of touching the man. Cody couldn't bear to look at him writhing in the flames, mere feet in front of him. Although a wall of flame separated them, Cody could sense the man's eyes looking at him, pleading for mercy. His screams drowned out all rational thoughts.

Cody took off his shirt, soaked as it was from the rain. He emptied his backpack and pulled out his sleeping bag. He had left his rain gear back at Aiko's house, as had Mia, yet he still had all the contents of his backpack. They were soggy, the bag itself not being waterproof. Cheap goods have dire consequences.

The only thing he salvaged was a black hoodie that was too small for him. It had been a gift from his mother: "Don't want you getting sick now," she had said as she hugged him too tightly at the airport. He slipped into it.

Cody had a full water bottle. Losing its contents wouldn't be a loss, as rain was abundant here. Despite drinking out of dirty puddles for days, none of them had gotten sick, not yet at least. Cody threw his shirt onto the flaming head in front of him. Tossed the sleeping bag over him and poured out the water bottle as well.

The flames hissed and began to die out. The sleeping bag was only somewhat burned, and the man's lower half was still burning. Cody grabbed the material (the process burned off his arm hairs), beat the bag against the man, and doused most of the fire. He stamped a few flames with his feet, and the lightly falling rain did the rest until it came to a stop once again. The man stopped screaming and didn't move; he froze in place. His body was a wet mess of grilled flesh, emitting thick smoke.

Mia snapped back to attention.

"What just happened to me?" Mia had eyes the size of dinner plates, widened pupils, and a breaking voice. Cody didn't answer. Instead, he was looking at the body in front of him. As the smoke cleared, he could see it clearly. A golden necklace with a large cross, draped across the neck. That meant nearby there should be... He felt behind him. The top right step had a hole in it. He had just missed tripping over this time.

The world spun around him. He almost lost his balance and fell down the steps. This was the same body they had seen, the one from Aiko's "funeral" procession. The cars below were the same. Instead of relief flooding his heart with the fact that they were closer to the cliff they had fallen from, terror gripped it. How had they traveled so far in such a short time?

"This man, he was dead this morning." *(Had it been just today?)* "I recognize the necklace; it's the same fucking one. Don't you remember?" Cody didn't wait for an answer. "And this place, it should have taken us hours to get here. And what has it been— one hour max?" He felt the familiar heaviness in his chest as his lungs began craving deep, rapid breaths.

"He's just like the one we saw at Aiko's place. Her father," Mia said.

"Does this mean they come back? To life, I mean. Like every night?"."

"At least it's over for him–" Mia began and paused.

The sky above grew bright. So bright, Cody could see the pores on Mia's face.

The light, now dimming to a hot coal-red, burned their exposed skin. Cody put on his hood and closed the drawstrings tightly. Mia pulled on the sweatshirt she had taken from Rick earlier. Thankfully, Rick was so big that she could easily hide herself in the sweatshirt's maze. This helped shield them from the burn.

The black skeleton moved. They jumped back off the platform and onto the top steps. The monstrous thing looked at them with hollow yet meaningful sockets. Cody felt sorry for the thing. Red light fell on the creature and illuminated it with both a fiery and silver glow. Flames erupted from nowhere and consumed it whole. It screamed again and fought fiercely to break free of its chains.

There was nothing that could be done.

This was a perpetual sacrifice. Fated to burn every night. For eternity?

Cody felt sick. He hadn't noticed it before, but in turning away from the thing before him, he could see another fire off in the distance. The screams were barely audible, yet Cody knew without a doubt what he would find should he dare venture out to them. Tears stained both of their faces as they walked back down the stairs. Cody wished for the rain to come again, if not to put out the fire, at least to drown out the howling.

Mia looked pleadingly at Cody. "Do you think that Rick... that if we get caught, this will happen to us?"

Cody bit his lip. "Not us. Aiko said that this would happen to Rick, but... what did she say? Something about us joining her."

"Screw that bitch."

They walked back into the woods, leaving the screaming torch left behind to its fate. There was one positive outcome from the grotesque discovery: the path that led to the pyramid, if they followed it the other way, would lead them back to the cliff. That was how they came here the other day, wasn't it?

"This is it," Cody said. "This is the way back, can't be much more than a few hours back."

Without the burden of carrying Rick, it could even be shorter than that. Mia whimpered in consent, and they hiked on. The way was bright and clear, thanks to the glow of the stars. The moon did not show itself. Everything had a ghostly glow. Trees that were green and brown by day took on a white and transcendental hue at night. It all seemed like a dream. The forest shimmered, and the light rippled in waves around them.

Cody wasn't sure if he was losing his mind at the sight, at the wavy appearance of the light, but seeing a dead man come alive (twice in one night) and burst into flames has a way of calling into doubt what he once called his sanity.

Fireflies appeared. Their lime-green sparks speckled throughout the silver cascades of light. They flitted at their feet and seemed to follow them on their melancholy hike.

"Cody, what's happening?"

"I don't know." He smacked an annoying bug off his cheek, and the trail of its blood painted his stubble. "But... it's something supernatural; we can't argue that at this point."

"I think that we're in hell."

He let out a scoffing laugh. "Yeah, it feels like that. But not literally, no. We're alive, Mia, and we're going to stay that way. We're going to get Rick help."

"If this isn't hell, then what is it?"

Cody looked up at the stars. "I don't know."

Mia followed his gaze. "They're so beautiful, the stars, I can't believe that something so pure could be behind this. If what Aiko said is true, that is. God of the stars…" She slowed her walk to a stop.

"Hey, you okay?"

She didn't respond. Her eyes remained fixed on the sky. Cody could see a glassy expression wash over her eyes.

"Mia," he said as he walked over to her. He shook her.

"S-sorry, I don't know what just happened." Wild fear decorated her face, like a child who got lost at an amusement park and just now realized that mommy wasn't by their side.

"This has happened a few times already." He held her eye contact, something he had never been good at. "Are you sure you're alright? Ever since we came here, you've been slipping in and out."

"I said I'm fine." She brushed his hand away and walked away.

They heard the screaming again. They had been pushing through tall grass and scraggly branches when it came.

The incandescent red of the fire pulsed through the dark. Cody looked over at Mia; her eyes were glazed over, staring out both intently and at nothing at the same time. A flicker streaked across her hazel eyes. For just a moment, he could have sworn that it was a silver light that showed in her eyes. A knot tightened itself deep in his stomach. He knew what it could mean now. They waded their way through the bushes and came out into the clearing and saw burnt-out cars, a stone pyramid, and a human torch atop the steps.

"This is the same place. No fucking way." Cody's voice faltered and cracked, something that hadn't happened to him since puberty.

He spun around and ran back into the woods. He had to stop momentarily to shake Mia out of her trance, and she followed. They ran past the shimmering trees and the mirage-like bushes, and though they ran in a straight line, they spilled back out into the same clearing. The same dead cars, the same monument of the damned.

He ran back out when Mia caught his hand.

"Don't you see, Cody? It won't let us leave."

"What won't?"

She looked up at the sky. Cody followed her gaze. His face trembled, and his blood froze. His eyes widened as red light splashed over his face, followed by an intense burning.

They ran.

Mia fell over a log. Cody stopped in his tracks, went back, and helped her up. Behind them, something roared like an out-of-control inferno. The ground shook in a rhythmic cadence, left foot, right foot. Trees fell. Cody ran without looking back. He couldn't bear facing it again. The shadow that walked in the red light. It had looked at him; the darkness had met his eyes. What he saw reduced his nerves to jelly. Anything would be better than facing that again, even death, even fire.

Behind them, a rolling wave of red washed over the forest. It crept towards them. A slow-motion tsunami of light. It wasn't just incorporeal light, though: the trees, the giants of the forest, bent before it, bowed before it, fell to their deaths before it. The ground became like water. The roar intensified. It shook his rib cage. The light was cool, the light burned, and the light pursued them.

In defiance of all common sense and the weight of his dread, he looked back and saw something moving in the light. The shadow. How such a thing could exist inside something so bright was beyond him. The dark thing moved with the light. Its shape couldn't be made out: the light forced Cody to shut his eyes soon after gazing upon it. One thing was for sure; it was alive and it was moving.

"Run, Mia, run!" Cody looked back at her as she gradually fell behind.

He had glimpsed the light, or rather, the thing at its center, the source of the light. What was using the light as a mask, a cover for what it truly was? The light had intention; it was alive, and it was getting closer.

The light, the living star, was mere feet behind them. Sweat poured off their skin. Their clothes blew against their bodies from the blast of its presence. They fell to the ground from its force. The light stopped. It was dark and silent.

Cody lifted himself onto his knees. In front of them lay the cracked stone toori gate of Inunaki.

The tall man stood in front of the gate, facing the town, his back to them.

He turned around.

16

Rick woke up with water dripping onto his face. He went to wipe it away, but nothing happened. His shoulder moved, but the water remained. He came to. The pain made him realize the awful truth that he could no longer use that hand to wipe water off his face, to hold Mia's hand, or even to wipe his own ass.

Electric pain shot through his nerves and fired through to his feet. Sweat and tears streamed down his face. He rocked himself into a sitting position and looked at where his arm used to be. It was bandaged up. Expertly so. The white cloth was stained red, but the bleeding had stopped.

Why on earth would they not have killed him? Why make sure that he was not only alive but cared for? He touched the wound, expecting a painful shock, but none came, at least not to the extent he had been expecting. He undid the bandages with his left hand. It was too dark to see the wound, but when he touched it, it felt smooth. No jagged bones, no shredded muscle, just baby-smooth skin.

What the fuck?

He was grateful, even let out an audible laugh, yet moments later fear gripped him. How was he healed?

He looked at his surroundings. He could make out some shapes from the light coming in from under the door to his cell. The floor was stone. The walls were a heavy earthen barrier. As he stood, he nearly slipped on the slick surface. He shivered.

For the first time in his life, Richard Davis felt genuine fear and self-pity. Those pathetic emotions never touched him when he was a kid. He was an all-star American football player, just like his dad, just like his granddad, Poppa. (Even if he did smell of urine and Marlboro, he was a damn star, a national treasure). Nothing could touch Rick in his heyday; he was fast; he was strong, and nobody hated him—he was sure of that. The only chink in his charismatic armor was his father's opinion. It was a spike that could wedge itself between the gaps and drive itself right down into the flesh.

In that damp and dark cell, a memory came to him.

He was eight. Standing on the pitcher's mound at Meyers Park. His team, the Flying Tigers, was tied with the Green Gophers at the bottom of the ninth, bases loaded. All he had to do was strike out the chubby kid at bat. Easy. Never been a problem before. With his shoulder wound up, his left knee bent up to his chest, he was ready to fire.

The spring wind hit his face and brought with it the sweet scent of jasmine. The sun lit up his face with golden pride. He bent forward, the ball feeling light as air in his hand. He hurled it at the chubby kid. Dad was cheering somewhere in the crowd—his boisterous shouting was unmistakable. His words followed the ball as it sailed through the afternoon air.

"Ball four!" the umpire announced.

With those two simple words, his world came crashing down. The Green Gophers cheered and ran at the fat kid, lifting him up and shouting in a frenzy. Rick's dad never let him live it down. He never said a word to Rick about, he didn't have to, the icy stare and the constant doubting of everything Rick did was enough of a message.

No problem. Nothing ever was.

Fuck the old man and fuck what he thinks of me. He's too busy working on his portfolio and fucking his secretary to even notice what I do, so why should I care about what he thinks of me?

He thought of his kid sister, Annie, and how she used to annoy the living shit out of him. He remembered the time she had run up to him crying and pointing at a scrape on her knee from falling off her bike. She must have been six and he twelve, and he was having none of it.

"Get over it, baby," he had said before turning back to Cody, holding a baseball bat.

"But Rick," she heaved and sobbed, "it hurts."

He was about to tell her off again, but stopped. Stupid sentiment tugged at him. He bent down and wiped the blood off her knee with his shirtsleeve. Not very sanitary, but it got the job done. She smiled and hugged his neck, threatening to strangle him then and there with love.

Alone in the dark cell, Rick began sobbing.

This isn't fair. I don't deserve this. Mia and Cody don't deserve this.

The thought of his friends unleashed more tears. He was going to marry Mia; that had been decided. Was going to help Cody get over that bitch Rachel. He always hated her and how she brought his friend down.

He needs to learn how to handle things on his own.

Yeah, that was right. Cody needs to stand up for himself and stop being such a leech. He felt bad about this thought, but it was true. He moved his attention back to the cell. There was nothing: no windows, no objects inside. The only thing was the door.

"Stop crying, pussy, get to work."

He pushed against the door with his left shoulder. Rock-solid. It didn't budge, not even in the slightest. Rick kicked the door with all his weight behind it. All the years of weightlifting (never skipped leg day) came to a single focused point in his foot as he kicked the door with his heel. It rattled but didn't move.

He kicked it again, and again, and again. His shins began cracking under the blows. He kicked it again. He heard another crack, not from his bones but from something on the side of the door near its hinges.

He saw that a few metal nails were coming loose at the hinges. Rick rammed his leg one more time into the door and shattered his tibia. He collapsed to the floor and cradled his leg with one hand, clenching his jaws tightly, but not allowing himself to yell out in pain. The pain racked his body in great tremors.

I just have to sleep, yeah, that's what I need.

He didn't even need to try; unconsciousness came to him effortlessly.

Rick woke to the sound of the door slamming against the wall. A shadow filled the frame of the entrance. Yellow and faded light rimmed it. Darkness shrouded the face, yet Rick could feel its eyes on him.

"What do you want?" he said in a deep and loud voice that nonetheless shook with apprehension.

The figure entered the cell.

It was a man with short, scraggly hair. He had a silver earring on his left earlobe and a scar across his left eye. His eyes glowed silver. He was skinny and much shorter than Rick. He smiled with his teeth while his eyes didn't move, not even to blink.

Rick tried to shove him aside, but the short man pulled out a long metal object and struck Rick on the closed wound where his arm used to be. The pain of his injury, despite his healing, turned into a vice crushing his body between its jaws. The man grabbed Rick's neck and lifted him off the ground, his feet suspended off the floor. The man smiled again, flashing a single gold tooth at him. He put Rick back on the ground and patted his head like one would a child's.

"*Momanaku kuru zo. Matte*," the man said.

"What the fuck are you saying, you little piece of shit?" Spit flew out of Rick's mouth, and he scrambled to his feet again. The short man brandished the metal pipe and slapped it in his hands, saying, "Try me" with his eyes. Rick tried him. He couldn't help it; that was who he was, not a man to back down from anything. Rick flew at the man and kicked him in the groin. He crumpled to the ground with a dry gasp.

Shit, I did it. Time to go.

Rick grabbed the pipe and was about to leave before regarding the man cradling his groin on the floor. He raised the pipe and brought it down on his shiny bald head. He went silent and slumped down on the floor. Blood flowed from his skull.

Rick didn't allow guilt to fill his heart. As with all things emotional, he closed himself off to the feelings. The man got back up.

The fuck?

Rick closed the door and slid the locking mechanism shut. To his surprise, the man did not attack the door, nor try to force it open, though Rick was sure he had the power to do so. He saw the shadow of the man's feet near the crack at the bottom of the door; the man just stood there.

Rick turned around and found himself in a dark corridor lined with barred doors and a few open, rust-colored cages. He walked down the hall, opened the door at the end, and came into another corridor.

More cages lined the walls. In them, Rick could see dried pools of blood and dirty rags. Some shoes. A baseball cap. A child's pink dress. They were all tattered and ripped to shreds. The cage directly across from his cell held a dead body. The smell of rotting meat, sweet fruit, and feces permeated the air.

The body was bloated and painted black and blue. There was no way to tell any specific details about what it once was: sex, age, and race were all erased by slow decay. It had to have been dead long enough to rot, but not so long that it would be reduced to a skeleton.

All these clothes, all those cars, those fires we saw at night. How long has this been going on? And the children's clothing everywhere... the sick fucks.

"Some are not fit for sacrifice."

Aiko entered the corridor at the end of the hall.

"Oh yeah, little girls not enough for you?" Rick's face was purple, and a vein pulsed on his forehead.

"You think us barbaric?" Aiko frowned. "Yes, it may seem that way. Were we to offer the unfit to Him, the consequences would be horrific, even worse than death. Death is a mercy to them. But those who are chosen to meet Him, such as myself and the people you have met so far, are the lucky ones. For we shall ever be in His presence, where there is no more pain or fear. As for you, I am beyond happy to see that your arm has healed. He does not accept sacrifices that have been tainted by blood."

"Fuck you and fuck your god."

"You say that now, Rick, but soon you will be begging him for mercy. And he will not give it to you." She smiled her perfect smile and winked at him. A strange attraction took hold there. Yes, Aiko was a beautiful woman, but that wasn't it. There was something else about her, something that shone. He thought for a moment what it would be like to have her eyes of silver, to be with a woman who spoke to a living god, to rule beside her.

As if she could see into his mind, she said, "You would like that, wouldn't you? It could have been yours, Rick; it still can be... if you kneel."

He shut out the thoughts and shook his head hard. Fuck the old man, fuck that bald fuck in the cell, and fuck this child-murdering bitch.

Rick charged her with the pipe in hand.

Her eyes went nova, burning his retinas. Rick didn't even have time to shield his eyes. He felt his soul leave his body. He smelled burnt hair and tasted nickel. All he could see and feel after that was the welcome warmth of the pale light that emanated from the woman at the end of the hall.

Oh, how he loved her then.

17

Cody and Mia ducked behind a bush full of dark, wine-colored berries. The tall man's eyes lit up the bush. The light passed quickly, though, and went towards the rice fields by the gate.

The monster of a man swiveled his head around the area one more time, and, appearing satisfied, went back to staring at the town's gates. The giant bent down under the archway and passed through it. His footsteps pounded away from them and moved away towards the center of the town. Although he moved further away, they could still see the top of his head just above the roofs of the buildings, like a shark's fin, alerting them to his location.

Behind them, somewhere deep in the hidden places of the forest, the trees shook. The stars were brilliant. The sky was crystal clear, smooth, and inviting. A red star was at the center of it all, seemingly directly above them.

As if sensing his thoughts, Mia said, "It—he—is not going to let us leave, Cody. I told you. There's no point in trying."

He looked at Mia and clenched his fists. "Do you think if we go back that way," he nodded into the forest from where they had fled, "we're just going to end up right back at the pyramid?"

"Yes. And the light will be there. You saw it too, right? That star came down; actually came fucking down from the sky and landed on that pyramid. It came down, and it followed us." She thrashed her arms as if she were fighting off invisible attackers as she spoke. Tears flooded down her face, washing her cheeks free of the grime and dirt of the past few hours.

"And you know what else I saw?"

Cody raised his open palm to her face and closed his eyes. "No, no, we didn't."

"I saw it, and you saw it too. We saw... *him.*"

"That's enough. We don't know what that was, but it wasn't a fucking god, okay?"

"Then what? What was it?"

Cody wanted to say UFOs, ghosts, government conspiracies, anything but what Aiko had told them back at her house. Anything would have been better than that. How could they hope to survive against something divine?

Before either could speak again, there was a scuffling sound from beyond the gate to the village. Someone moaned, but it wasn't human. It was deeper, filled with sorrow and pain. A pot fell to the ground and broke.

"Let's go back to the woods," Cody said and turned around.

The trees bent and cracked. A deep growl emanated from the hollows of the dark places. No stars showed their light there now; it was pure blackness save for one spot deep in the woods. They could see it—the red light that walked in the shadows. It was out there, and it was waiting for them.

"Cody." Mia put her hand on his back. "It's in there and won't let us go back that way. If we try it again, we're dead, I just know it."

Cody hung his head. "You're right; there's no leaving here."

The moaning from beyond the gate rose to a lamentation. Feet scuffled, and the sound began moving towards them. It was not the quaking of the giant's footsteps. It was the soft scraping of more humanlike feet. The moan was a violence breaking upon the still night.

"So, what do we do? We can't just sit here all night. We have to move," Mia said.

The choice was made for them. The voice of an ancient being, of some old man chanting an incomprehensible language, came from the direction of the light in the forest. They couldn't see what spoke those scattered words. They did, however, see the trees quake before it.

Something was coming. Something big. Its footsteps picked up pace and moved towards them.

Stuck between two unseen threats, Cody motioned to Mia and mouthed, "Follow me," at her. He walked out of the tree line, crouching low and glancing around furtively down into the rice paddy that lay just beyond the obscurity of their hiding place. The rice field was the same one that the two farmers who greeted them with smiles were in when the friends first came to Inunaki. When they thought they were saved.

Cody moved toward the middle of the field in nearly waist-high water. Mia followed, the water coming up to her chest. She floated and swam rather than walked. The smell of something foul rose from the water, and gnats clamored near their faces. Cody sank to his stomach, submerging most of his body under the water and the stalks of the rice. Mia floated along, already nearly hidden under the water.

The gnats were at their eyes now, getting stuck in their lashes. Cody's glasses acted as a shield to some of them, but his breath fogged up the lenses and blurred the world around him.

A man holding a flaming torch walked onto the road leading from the town to the rice fields. He held a curved blade in the other hand. He was scanning the area with eyes that glowed white-hot and fluorescent. Everywhere he looked, the area lit up as if melancholy daylight exposed it.

The cold light skipped across the field to the far end of the rice stalks and landed near them. Tall rice protected most of their faces from the light, and water covered their bodies. The man made no movements or sounds, apparently not seeing them. Cody moved his head parallel to the water and submerged it, leaving only his nose out. Mia followed suit.

Something large emerged from the forest. Branches cracked and gave way before something massive. From it came that prehistoric speech, distant and ancient and aggressive, muttering to itself. Cody heard it come near the man with the scythe, who responded with the same low voice and fractured language.

More branches snapped, and the sound of heavy steps grew louder until it passed and faded in the direction of the town.

For a minute, neither Cody nor Mia moved. They breathed slowly through their nostrils.

Then a sickening sound of something stretching itself out came from the path. Cody dared to move a rice stalk to its side and saw the farmer; he hadn't moved from his spot. At least whatever beast that had emerged from the forest had gone. The stretching sound came from the man's neck as it began growing.

The neck reached out, tripling its size, like a rubbery python. Cody let out a gasp, sending bubbles to the surface of the water and dirty water into his lungs. He concentrated, clasped his hand over his mouth, and slowed his breathing. He fought the urge to cough up the water and just swallowed it.

The head, attached to a serpentine neck, slithered down to the water, now at least four feet long and counting. The man's breath caused the water to ripple. The tiny waves from the epicenter crashed into Cody's eyes, washing off a few insects.

The giraffe-like neck guided the head around the perimeter of the field. Cody could see his teeth in the light of his eyes. The teeth were broken, shattered, and made sharp in their disfigurement. Drool flowed out of the gaping hole. The neck grew longer and came nearer to his position. Cody looked over and saw the whites of Mia's eyes.

He reached out and grabbed her hand underwater. She looked at him; he sank his head under the surface, and she followed. They lay still, fully submerged, and covered their noses. A face hovered above them, distorted through the water, pushing through the rice stalks, its searchlight eyes looking into the pond and missing them by inches.

He saw the light in its eyes move away. Cody stayed still a moment more. He could see nothing above him and did not know if it was still there. Then, when he could no longer hold his breath, he surfaced slowly. Mia was already sitting up. The farmer was looking away from them and at the forest on the other side of the path that lay by the field, scanning the foliage.

A branch snapped. In an instant, the man lunged into the trees. Some animal shrieked and went silent. Cody could hear him eating whatever he had found. The curved blade remained on the bank of the field as the thing that was once the farmer fed. Cody moved through the water over to the weapon, careful not to make any noise. The man was in the woods and out of Cody's sight, partially hidden by the embankment. He got to the edge of the field and took the blade.

Now he could see the monster in the shade of a tree feasting on whatever unfortunate animal it had found. The monster's neck coiled several times over, exposing it and leaving it unguarded. He had dropped his torch on the ground, its flame snuffed out in the dirt.

He was close, no more than five or six steps away. Nothing would have stopped Cody from bringing the blade down on it. He gripped the handle and stood. His hand shook. All he could hear was a ringing sound in his ears. He breathed fast and deep and became lightheaded. Cody shivered from the cold, his hands shaking. He lost his grip on the blade. Dropped it. Picked it back up. Crouched down, and went back into the water and back to Mia.

He couldn't do it.

As he lowered himself back into the pool, he wasn't altogether silent. A slight splash greeted him as he entered the water. Cody was quick to lie down amid the tall stalks. The farmer, or the thing that was once a farmer, that was once a human being, that was once the kindly face that greeted them as a sign of salvation from being lost, turned its serpentine head towards the field.

The wild animal's blood flowed with the man's drool, creating a cascade of gelatinous red that dripped down. The man entered the water. His head dove under the surface and glided through the rice stalks just as a python or alligator would through the Everglades. The lower half of his face was under the water. His eyes were like silver searchlights on a ghostly ship sailing through the dark water.

Those lights landed on the stalk in front of Mia's face. She dove her head under the water, making a splash.

The monster darted toward her. At this moment, Cody still held onto the blade. As the creature struck, Cody sprang up from his prone position, swiped the weapon out blindly in front of him, and made contact. The curved edge sank into the right eye of the monster.

It shouted and retreated to the land. Its neck cracked and squelched and returned to its original size. The farmer stumbled to his knees as he struggled with the blade that Cody had jammed into his face.

Cody jumped out of the water and ran, yelling at Mia to get out of there. He heard the splash of her frantic footsteps behind him. Cody sprinted for the woods but froze when he saw the red light was still there, moving in the darkness, stalking between the trees, moving them aside like blades of grass. He turned around and ran for the stone gates of the village. Cody had to pass by the farmer to do so. He—it—was still grappling the blade and pulling it out of the eye socket.

In front of them lay the road that would take them to the heart of the town. That wasn't an option; that way lay both the tall man and whatever monster they had heard emerge from the forest. Yet, going back would bring them face to face with the red light once more.

To their left, there was a trail, half-hidden by fern leaves, that looked like it wound its way around the town by going up a slight hill, a bypass to the whole place. Small stone rectangles dotted the path. They took it and ran up the hill.

They made it to an open area with more stones laid out in a circular pattern, clustered tightly together. Pictures of people, mostly of the elderly, were attached to the stones. From here, they could see the town down below. Cody looked back down the path.

The farmer was walking towards them. No blade in his eye. No trace of blood or injury. No dimming of that accursed light. It looked just as it had before Cody stabbed it. The farmer's neck was already growing out again, causing his head to flail and bob wildly.

They dove into the bushes on the far side of the graveyard and ran through thick vegetation until they came out to another clearing. A hut riddled with holes from countless termites stood in front of them.

Chest-high grass filled the area surrounding the hut. They went through the open door of the hut and closed it. They could see outside through the holes in the wall. They waited. Cody began hyperventilating.

"Shut up," Mia whispered.

He struggled to form a sentence but couldn't through the gasping and breaking breaths. Mia put her hand over his mouth and clasped it shut. Cody felt like he was being smothered, but gave in to the feeling, knowing there was no other way to remain quiet.

The near-murder of the man was unnecessary. No one came crashing through the thick bushes between the cemetery and the hut. They waited another minute, Cody's breath calmed, and nothing sounded outside. The only thing that registered with their senses was the musty odor of countless decades of mold that must have been hibernating inside the hut.

It wouldn't be so bad, Cody thought, *to just hole up here forever.*

To avoid moving, to escape the horrors outside. Just live here in this hut with a woman who hated him. Or just die of starvation. Yeah, that would be better than having to look into those bright eyes ever again.

A cry filled the air. Cody and Mia looked at one another.

"That's..." Mia began.

"Rick," Cody finished.

They said nothing more. The choice was obvious. Stay here in relative safety, or try to aid Rick. Mia opened the door and left. Cody followed tentatively.

They crouched down and tiptoed through the bushes. When they reached the cemetery, the farmer had already gone. The screams had ceased. They moved to the edge of the graveyard, where they could look down into the town.

Cody saw something on the side of a building. White bandana on the head, pink blouse stretched to its limit over the bloated thing wearing it. The woman who, but a few hours ago, had been hanging her laundry in the sun. She was crawling up the side of a house. She came to the roof and perched herself on its edge, her head twitching from side to side, like a praying mantis searching for flies. She leaped off the roof and scrambled up a tall tree nearby.

Or did she fly up it? Thin, nearly translucent wings protruded from her back. She sat perfectly still in the tree, scanning the ground beneath her with intent. Had they been walking underneath that tree, they would never have known the horror waiting for them above.

Cody's spine tingled with the sensation of cold needles being inserted through his skin down to the bone. He didn't want to, but forced himself to look up into the trees. Imagining a monstrosity falling upon him was too much to bear. He saw nothing, save for the branches of a great cedar bouncing softly in the wind, thank God.

The screams did not come again. Cody strained his eyes to see if he could find where they had come from, to no avail.

There was no reason to move at the moment. No one had seen them yet; they had cover, and there was nowhere they could think of moving to. Beneath them, the townspeople had packed into the courtyard before the pyramid. The crowd's silver eyes glowed and swayed in the dark like cell phones at a concert.

They were waiting for something, torches in hand. The tall man moved through the back of the crowd like a bouncer. His watchful stare washed the entire village in light. He occasionally flashed those eyes up to his left, in the hills where Cody and Mia were hiding. They could feel it as it passed over them as if it were a cool breeze. Drums picked up, slowly at first, and gradually beat faster.

Mia whispered, "What do we do?"

"I don't know, but I think I understand something now. It's not that they're dumb, but I think they lose focus quickly. The thing that chased us up here, it went away when it couldn't see us anymore. Same with that giant and that girl we saw in the woods. I think if we just stay hidden, they won't find us." He remembered the glazed expressions of the people from the afternoon. He hoped he was right, that they were not altogether "there."

He went on. "And Rick, he has to be down there, right? We heard him. Maybe we should just wait until sunrise, head back to the hut? These things—the people — they changed once it got dark, right? Maybe if we wait until daylight, they might change back. I mean, they could have killed us when we first came here, but they didn't. When Rick was asleep at Aiko's house and I was in the bath, that would've been the perfect time to do something. Maybe they had to wait until it got dark."

"If they don't want to kill us, then what do they want?"

Cody remembered Aiko's words: "*In his world, there is no more pain.*"

"It doesn't matter, because it will not happen to us, alright?"

"But what can we do about it?"

He hadn't a clue, not even the barest sliver of one.

Just then, the tall man walked over to their position. Had he heard them? His face drew near the hill and deluged the area with its torrent of light. They were under the bush, looking up at the giant face. Were it to look directly down, it would see them clearly. The tall man continued walking, marching a perimeter around the entire town.

They looked out at the festival of chilling lights below. Their eyes reminded Cody of the fireflies in the forest from earlier. Those had provided a modicum of comfort. These drained him of all hope.

Mia's voice startled Cody out of his thoughts. "You know, I'm not as happy as I look."

Where the hell is this coming from? He thought.

She looked at him knowingly. "If we're going to die tonight, I may as well say it to somebody. I've been depressed for years, not like super-serious, but, you know, bad," she let out a sigh, "but Rick really helped me. I know he's an oaf, but he's a good guy. He never judged me; he let me be me. I don't know if I can go on without him."

Cody sucked at heart-to-hearts, but gave it a shot. "Yeah, he's a good guy. But whatever happens, you're going to be fine. I mean, you killed that monster girl that almost killed me, right? And with a fucking metal pole. That's badass."

"Even if she didn't actually die?" She laughed.

"Especially because she didn't die. Not many people can say they took on a demon and lived."

The ripples of their stifled laughter gradually died down. They went back to silence and watched the scene below, hoping their path forward would reveal itself.

It would, in the most devastating of ways.

Aiko appeared. She still looked human, with no tight skin, no sharp teeth. The only thing about her that would give one cause for uneasiness were the glowing eyes. A minor issue, all things considered. She made her way to the steps of the pyramid, turned to face the townsfolk, and began speaking. She wasn't shouting, but Cody could hear her voice as clearly as if she were whispering directly into his ears.

Her words were beyond their understanding, but their intent was unmistakable. Hate filled them. As she spoke, the creatures didn't move. They all stood slack-jawed, mouths agape, and dumbfounded. Two men walked in front of Aiko, carrying something in their arms.

It was Rick.

18

The men dropped him on the ground in front of Aiko. He seemed to be unconscious or dead. Mia let out a choked sob. Cody held her hand.

The thunder of drums reverberated throughout the town. Cody could feel the vibration in his skin. It caused his heart to skip a beat or two. A conch shell sounded out over the town from an unseen location. Aiko bent down and said something over Rick's unmoving body. He rose to his knees. Cody could now see a bright white cloth bandaged where his arm used to be.

That means they want him alive, right?

A fleeting moment of hope crossed Cody's mind—a solitary island of light and warmth amidst the sea of death and terror they now found themselves in.

Cody was about to be proven wrong.

Aiko went up the steps, and Rick followed her, stumbling as if he were drunk. From their vantage point, they could see the top of the pyramid clearly. Aiko walked to the far end of the platform, while Rick stopped at its center point and turned around. His eyes half-closed, and he cocked his head to the side. He bit his lip, a remnant of his former self showing through whatever hypnosis he was under.

The drums beat more furiously, an ecstatic dance of some wild pagan orgy of delight. Aiko fastened a chain to his remaining wrist and a second one to his right ankle. It looked as if someone had solidly secured them to the platform. After she finished, she walked purposefully down the steps.

Rick woke up. He shook his head. Looked like a terrified dog. He thrashed about in his chains. Rick yelled out, "What's going on?! Cody, Mia, where are you?"

Their names were being shouted across the town with sad desperation.

Mia squirmed in her spot, so much so Cody thought he might have to restrain her from running down to Rick. She didn't move, but her chest heaved violently as she stifled her screams. Cody's breath came out in fast bursts. He gripped the dirt in front of him for some kind of stability.

Rick yelled obscenities and rage into the sky.

Aiko also shouted into the sky. All the villagers went silent and bowed to the ground. Even the tall man, who stood at the back of the crowd. Aiko herself bent her face to the pavement like a folded-over piece of cardboard.

Rick started crying. He struggled with his one arm against the chain. He flopped like a fish against the steel and paused.

He cried out, "You fuckers! You'd better not touch my friends. I'm going to get out of here and shove your deformed, freakish hands or whatever you have up your asses!"

His face was fiery red as he bellowed down at the monstrosities.

Then he went silent. The red left his face. White glossed over his expression. He looked up at the sky. His eyes were wide with terror. He fell to his knees. It didn't seem like he could help it; more like something pushed him down and held him there. Something held him glued to the platform at his knees. He shook as he tried to stand but could not do so. His head snapped back, looking directly upward.

The stars went out. As did the torches held by the townspeople. The dark sky seemed to fold back on itself. Like the parting of storm clouds, though none were present. A red star appeared off in the forest, to Cody and Mia's right, near the town's main entrance. It rose into the sky and sailed high over the town. The color shaded everything in massacre-red. The scarlet light moved. It searched from one face in the crowd to another.

Dear God, don't let it see us.

Cody felt exposed, no matter where he was hiding. The light focused itself solely on Rick.

The star descended and came to rest closer above the town, a stone's throw away. It looked no bigger than one of the nearby buildings. The star disappeared and snuffed itself out. Full dark. Silence and expectation weighed heavily in the blackness.

Rick erupted in flames.

He screamed with a voice ripped straight from his marrow. He lifted his left hand towards the sky and began shouting, "Amatsu! Amatsu!"

His body was perfectly still, as if held in place by some unseen force. He screamed. Mia reciprocated. Cody dove on top of her, covering her mouth with his hands. She bit him. Cody winced but held on to her. It was sick to say, but thankfully Rick's screams and the inferno of red light were louder.

As he burned, a dark cloud swirled high above Rick. It writhed about as if it were made of tentacles or snakes, all jostling over each other, twisting their way into one another. Aiko and the townspeople turned their faces away from it and bowed even further into the ground.

A shadow descended from the cloud. It was large, the size of the pyramid itself. It was too dark to see, but Cody could make out some details in the fire's light. A face. It was a fleeting moment, but he saw it: a face emerged from the darkness. It was as large as Rick's whole body, but covered in shadow. He couldn't see any details. It looked like it was inhaling the smoke of the fire. The shadows covered it fully once the mass retreated into the cloud.

The red star reignited. The blast of its light was a maelstrom of radiance.

Everyone, Aiko included, had to shield themselves from it. The star climbed back into the sky and dispersed itself back into what Cody thought had been a constellation, what he now knew was a facade. It looked like a normal star shining in the sky. It was right next to the North Star.

Had he been paying attention, he would have noticed something odd about it. Its color was off compared to the rest of the stars. It held a reddish tint, but nothing overt. It covered the North Star, masking itself over it. But it was there. How long had it been watching them from the depths of space?

Rick's screams reached a pitch that broke Cody's train of thought.

Cody looked on as Rick burned.

Minutes passed, and he kept on burning, kept on screaming.

He did not die.

19

"Oh, my God." Mia broke free from Cody's grasp.

She started climbing down the hill towards the pyramid.

She knocked some small rocks off the ledge, and they rolled down to the street below. Seconds later, her feet slipped on the dirt that began spilling out beneath her. She tumbled down and landed with a thud. A solitary nearby towns person turned and spotted her. It was the farmer, the one with the snakelike neck. His eyes glowed as they rested on Mia, and he charged her. She raised her hands to her face.

The creature stopped mid-charge.

Pink rays of sunrise cut through the night. They were weak and faint at first, the sun just rising. Clouds came rolling in, desperately racing to cover the valley. No, not clouds. It looked like smoke pouring out of the mountain that overlooked the town. Flowing out like an eruption from a volcano. It spewed down to the ground and rose to the sky, covering everything in its gray obscurity. For a moment, Cody saw the unblemished sky of the morning, painted in frosty blue and pink.

The feeling of unfiltered daylight raised his spirits, despite his fatigue, if only just for a second.

The man with the long neck saw the sunrise as well. He hissed and cowered against it, taking refuge under the eaves of a nearby home. As soon as the smog covered the sky, he straightened up again. The light in his eyes disappeared. The jagged teeth set themselves straight with a crack. The neck retracted back into the shoulders. His mummified skin softened, returning to a more human, meaty look. He stood there, disoriented.

Cody looked out over the town and saw a similar metamorphosis take place with the others. The light in the silver eyes went out. The woman in the trees fell to the ground, her wings jamming themselves back into her body. The tall man shrank until he was no taller than an average-looking man. He looked familiar now; it was the man who carried the conch shell. His locks of gray hair made that obvious. Someone must have specifically made the robes he had worn as the tall man for him, as a much smaller man emerged naked from the comically oversized cloth.

The red star descended once more. It fell on top of the hill that spewed out the smoke. It seeped into the ground and seemed to enter the mountain. The moment the sun rose, the fire on the pyramid went out, and Rick stopped screaming.

Cody scrambled down the hill and landed on his feet next to Mia. He helped her up. He picked up a softball-sized stone that had fallen with him and cocked his arm back, facing off against the man who stood some distance in front of them under the eaves of the house. That man stood still as if in a trance.

From their position, they were alone with the man. The rest of the community was on the other side of a house. He didn't move, aside from swaying from side to side as he stared up at the sky. The man lowered his head and fixed his eyes on them. He was miles away, but a faint flicker of recognition was returning to him, like a drunk just sobering up. He focused his pupils and raised a finger at them. A sound escaped his throat.

Cody ran across the street, rock in hand. He hurled it against the man's forehead.

The stone made a sharp smacking sound against his skull. The man fell to the ground and hit his head on the pavement.

Cody stood over the body and saw the blood spread red over the dull tone of the street. The world spun around his field of vision as he reeled and lurched forward, vomiting over his shoes. When he opened his eyes, he saw Mia lifting him to a sitting position.

The farmer lay on the ground, motionless.

"Come on, get up. We have to get out of here before anyone else comes by."

Cody stood.

"Rick. We have to go to him now," Mia said as she grabbed his sleeve and began dragging him towards the town square.

"Hold on." He ripped his sleeve back from her. "We'll get caught for sure. We have to think about getting out of here. I think the light, I mean sunlight, means something. You saw what happened. Everyone changed back to normal or whatever the fuck passes for that is. They changed when the sun came out. Maybe we can get through the forest now. That red light went into the mountain, maybe during the day things will change back to normal."

"But we saw it, that light, in the daytime. Well, it was dark out, but you know what I mean."

"Yeah, but it's in the mountain now. Maybe it'll come out, who knows. But it's something to go on. Let's move."

She took a step back from him and crossed her arms. "And leave Rick?"

"He's... he's dead, Mia."

"I know." Her lips wavered, and her face lost its color. "I know, but... if it's the same as that body we saw at the pyramid last night, he's not completely dead. I mean, he's going to come back and... and keep on burning every night. And for how long? Forever?" The last word was barely audible because of her voice cracking.

An image of the closed bathroom door came unwanted to his attention.

Cody knew she was right. Rick was dead. Of that, there was no debate. But he wasn't completely dead. Cody saw it. He heard the screaming the entire time, far longer than should have been possible for someone to survive being consumed by flames. It all stopped the moment the sun rose.

"You're right. But we have to be careful."

"I want to kill her," Mia said with dead eyes. "I want to kill that bitch and set her on fire. If that would even do anything."

Would it? Cody wondered if anyone could kill Aiko at all, let alone with fire. He saw the head wound Rick had given her. There was too much blood for her to have gotten back up as fast as she did. He looked down at the man with the cracked skull. Was he dead? Sure, any reasonable person would say he was. But given the horrors of last night, he was up for believing anything now.

"If we killed her, would all this stop?" She looked up at Cody with expectant eyes.

"Like a sci-fi movie where you kill the head alien and everything else dies?" Her face was clueless in response to his words. "I don't think it works that way. But she is the leader, the priestess of that thing. It might work. At least as far as helping Rick."

"We have to do something. I'm not leaving him like this."

Cody nodded. They walked towards the center of town, keeping themselves pressed to the sides of the buildings.

On the other side of the house in front of them, they could hear some people speaking.

Not people, he thought, *can't think of them as people, can't think that I just killed some-ONE.*

Their voices were muffled, but they were coming near. There was an open door to the house. Cody and Mia ducked inside and crouched behind a bundle of rice at the entrance. Two men drew near. They looked completely normal. The one nearest the house even laughed at something the one on the right had said.

There were knives and some farming tools on the wall where they were hiding. They each grabbed one, Mia a dull scythe, Cody a short blunt knife. As the men outside were within arm's reach, Cody tensed his hand around the handle. He had done it before. Just five minutes ago. Sure, he didn't know that he would kill the man before he acted, but the result was the same—death. The men in front of him looked human. He knew they weren't, but that didn't change the visceral feeling in his gut that it would be murder. His heart beat so hard he felt it in his wrists.

The men continued on and walked away from the house. Cody let out a pregnant sigh.

"How do we get to Rick with no one seeing us? And before it gets dark!" Mia half-whispered, half-shouted.

"Yesterday, when I was walking around before things went bat-shit-crazy, I saw some people, like the flying thing in the pink shirt. She was doing her laundry kind of absent-mindedly. Like she wasn't fully aware of what she was doing."

Mia's puzzled face spurred him on. "I mean, they were doing things like it was all on repeat. They weren't present and focused. I think that means that they aren't that smart and observant, like the things that chased us last night. We could take advantage of that."

"Not Aiko."

No, not her. If anything, she seemed more awake, more "there" than the others. She possessed knowledge and power that were beyond the others. Cody doubted she had ever actually learned English through a stupid radio program. Hers was a wisdom given to her by something beyond this world.

Cody did not know what to do. Thoroughly stumped. He looked away to the wall.

"The chains!" Cody exclaimed, causing Mia to jump up in surprise.

He went on, "The bodies are all chained up, right? You only do that if you want something to stay where it is. Maybe they have to be on those pyramids for the fire to burn them. If we take his body away, we can-" Cody nearly broke down in tears. "Then maybe something will happen. Maybe it will break whatever hold this god has over him."

"And then what? Leave his body on the street?"

"Hey, I don't know what the fuck I'm doing here, okay? This is all I've got."

Mia went silent. Cody looked away.

Mia spoke up. "What about all those other people? Aiko's father and the one with the gold necklace?"

"No, we'll probably die trying to help just Rick. No way we can do anything for anybody else. If we succeed with Rick, we just hit the road that you saw the other day and get the fuck out of here."

"There's one more thing we can do."

"What?"

"I'm going to slit that bitch's throat."

Cody nodded his head in agreement, though in his heart he knew that wouldn't be possible. They stood up and looked around the home. Everything was neat and in order, with not a trace of dust to be found.

The home looked just like Aiko's with some minor differences. It had the same red door, and the same Jesus-esque painting of the man in the light, but there was a different portrait on the wall. It was of a man and woman—in their fifties, by the look of it. The year of their deaths was 1968. Around the same time as Aiko's father.

Not a coincidence, Cody thought. *I wonder if they're behind that door as well. Does everyone in this hell have a parent chained up outside, undergoing everlasting punishment? Quite therapeutic in dealing with your problems.*

On the same wall where Cody grabbed his dull blade (now resting in his pocket), there was a saw. It looked functional, so it would have to do. The chains weren't coming off through brute force.

There was a ladder leaning against the wall opposite the red door. Cody pointed it out to Mia with his eyes, and they climbed it. It took them to a verandah that overlooked the street below. There was a lattice large enough for them to crouch behind and remain hidden. Below, several people walked by. Poking his head over the lattice, Cody could see three houses separating them from the town square. A black figure stood atop the stone structure, wisps of smoke rising off it. Behind Rick's body, the looming mountain sent its smoke into the sky.

Cody knew what that meant now: whatever this thing was, it hated the light of the sun. Good to know, but hardly the thing one could control and leverage.

The home next to where they stood was close. So close that was almost within arm's reach from the veranda.

"It'll be easy to jump over to the next house from here instead of being down there with those people walking around. If we can do that a few times, we'll get close to the square without being noticed, hopefully," Cody said.

Mia looked over at the next house doubtfully. "I guess so…"

The men below had moved on and were out of sight. Cody stood with one leg on the wall and catapulted himself across the gap to the next house, landing softly on the verandah. He was a light man, after all. Mia came next and jumped. She slipped on the edge of the veranda as she landed, but Cody caught her hands. They moved to the other side, and the distance to the next house was the same as the last, all these homes so tightly packed together. Cody jumped first, turned around, and waited for Mia. She slipped again, but this time Cody was ready to catch her. Her short legs were not cut out for this. They could repeat the action one last time, with minimal slipping, and got to the final veranda.

This was too easy.

There was no one in the courtyard. Cody could hear voices from a hidden alley or maybe from beneath their feet. The laughter he heard caused Cody to hate them. Looking up at what was left of Rick, he hated the people of this town all the more. His palms were sweaty from all the emotion stirring inside him. He thought about wringing Aiko's neck and chaining her up outside. Maybe he could free her father and have him do it.

It seemed like most of the townspeople had left the area and were milling about near the fields in the outer parts of the town. Cody could spot a solitary individual walking aimlessly in the courtyard and leaving from time to time. It seemed like no one was searching for them. Come to think of it, it never really seemed like they were being chased. Sure, they had a few run-ins after Aiko's house, but none of the people ever actually *ran* after them.

He locked those thoughts away for later pondering, assuming he would ever have the chance again to do so.

Cody gestured at the pyramid. "Okay, this is our only chance. I don't think we'll get so lucky again, and there's no way we're surviving another night here. We slide down this rain pipe here. I'll go first and help you land after. Then we run to Rick, cut his chains, I'll carry him, and-"

"It's not going to work, is it?"

Cody sighed. It was a ridiculous plan. "No, it's not. But what choice do we have?"

"How many people would you say are in this village? Thirty?"

"Twenty-nine if you count the guy without a solid skull back there."

"Okay. What if we just kill them one by one? Move from house to house and bash their heads in?"

Cody's mouth hung low, and his eyebrows arched. "I'm no fucking James Bond here, and no offense, neither are you."

"It's an option, though, isn't it?"

"Even the kids?"

She didn't answer, but Cody could feel her intent. She was silent, but not out of shame. Her face beamed a cold, determined calculation.

"How would we even go about doing that?" He asked.

She eyed her scythe and passed it from one hand to the other. It was dull. How many throats could it cut before it became useless? How could a 100-pound girl hope to kill an army of supernaturally charged creatures with a defunct farming tool? Fuck, how could *he* do it? Even Rick was no match for one of them. Sure, it was day now, and they looked normal, but even so, it was two against dozens.

Indecision paralyzed Cody until he remembered the bell tower. "The bell at the entrance to the town. If we ring it, we can lure them out to the sound. Then one of us can make it out to Rick and get him free."

"You should go for Rick. You're stronger, so you can carry him. I'm smaller, I can get around better."

"We probably won't be able to meet back up after shit hits the fan. Once you ring the bell, run back up the path to the cemetery, go down the hill you fell from earlier, and book it to the road. You ring the bell, get to that spot, and just run. I don't know if I'll be there before you or not, so don't wait for me."

Mia hugged him. "All the things I said earlier... I'm sorry."

"It's okay. I'm sorry too. If I had done more earlier, we wouldn't be here. If we make it out of this, I'll make it up to you, I swear."

"We will make it out, both of us." She smiled at him. He hadn't even realized he missed seeing that electric smile. It had only been a day or so since it had failed to appear on her face, but that seemed like a lifetime ago. Glazed-over eyes and a dead smile had replaced it, most often when she was looking at the sky.

She's going to be okay.

They waited until they couldn't hear any voices from below. Cody watched as Mia entered the house and went down the ladder. When she disappeared, he hid behind a large basket on the veranda. He had a clear shot at Rick. All he had to do was wait for the bell, watch everyone leave, shimmy down the drainpipe, run up the steps, saw through the chains, carry Rick's body down, and find a place to bury it.

Maybe if I can make it back to the woods, I'll find a spot by a large tree. Easy.

20

Mia had always hated her size. In middle school, the other girls called her "Minnie Mouse." And not out of affection. Flat chest, big ears, short legs, short stature.

The words of the other kids at Gladstone County Middle School hurt like thin razor blades across her wrists. It was during this time that her father started drinking and taking out his insecurities on her. She had always wanted to hide, to go about life unseen. She wanted to become an actual mouse and tuck away somewhere where no one could ever find her. Now, her small size was an advantage as she crawled and tiptoed around the alleyways of the village. She rarely needed to go prone or squat behind an obstruction to hide. She was made for this.

She was several blocks away from where she had left Cody. *Not a bad guy*, she thought. And though she apologized to him, she thought he was a pussy. Not that he couldn't grow out of it. He cracked that thing's skull earlier. There was hope for the boy indeed.

A lingering sadness crept into her thoughts. Rick. He was an idiot, of course; she knew that. But he was a good man, funny, charming, and painfully handsome. He made her feel okay in the world, like she wasn't the mousy kid she always felt that she was. Ever since she ran away from home at eighteen, she bounced from guy to guy, trying to replace her lack of parental love, or at least that's what her therapist said. She had to agree, and she hated that fact.

She never knew her father, and the man that replaced him was mean and reeked so strongly of alcohol that a single match could light him up. Even if he hadn't been drinking, the aroma of spirits steamed from his mouth regardless, night or day. It had bled into his core. Her mother was no better—not in her meanness, but in her complete absence in Mia's life. Sure, her mother raised her, as in let her live at the house. Aside from that, Mia hardly ever saw her, let alone spoke with her.

She was good at hiding what went on at home. From an early age, she learned to cover up the purple blotches on her face with the right shade of foundation. At thirteen, she used the cakey cheap shit that made her face look like a dusty antique doll. She quickly learned better. Never had she shown what her life was really like to anyone, not to any of the many men she had dated. Not until Rick came and demolished all those walls.

She smacked herself before she could cry. There would be time for all of this later. For now, they had to save him, not from death but from something worse. Then, get the hell out of here.

She hid behind a basket full of fish. The smell of decay made the air thick. Never eating sushi again, that's for sure. Behind her was a wall of a house; on the other side of the basket was a street with three people on it.

Cody was right. They were not fully aware of the world around them. Two of the men were rolling up their fishing nets and talking, but their eyes were out of focus, wandering off to some far distance. An older woman in a white bandana and pink blouse chopped the heads off the fish that were piled to her side.

No way, she thought, *the bug lady from last night.*

The woman cut and stacked the fish heads, then looked off into space like she was stoned. A minute went by before she shook her head and went back to the fish. Once or twice, she brought her cleaver down on an already headless fish but didn't seem to notice that she was slicing into the empty air.

Beyond these zombified people was a stretch of no cover, at least half the length of a football field, until she could reach the bell tower. She thought about whether she could outrun them to the tower. Maybe. But then what? They would be on her ass and waiting for her to get down in a second.

She scanned the environment, looking for something to use to her advantage. Some rocks by her feet. A clay pot next to the fish basket. The fish themselves? The cleaver the woman was holding looked nice and sharp. But who was she kidding? Even if she had a better weapon on hand than her scythe, they'd overpower her in an instant, regardless of anything supernatural. Clay pot it is. She took it in her hand. She would wait until they faced the other way. The two men looked down at their nets. The woman was looking up in Mia's direction.

Come on, look away, bitch.

After splattering a perfectly good fish on the cutting board, the woman looked up in a daze.

Now.

Mia hurled the pot behind her, against the side of a house down the street. The breaking sound was sharp and satisfying.

The men tossed their nets aside and rushed over. Mia kept the basket between their line of sight and her body. The woman, where is she? Shit. She came over but was standing right on the other side of the basket. If Mia moved now, she'd have to run right into the bug lady. The woman moved around the basket and towards the men. She stopped in front of Mia with her back to her, so close Mia could have touched her. The cleaver was in her hand, held with a loose grip, her fingers barely curled around the hilt.

Mia looked the other way towards the bell tower. No one around.

Do I take the cleaver or just run for the bell?

The men left her sight and walked down the alley to their right. It was just the two women alone on a silent street.

Mia's heart was beating in her throat. She shook as she stood. Thank God she was so small, so light, so quiet.

Mia kicked the back of the woman's knees and swung the scythe into the side of the woman's face. It stuck in her flesh. Mia grabbed the cleaver fluidly, and before she ever knew what she would do, the weapon swung from her hand and she buried it deep in the woman's neck. Mia lost her grip on the handle, and the blade remained lodged where it struck. The woman let out a gasp and twitched; the embedded scythe and cleaver rattled on the ground. Mia placed a foot on the woman's shoulder and pulled the cleaver out. Blood splashed over her pink yoga pants, blotting out the mud stains and adding a new psychedelic glow to them.

After freeing the weapon, Mia hacked at the woman's neck several times until the woman stopped moving. The head remained connected to the exposed sinews and muscle and did not separate from the body. Mia felt the fury of a lifetime in those hits. She was out of breath, sweating, covered in blood. She was afraid the two men would return, but the street remained empty. Mia wondered if her attack had been silent in its violence.

She ran towards the tower, cleaver in hand. Made it to the ladder. Tucked the blade into the back of her pants. Climbed up the rungs with her blood-covered shoes, yet did not slip. At the top, she came to a platform with the bell hanging over it. The bell was high up, but had a thick rope attached to the bottom. She grabbed the rope.

She stopped.

If I ring this, what's *next?*

She looked around and saw no one coming, the nearly headless body of the woman sprawled out in the street.

Did I really just do that?

For a moment, she thought about leaving right now. Just forget Rick and Cody, and book it. Her chances would be better alone than in attracting the whole town to her then and there. How fast could she descend the ladder before the two men were on her?

She went down the ladder and back to the ground.

There were several stones nearby. She picked up five. Backed up and aimed at the bell, sizing up the target. Mia threw a stone. Missed. Not high enough. She tried again. Missed. One more attempt. The bell rang out and swung. Not enough. She threw another rock. The echo of the bell sounded out over the town. The bell itself swung a bit. Just one more to be sure. She didn't need to. The two men with the fishing nets had returned to their posts and were now bent over the mangled woman. They looked up and saw Mia. They ran towards her, shouting as they approached.

She turned and ran down the path, past the rice fields where she had lain hidden the night before, and dove into the forest. No pulsating red light blocked her path. It was clear. She had only a vague impression of where to go. The road in the mountains was in the opposite direction from where she was running, back near the town's courtyard. But if she made a wide right turn and doubled back, she could skirt the entire town and would have to hit the mountain road anyway, or so she reasoned.

She rounded a bend and nearly crashed into the ruin of a car. Its blackened hull and serrated edges were inches from her face. Backing up, she surveyed the field she had just entered. Dozens of vehicles were strewn about. A stone pyramid in the center. Smoke rising from the top.

She was back at the first sacrifice site.

No, no, no, *no.*

This should have taken her hours, if not a whole day, to reach. But here she was in mere minutes. She turned to run back into the forest, but some part of her knew she'd only end up back here. There was no running away from this; there was no escape, even by daylight.

"What do you want?" she screamed into the ash-colored sky.

"Mia," an ethereal voice sang out. It wasn't spoken out loud. It wasn't even in a human language as far as she knew. It was just... there. At first, she cowered at the voice, making herself even smaller, into a little ball against the floor of dead grass.

The voice came to her again. She didn't tell Rick or Cody that she had heard this voice the first time it had come to her, the first day they entered the valley. Instead, she bottled it up and hoped it would go away. The voice wasn't human. She wasn't sure exactly how she knew this, but she did. It was deeper, rougher, older. It spoke out of the infinite chasm of history. That voice alone brought terror to her heart. It spoke to her often while she was in this valley. It told her things, promised her things that until now she had shut out of her mind.

"Mia, come."

The voice was drawing her, pulling her towards the pyramid. A black hole of an unexplainable force. The voice terrified her. The voice excited her. The voice promised her peace, love, and safety.

She took to the steps. Each one was an eternity. With each fall of her gore-covered sneakers on the stone, she could feel the old world she had known was fading away.

All that remained was *his* world.

She came to the chained and burnt body. Mia looked into the places where the eyes had once been. She was suddenly aware that she could no longer remember her father. His face, his voice, what had he done to her exactly? All these details were washing away. She forgot the names of the two men she had been traveling with. Their faces blurred into the past.

She forgot her own name.

A vision passed through her mind. A man who reeked of cigarettes and alcohol sat in a beat-up armchair. He was wearing a yellow-stained shirt that had once been white.

What was his name? Who was he? Although she could no longer remember those details, she could feel what he had done to her. Rage filled her heart and overflowed onto her face.

A voice came to her.

"If you wish, I will make him go away."

"Yes, please," she responded.

The man was gone, as were the lingering feelings of dread and shame. The most beautiful light she had ever seen in her life replaced them. It lit up her soul.

She cupped the corpse's skull under its chin. The ashes fell into her palms as if responding to her desire. She brought them to her lips.

She ate.

She swallowed.

She lost herself.

Black ash painted her face, her forehead sweat fell, and cut streaks across her cheeks. She stood tall. She *felt* tall. No more fucking Minnie Mouse.

A hand on her shoulder. She turned and saw a woman clothed in red and white. The woman's smile filled her heart with joy. She wept and didn't know why she was so happy, so lucky to be in this woman's presence.

The woman spoke, "Dear child. No more running. No more pain. Come, let us meet Him."

Mia took the offered hand.

21

Cody watched as the few people who had gathered in the square ran towards where Mia had gone. He couldn't hear the bells, but assumed Mia had made it work somehow. Cody waited until he was sure that everyone had left, stood, grabbed onto the drainpipe, and wrapped his legs around it. He dropped the saw onto the street below. Slid down, cutting his hands on the rusty metal as he slipped to the ground. Squeezed his hands into fists until the pain went away.

Cody realized here and now that the cuts from the window last night had healed over only to be replaced by new ones. Maybe it was the adrenaline or the laser focus on what was happening around him, but he never noticed. These fresh cuts hurt, but the pain quickly subsided and the blood stopped flowing almost instantly. This caused his heart and his mind to race.

The courtyard was silent. He grabbed the saw off the ground and made his way across the open square with his shoulders hunched and back bent, half-crawling, half-running. He got to the steps, looked around, and, satisfied that he was alone, ran up them.

The sight that greeted Cody wrenched his stomach. There Rick was, right in front of him. His best friend of twenty-five years. Rick's jaws were open in a horrifying chasm of despair. His black and flaky skin sent smoke up into the sky. He didn't move, but Cody could sense life in there somewhere. Somewhere within this display of cruelty, his friend was still there. He would come alive tonight, and he would burn. For how long? An eternity? And for whom?

The god of stars.

These fucked-up people.

That woman who invited them into her home.

Cody clenched his hands tightly around the saw's handle and went to work. Chains kept Rick's left arm and right ankle to the ground. Cody grabbed the chain that was linked to the arm and sawed away. Decades of pent-up frustration worked their way into his hands as he cut at the chains. Cody had never been in a fight before. He had never even raised his voice at another in anger. These last few days were breaking something open inside him, and he wasn't sure that he liked it.

Maybe he did like it. The rush felt good, didn't it? Hearing the crack of that man's skull against the rock. Well, he (correction—*it*) deserved what happened.

I'm not a bad person. *I'm not a violent man.*

But what if I am?

What if I need to be exactly that right now?

Cody looked down and saw that he was making almost no progress whatsoever. The saw had barely cut into the chain. He tried to not look at Rick's face. He could feel the empty sockets staring at him. Boring into his skull. Was it accusation he felt in that lifeless gaze? Was it his own guilt and shame? Cody kept at the saw.

"I fucking told you, didn't I? I said that we needed to stay where we were and wait for help. But no, you had to do what you always do and act without thinking. And look where it got you, and me, and Mia."

The dead face hung in a slump and looked off into the endless distance. Cody could feel that hanging head was nodding at him.

"And another thing. You say that you did all this for me. Coming to Japan, coming out on this hike, it was all for me, right? Then why did you never ask me if I wanted to go in the first place, huh? You were always so fucking selfish, and I let you be that way to me."

Cody's lips trembled.

"But you were always there for me. Even if you were a dick. I'm going to miss you."

Arguing with and confessing to a dead, not-dead, man. It was the first time Cody had been so blunt with someone. What is life if not progress?

The saw was useless. Cody threw it down. He sat there, staring at the chain, nearly hyperventilating. He looked at Rick's ankle; it was thin now that all the flesh had been burned off. Thin and brittle.

"I'm sorry, man," he said as he raised his foot over the ankle.

Cody stomped down on it and heard a crunch. It wasn't severed, but he could see the fault lines. Another stomp, several more cracks and crunches. He brought his foot down one last time and broke the ankle, separating Rick's body from his chained foot. Cody grabbed Rick's left hand, put his foot over the wrist, and smashed his foot into it until he broke it off.

Cody squatted down and put the body over his shoulders. The ash rained down on his face. The burned skin was rough to the touch, like sandpaper that easily fell apart. Cody stood up. It was easy considering how little of Rick's body was left. He turned around and started going down the stairs. He knew the way out of town and into the forest.

Just get to the woods and bury him under a large tree. Would that be enough to keep Rick from coming to life tonight?

No way to know, but there's no time to lose.

Cody carried the body down the steps and hit the pavement of the courtyard. So far, so good. The moment Rick's body left the structure, the pyramid quaked. The shaking did not affect the other buildings. Cody ran from it. Whatever he'd just done, it felt like he'd angered something.

He ran with the corpse across the street, pieces of it falling off. Bits of Rick would forever be left on the center road of Inunaki, his right foot and left hand somewhere atop the pyramid. He hurried down an alleyway between two homes. At the end, he could see a wall of dirt, probably man-made, more of a compacted mound. And above that, the forest. This section of the town must have been dug down into the earth.

Cody readjusted the body to better situate it (correction—*him*) on his back. When he arrived at the dirt wall, he surveyed it for a way up and over. He wouldn't have the time to figure it out.

From his peripheral vision, he saw on both the right and left sides of him, shadows encroaching. With a quick double take on both sides, he figured at least a dozen of the townsfolk were closing in, but had yet to appear around the corners of the homes. He had no choice. He dropped Rick's body where it was. Launched himself at the dirt wall and began clawing his way up. The wall's exterior came tumbling down as his hands dug into it. He feverishly swam up the torrent of rocks and dirt, eventually finding his footing on a solid tree root sticking out of the ground. He shot himself up the mound of dirt until he scaled it. On the other side, there was a drop of about ten feet. He leapt down and landed like a sack of flour. Cody got up and ran into the woods.

He hiked through the forest. His mouth was dry, and his stomach ached. Cody walked through a dirty puddle. He drank from it. Sat down. And nearly collapsed from exhaustion. He wondered where Mia was. He strained his ears for any sound that could be her running through the forest. Nothing. Cody had the vaguest idea where the road should be. If he kept to his right, then maybe he'd skirt the town and hit it. If Mia could make it, that's where he could find her.

He got back up and walked on. Slipped on muddy paths. Bruised his knee falling on an overgrown root, and became a feast to the swarms of gnats. The trees looked familiar to him. Then again, how could they not? Every single one was the same to him. A monotonous blend of brown trunks and green moss. Cody was always a "see the trees and miss the forest" kind of guy. He desperately wished to trade places with somebody who could organize the chaotic mess before him and figure out where to go.

He walked into a bush and tripped on a log that was hiding behind the vegetation. He no longer felt pain or cared about the mud in his face. Hell, it could have been shit and he wouldn't have minded. He just took whatever came at him. If it meant he could survive, he resolved to take anything.

He lifted himself from where he had fallen. To his utter horror, he saw a clearing, abandoned cars, and a stone pyramid with smoke rising from the top of the platform. He had only been in the woods for what seemed like an hour, going in the opposite direction—no way he could be here. But here he was. As was Aiko. She was standing at the bottom of the steps facing him as if she knew he would be there. She said nothing.

A voice came to Cody's mind. Since his arrival in the valley, he had not heard this voice, but it felt as though something was trying to worm its way into his thoughts. Now it was there, alive and in his most private of sanctuaries.

"Cody, come."

He felt his body move toward the pyramid.

No, no, I don't want to.

Cody tried to flex his muscles and move his limbs, to no avail. He was on autopilot. He saw the closed bathroom door. Blood and pills flowed from the gap under the frame in waves that soon came up to his chest. He started hyperventilating.

"Leave the door closed. Turn and come to me, and I will make it go away."

Yes, yes, yes.

Cody was crying as he walked up the steps and passed Aiko's smiling face.

"Soon, dear child. Soon you will know His love. All this fighting and running, and for what? I am glad we did not have to sacrifice you. I am filled with joy that you can know what it is like to be in his family."

She kissed Cody on the lips. She spoke not with cruelty but with genuine affection for the man. Cody had never felt so loved before.

He went up the staircase, and Aiko stayed where she was.

Mia was there, standing next to the burned body with the golden necklace. Ashes covered her face, her braid was undone, and someone seemed to have taken a weed whacker to her hair.

She stood there looking at him, but her mind seemed to be worlds away. There was no feeling in those eyes. Before, those eyes telegraphed every emotion of hers, even when she did her best to hide them. Cody was learning to read her the more time they spent together. Now they were vacant and revealed nothing, though for the briefest of moments, there was a slight flicker of recognition in them. Her face seemed to want to speak; the muscles of her cheeks tightened, and a sound barely escaped her closed mouth before returning to her motionless, plastic expression.

No, no, no. I don't want this.

He knelt before the burned body, staring into the dark abyss of its eyes. The bathroom door remained shut, but he was no longer feeling the weight of guilt for closing it. A bright light was burning through the door, reducing it to nothing. He cupped the skull in his hands. Ashes fell into them. He brought the ashes to his lips.

Before he devoured the remnants of what used to be a human being, Mia pushed him to the ground. The ashes spilled out onto the platform. The light faded, and the door remained as it always had been. Cody shook his head and jumped to his feet.

"Go... I can't... control..." Mia was holding onto her stomach as she yelled at him. Silver light burned in her dark eyes. Her skin tightened, and her teeth broke into jagged shards.

The sky went dark. Not the darkness of night. The mist in the sky grew black. It filled with a noxious dark ink as if injected with it.

Mia pushed him one more time and shouted at him to go. He could hear Aiko's cry of fury as she raced up the steps, the jangling of her ankle bells telegraphing her malice.

"I'm sorry," Cody said as he ran down the opposite side of the pyramid. In his haste, he stumbled on the first step, and his glasses flew off. They fell somewhere on his right. He did not turn around to grab them.

He ran into the midday night.

22

Well, shit.

Ms. Tanaka stood outside the car with her hands on her hips. The car's flashing purple lights blasted out from under its frame, illuminating the scene before her: several large boulders blocking the road.

"Tanaka-sama, let's go back already, okay? It's getting dark." The pretty man behind the wheel asked her, flashing her his credit card smile.

"Taro-kun, shut up and let me think."

She liked that pretty head of his, the straightened blond hair, the artful highlights. It probably cost more to style it daily than she spent in an entire year at the salon. But sometimes he would grate on her nerves. He was very naïve and very young, and though she liked that, at this moment she was painfully aware of how useless he was. Save for the car, of course; that had come in handy in getting her out here.

She surveyed the scene. Across the valley, she could see the general area where she had stood with the police officers the other day. She could almost make out the rivets in the cliff that marked where the three foreigners had most likely fallen.

The police sent out their search party, but she knew they would only check the surrounding hills, not the valley itself.

Here, on the opposite side of the valley, there was a single road that fed down into the mist-covered forest below. And now it was blocked. And now she was feeling the urge to go home and give up. If the police wouldn't do anything, why should she?

"Tanaka-sama, don't be so mean," he crooned like a young girl pleading with her father.

She could sense that what he wanted to say was, "Bitch, I don't want to be here; let's go," but she knew he wouldn't dare. She was his number one customer. And as long as she kept on racking up that credit debt at his shop, he would cart her off anywhere.

"Then get out here and help me look around," she commanded.

He groaned as he got out of the lowrider. Why, oh why did she not find somebody with an off-roader? A Jeep or even a Jimny would have been better.

She climbed up one rock, which stood at about her height. She slumped her considerable frame over the rock and, with the help of Taro pushing her feet up, plopped onto the top of the rock.

The road on the other side looked clear. If they could clear this mess, then they could make it down to the town she saw in the distance, poking out of the mist like rocks in the sea.

"Tanaka-sama, let's just give up and go. We could go drink at the club some. Tonight will be on the house." His smile stretched out too thin to conceal the impatience boiling inside his mind.

The clouds below suddenly went dark as if a chemical fire in an industrial plant had broken out. It happened in an instant. She could see the source of the smog; it was coming from the top of a large mountain. Was it about to blow? Despite the sun maintaining its position in the sky, she could see some faint stars appear.

"What time is it, Taro-kun?"

He looked at the hunk of gold on his thin wrist. "It's almost noon." His voice quivered.

"Something's not right here," Ms. Tanaka said with determination.

Down below in the distance, two lights appeared. Lights from the homes? That didn't seem right. These lights flickered and danced like a bonfire.

Could it be the lost tourists?

She heard an echo bounce off the cliff faces from the valley floor. At first, she thought it was the wind. Sometimes late at night, the wind sounds like the screech of some demon as it funnels through tight places. But this wasn't the same. It was more human. The screams boiled up from the valley floor like the coming onslaught of some titanic flood.

She flipped out her phone and dialed a number.

"Hey, yeah, it's me. Do you still work in construction?"

<h1 style="text-align:center">23</h1>

As Cody sprinted through the forest, he could hear shrill cries ripping through the night air. He could barely see the way in front of him, but it was fast becoming a gray haze.

I almost did it; *I almost ate those ashes. Then what would have happened? Mia, oh my God.*

The cries were closer now. Were they her cries? Of course, they were. His friend was now hunting him through the dark forest. The sky was pitch black now. Cody knew it was still daytime, so either the sun had set or the clouds had changed color. The only comfort is that there were no stars out. Did it—that god—make the sky dark so that Mia could transform? She changed in tandem with the dark and with Cody's failure to eat the ashes.

Branches snapped behind him, and the tops of trees rustled with force.

He ran harder, so hard he nearly coughed his lungs out of his body. He could see the light of a fire on his left. Not going that way. Before him, he could see smaller lights coming from the windows of homes. He had to be closing in on Inunaki once again. There was no choice.

Behind him, Mia. Before him, more creatures. To his left, it was probably the same pyramid he had just escaped from. And to his right, a steep rise too sharp to climb quickly. He would have taken his chances with just Mia, but the fear that gripped him prodded him forward. He couldn't bear to see what a hideous malformation of nature she had become. But he could hear her footsteps coming in quick succession on the floor of leaves; they sounded close and almost on his heels. Better to keep running forward.

All lights went out.

The torch lights in the village.

The fire of the pyramid.

Absolute, tangible, thick darkness. Even with his eyes closed in a dark room, never could Cody have imagined total and complete blackness. The only senses he could rely on were his hearing and touch. And what he heard froze him in place faster than the sudden darkness.

Mia was close by. He could hear her scuffling through the undergrowth and bumping into trees. He couldn't see her silver eyes.

Without the stars, no glowing eyes?

"He is angry," Mia hissed. "Angry must have you. Light need light. Why no light, please."

It was Mia's voice at one point. Now it was garbled and oscillated between both deep and high with no rhyme or reason. It slipped between her twenty-eight-year-old voice and that of something far older.

"Cody… come. Then no anger light comes… need light then no pain."

She cried out in frustration, and Cody could hear something being torn out of its roots. He imagined trees being ripped right from the soil in her fury.

Mia, I'm so sorry.

Cody lay down quietly on his back. Mia walked nearby. He heard her footsteps approaching. Then he could feel the leaves touch his face from the plant she must have brushed against. He remained still, his breath under control. He focused on nothing. His heart didn't even feel like it beat at all. She walked right over his body, narrowly missing stepping on his stomach. She walked off, screeching her broken words away.

When all was silent and stayed that way for a good while, Cody stood up. Everything was still tar-black as Hades. He moved slowly with his arms out in front of him. Every step felt like it would be his last. He had played hide-and-seek in the dark with his brothers back in his father's apartment before. Then, even with all the lights out, he could still make out ambiguous shapes: a sofa here, dad's drum set there.

Now, in the depths of this unnatural forest, he could see nothing. No shapes. No hints at form. Would the next step be as simple as bumping into a tree? Falling off a cliff? What if Mia stopped moving and remained silent? He could walk right into her open arms, and that would be it, no hope of escape.

He tripped over something and fell. Shielded his face from most of the impact, but sharp pain still lit up his hands. He crawled over something wet. Whether it was mud, blood, or even shit, it didn't matter. All that mattered was getting back up and to keep going. Towards what? Fuck if he knew.

It was here that Cody reconciled himself to never getting out. Not surviving. Never seeing his mom again. He thought it was cliché for someone on the verge of destruction to cry for their mommy. With frightening clarity, he found that was true. To sit in her living room and pet that dumb, fat, orange cat of hers. He would gladly have traded a lifetime of being the loser who lived in his mom's basement for his current predicament.

As he crawled on the ground, he felt a puddle in the mud. He made a slight splashing sound and froze. He heard nothing. And in that stillness, exhaustion took him. He shut his eyes and let sleep carry him away.

"Cody."

Cody woke with a start. It was still black as hell out. The voice was clear to him. No mistaking it for a hallucination. It didn't come from any source he could pinpoint; it was as if it were in his head.

"Cody, come."

He fumbled the cheap shell charm necklace about his neck with both hands.

That voice stilled his blood. That feeling of someone up there in the sky watching over him. He had always felt it, even when he was young. Had always known. This truth, more than anything, nearly tipped him towards insanity. There was somebody up there watching over him his whole life.

He was the god of stars.

And he was talking to him now.

The fuck does that even mean? It can't be true.

What was a god? The picture he had seen on Aiko's wall came before his mind. The image of the light-skinned man, surrounded by golden light, descending to greet his devoted followers. A floating Messiah. Another image immediately replaced this one. A young man, missing an arm, chained to a stone platform. His eyes fixed on the red sky as its light bore itself into his eyes. The fire that consumed him, that sacrifice, was that pleasing to this god?

All the horrors of the valley flashed before his eyes. A man too tall to be possible, a man with a snake's neck, the dead rising back to life only to be consumed by flames each night. This was hell.

A god? No, not a god. A demon? Maybe what men had labeled as gods throughout the expanse of history were not things that could be painted on a wall in beautiful pictures. They were not things that the human imagination could capture or explain. They were older; they were beyond and outside of human experience or classification, they were something horrible and eldritch. We just give them names and mythologies to make them more palatable for the mind to accept.

Cody never felt more alone in the dark tides of the universe than he did at that moment. There was no one to call out to for help. Because what might answer back was too terrifying to allow into one's safe and hermetic life.

Once more, that voice out of time spoke: "Cody." This one differed from what had beckoned to him at the pyramid. This too was ancient, yet Cody could sense something in it: not darkness, but light.

He didn't need to respond to that voice. He felt pulled in a direction to his right. The voice guided him like the force of gravity. Cody missed all obstacles. No bumping or tripping and crashing. He just knew where to place his feet.

Cody was standing before the mountain, the one that dominated Inunaki's skyline. At its base, an entrance. Its grotesque shape beckoned one to imagine a great jaw opened and ready to engulf all life. Sharp-angled rocks and sizeable gaps in the sides rimmed the open entryway. Deep darkness filled the mouth of the cave. The unnatural blackness that had consumed the sky faded, and the stars came out; by their light he could see his environment again. No townsfolk, no Mia, no red-and-white-clad woman. Just him before the great black mountain. The mountain's sides were charred, devoid of all life. Not a single tree, bush, or even weed grew on its banks. It resembled a volcano with its active lava flow, sanitized of life. It was dark, though no smoke poured out of it as it did during the day.

That's because it isn't inside right now; *it's out there, above me somewhere, searching for me.*

There were no other options. He couldn't fight his way out against the monstrous townspeople. Even if they were just human, they'd overpower him. Escape was moot as well. Twice now he had tried to run, and twice the geography had bent and led him exactly where it wanted him to be.

The only way out is through.

He walked into the darkness of the mountain. He kept his right hand on the wall to keep his bearings. The stone was smooth to his touch, as if man, not nature, had made it.

He felt himself moving downward into the abyss. His pace was slow yet methodical, though he entertained thoughts of tumbling off some unseen precipice. Surely that end was preferable to Rick's. However, the people of the valley had not seemed intent on killing him, or Mia. The way Aiko had looked at him when she said, "No more guilt or shame," stuck with him. Mia's fate was to be his as well. To become a mindless slave of the night sky.

Yeah, not so bad. Just fall and crack my head down below. Deep underground, away from the open sky.

The voice, the one that was tinged with light—no longer guided him. It didn't need to: a warm light soon revealed itself as he rounded the first corner. It was deep-orange and streaked with red. The kind of light that could be found in a snug cabin during a snowstorm. Yet instead of warming his resolve, he felt it sapping away. The light felt somehow cold to him. He crouched to the ground and approached.

A chamber opened up before him. On its walls was the same proto-Japanese script he had seen the second day in the valley. The orange walls displayed images of stars, great fires, and masses of people with outstretched arms pining for the heavens, splashed with white paint. The people stood before pyramids with a single person at the top. A bright light shot forth from that individual. In the next relief, the light of the pyramid cascaded out, over a group of people. Here, the drawings showed those who were injured or dead previously alive, strong, and renewed.

Eternal life and better health. All for the price of a few sacrifices. Oh yeah, also being a slave to some demonic entity.

Whereas the script at the pyramid looked relatively new, maybe done within the past few years or decades, the writing on the cave walls was much more ancient and faded. Cody wondered if it even predated Japanese civilization itself. It reminded him of some prehistoric cave paintings in France (or was it Germany?) he had seen on a slide in high school.

He walked further into the chamber and stopped before a great mural. The paint here was fresh. The reds and whites of the images reflected the subterranean firelight from further within the caverns. At its center was a woman dressed in red and white.

Her eyes flashed silver and seemed to watch Cody as he approached. It was Aiko for sure, forever immortalized in an artistic expression like some modern-day Mother Mary. Flowers formed the base of the mural. Lit candles were stationed on various ledges in the rock wall, surrounding the painting. A deep red star shone above Aiko. Its light descended on her head, forming a slight halo, or crown.

The village is her own personal fiefdom. Queen of the dead.

Stripping his eyes away from Aiko's vacant expression on the wall, Cody ventured deeper into the cave, towards the light.

24

The earth beneath his feet growled. It shook in cadence, from something that almost knocked him down to a slight tremor and back again. It was as if the world beneath him breathed with great lungs of stone. Like it was alive.

He held onto the rock wall as he entered the second chamber. As he approached the orange light, sweat beaded down his forehead, and he shielded his eyes.

This chamber was the brightest thing he had seen since entering this valley with its muted colors. Rivers of lava flowed to his left and right, with a stone bridge straight ahead. The path was narrow. The furnace heat nearly made him pass out. There was a strong odor of sulfur. Cody crossed the bridge on his hands and knees, not daring to look to either side at the flaming rivers.

He couldn't help it and found himself entranced by the flow of the magma. The smooth and solid waves of melted rock were almost soothing, meditative. It was fire; it was the blood of the earth. Something Aiko had said earlier came back to him.

"Born of the blood of the fire god."

If that was true, did this god come from here? From the deep and forgotten places of the world? Then why would it be called the god of stars? How could something that ruled the sky come from such a hidden hell?

Above the chamber, there was no roof. A hole opened out onto the black sky. Cody could see no stars, and for that he was glad.

"Does not need the sun nor the moon."

That would explain why the valley was under constant cloud cover. A cracked skull flashed before his mind. He had murdered that man (no, that *thing*) with the rock. How could he have killed it so easily then, when at night these things were invulnerable?

The sun. Something he never knew he could miss so badly, more than his own family. The reassuring light of day had been absent these past few days. Did the sun somehow weaken Amatsu's power? Cody imagined the sun rising on the village and burning everyone to ashes, like vampires. Only classic vampires were much preferred to what Cody had now: a cult of unknown horrors that could shape the very reality around him. And how could he fucking bring the sun out through the clouds? It was obvious the gray cover wasn't natural. It was here that Cody became convinced direct sunlight might actually harm, if not kill, these things. Given the circumstances, a simple stake through the heart seemed easy by comparison.

He made it to the end of the bridge and came out onto a large rock platform. At its center, a stone larger than a city bus. It was oblong and egg-like. A great crack split down the entire length of its middle, giving the impression it had hatched. Black slits were carved all over it. A script of some kind. Different from what he had seen on the walls of the cave.

He had no rational justification for this thought; he just knew it, felt it. The markings on the wall filled him with dread and unease, as if some violent and chaotic beast had formed them. The markings on the stone were as elegant and beautiful as they were mysterious. He felt drawn to them.

He touched the stone, and a flash of light blinded him.

His eyes rolled up into the back of his head, and his mind was taken to the past.

25

Aiko Koike opened her swollen eyes to the sunrise peering at her from the open window. She grasped her head like a vice and closed the curtains. Her throat was dry, her head pounded, and she needed to wretch.

Hangovers were the worst. Never again, I swear.

After taking care of what had become her morning routine of painkillers accompanied by lukewarm tea, she sat in front of the mirror in her bedroom.

Her hair stuck out in multiple directions and looked as if she had mixed sap into it. Eyes stood above deep purple rings. Puffy flesh surrounded her left eye and was a deep blueish black. She had some minor cuts scattered across her face. She looked down at her wrists and thought about doing it again. The scars had faded some but were still there, just like her past, just like her present demons. That asshole was just outside her door now. Probably asleep in his own piss, sweating off the previous night's deluge of sake and target practice.

Why did I come back?

She knew the answer. It was out behind her home in a shallow grave. Her mother's body had lain buried not even two weeks ago. The bastard couldn't even afford to have her cremated at the temple. Aiko swore she would never again enter this house and live with this man, this animal she once called Papa. But she couldn't stay away from her mother's funeral. Mama was the only person in Aiko's life who treated her with even a fraction of kindness. She used to smear Aiko's face with cake batter when she was a child and pretended to put her into the oven to make Aiko-cakes. How she would laugh and scream as her mother chased her around the house with the spatula.

Now she was gone. Never coming back. She wasn't given the dignity of being interred at the temple with her ancestors. She was rotting out back in a shallow grave.

Aiko always doubted her mother had died of natural causes. Cancer never seemed like something she would succumb to, and if she did, Aiko never heard a word about her having it until she died. There had not been a visit from the police or any medical professional to determine the cause of the sudden death. When Aiko inquired at the nearby police station, all they told her was, "It's a family matter. You need to see to it yourself."

A family matter in a small town in the middle of fucking nowhere. She laughed just then. How stupid she was to believe that anyone would help her. Now, she had no money and couldn't leave. She was also determined to out the old man for what she knew deep down to be the truth: that he murdered her mother. Nineteen years of life had taught Aiko one brutal truth about her father—not only that he was violent, but that he savored the pain that he caused.

No one in the town liked her, and she didn't like them in return. It was a good arrangement. But no one would take her in if she left. She had no choice but to live under this roof. Aiko got good at weathering the abuse as a child. She could hold out a little more until she figured out a way to fuck over her slob of a father, the useless monster of a man—no, the shell of what used to be a man. Yes, that was better. He wasn't human. He was nothing.

The sun shone brightly above, set in the deep blue sky. Rings of light radiated outwards, birds chirped and flew in V-patterned flocks, and butterflies danced between the freshly opened petals.

What a sickeningly beautiful day.

Aiko held an umbrella and wore a pair of sunglasses. The hangover and head injuries conspired together to split her skull open. Even the faintest light seared its way into her brain. But she couldn't stay at home today. Dad was in a right rage. He would spend the next six to eight hours searching for solace at the end of a bottle, or two, or twelve. Best not to be there when he failed to find what he was looking for.

She drifted through the town. Flocks of children came running down the road, chasing each other. A few cars rolled lazily through the main street. She followed them to the town square, where dozens of booths were set up.

Old man Tada had his dried fish hung over a wire; the thick aroma permeated the air. He used to come over and drink with Dad until he too left one night with a black eye.

Ms. Satoshi sat on the ground with a blanket stretched out in front of her. Old trinkets from the war lay scattered about. A beat-up flask. An imperial Navy officer's uniform, yellowed with age. She had lost her husband somewhere in the middle of the Pacific. He was a grunt, a foot soldier, who probably got mowed down by a machine gun the moment the Americans touched that beach. Aiko smiled a bit at that thought.

Not at the man's death, but at his widow's desperate attempt to reclaim what was forever lost.

Most of the town must have been out. Laughter, vendors calling people over, and kids screaming in delight. Inunaki was a festive place today.

Aiko floated past the activity like a ghost and took in the details, but gave them no thought, no emotional importance. She drifted on like a lost soul, bound and ready to be forced to walk the plank to the icy depths below. She had lived in Tokyo for a few years, working as a hostess. The money was easy, but her lifestyle drained any chance of savings. Flirting with rich old men certainly brought in the cash. Her paternally inherited drinking habits bled it out just as fast. Her choice of men painfully reminded her of her father. Not all the scars on her face were from that old bastard's hands.

Inunaki was a place of joy in her childhood. As she strolled through the open market, she smiled bitterly at the memories. Fishing with the neighborhood kids out by the stream deep in the forest. Those were the days of innocence when parents never worried about their children playing alone in the valley's heart. Especially in the ruins of that old stone structure. No one knew who had built it long ago. Now it was used as a drinking spot for the few teenagers left in town; no one else dared venture out that way. Soon, those carefree days would be overshadowed by the visage of a drunk and angry man, who possibly, no—probably—murdered her mother in a fit of despairing rage.

Aiko sailed past the open square and headed towards the mountain that oversaw all the joyous activity. Mount Hinokami was abnormally close to the town square. Instead of planning their town away from it, whoever had settled this ancient land used the hopefully dormant volcano as its center point.

Aiko had always hated Mount Hinokami. Its shadow chilled her bones even in summer. As a child, she would look up at it in fright: at its rough exterior, its lack of green, and its strange shrine situated towards the summit. Of course, she'd been there before—all the bored youths had. But every time she'd sneak off with her friends to drink at the shrine, she always felt that same coldness of the mountain's shadow. No matter what fiery toxin she forced down her throat, the latent ghost of the place left a chill.

The last time she had visited was with her boyfriend when she was sixteen. They had hiked to the summit, lit up their *cigarettes,* and started ripping on their neighbors, who they could see scurrying around like ants from their vantage point. Riku, her boyfriend of an entire two weeks, wanted to make out.

He puckered his lips like a fish and leaned in. Aiko had pushed him off, called him a loser, and promptly ignored him. Riku stormed away down the mountain, sure to spread rumors about her like the plague. She didn't mind. What bothered her was why she had reacted like that to him, pushing him away when what she wanted was to kiss him back. As she sat there alone, a frigid chill made her stand up straight and hug her arms around her bony frame. She didn't know why, but she got the sense she was being watched.

Her arm hairs stood like pins, and she ran back down the mountain not far behind Riku.

Today she felt different.

Maybe it was the hangover or the noise of the crowd, or maybe it was just because it was the furthest point in town from her father's house, but today she felt like climbing that mountain again. Getting away from it all. Maybe it would be nice to jump off the shrine and make a guest appearance in the town square, all flat and bloody and spectacular. That would show them all.

No, that's not what I want. Why should I suffer because of their fucked-up decisions?

They're the ones who deserve to die; they're the ones who ignore men like my father and what they do, all to not make a fuss and shake things up.

She started climbing the steep trail towards the mouth of the volcano.

It was almost like it was asking her to.

The shrine was in disrepair. The toori gates were wooden. The ages had rotted them down to chewed-up apple cores.

The *shide* were nothing but tatters; the *shimenawa* were reduced to threads. Beer and Boss coffee cans were strewn about the grounds. The holy was replaced with the refuse of common addiction, the sanctified with immediate gratification. There were cherry trees up here, but they never bloomed. Skeletal limbs that clawed their way towards the sky.

No one in town knew what god this shrine was built in honor of. There were no names or images to guess by, no local historian or tale to follow up on. The main shrine in town, by the large stone entrance gates, was Amaterasu's, goddess of the sun. Her sanctuary was bright, her servants dedicated, flowers bloomed there, and no one left it to the waste of neglect.

Up here, before the shrine to an unknown deity, one whom the people had forgotten, and no longer cared for, Aiko felt a sliver of shared isolation. She walked over to the ledge. A clear drop from here to the busy marketplace below.

Maybe I will do it now. Or just stay here and live among *the forgotten.*

She turned back from the edge of the mountain. On the opposite side of the shrine, there was a small opening in the ground. It was where, countless eons ago, Hinokami had last erupted, cracking the stone and pouring out the flame that shaped the valley. Now the volcano was dead and hollow. She couldn't remember any talk about when it would erupt again, probably because there was no chance of it.

The hole was just wide enough for a person to enter. No one had dared do so since she had been born. She had heard stories about her parents' generation. Some young guy took up a dare from friends to scope out the caverns below. His friends had tied a rope between his waist and one of the skeleton trees on the surface. From the moment he had descended into that darkness, he stopped responding to his friends calling his name. They pulled at the rope and found that it had been cut loose. The body was never found. That hole was the only entrance into the mountain and was deemed too dangerous to enter. A search was never even attempted.

The last time Aiko had prayed was with her mother during the New Year's holiday. She was ten. Mama took her to the sun goddess's shrine at midnight together, bowed and clapped their hands twice. Aiko had asked her mother if she believed in the goddess, to which Mama said it didn't matter, do it just in case. Now, in the barren waste of a once sacred place, Aiko approached the altar atop Hinokami.

The wind blew harder up at the top of the hill. Her hair fluttered about wildly. There was no bell to ring—time and vandals had seen to that. Instead, she pressed her hands together in front of her chest in prayer. She bowed her head. Tears squeezed between her tightly shut eyes and fell down her face. She offered a silent request, a plea, a cry for her pain to end. She lifted her head, clapped her hands twice, and turned away. For some reason beyond her comprehension, she clapped once more. Not the usual way of doing things, no, but she felt compelled.

A voice came. Not in actual words. Even so, she knew it was a voice. Not out there in the world, but somewhere in her mind.

I'm losing it.

The voice, the feeling, was weak. She felt the urge to ignore it. With that voice came the chill of the mountain's shadow once again, the same chill that made her run back into Riku's arms. She wanted to sprint back down the trail. Run back home, open up her father's stash, and get hammered.

And then what? Wait for him to kill me, day by day. Or just do it myself?

She turned back towards the chasm. The voice drew her to the mouth of the darkness. She leaned down towards it and could hear the low whistle of the wind as it rushed out from places unseen and unknowable. In the depths of that still black space, she heard it. A low growl that sounded like the ignition of a furnace.

She didn't blink. Her heart beat faster inside her chest. Her head pounded like a hammer struck against a rock. She almost turned away.

The growl called out once again.

She bent down and reached inside the pit. Felt a flat stone, like a step. Put her feet on it and descended.

In the dark, she could make out writing on the cave wall. It was as if the words were under a light, despite none entering the cavern. The words were beneath the staircase, chiseled into the rock. She couldn't believe such a structure existed inside the mountain. Years of fear and paranoia surrounding the mountain had kept the stairs a secret from everyone.

She walked around the cavern. There was a large egg-shaped stone and a stone bridge over a dark and cold emptiness. She returned to the words on the wall and placed her hands over a pictograph that looked like fire.

The words danced in Aiko's mind. She couldn't read them, but their meaning came to life inside of her. More than that, something transported her mind to a realm of images. She was standing in a void, witnessing something so real, she could feel the cold of the space before her despite the sweltering air inside the cave.

She sensed two beings creating the world. The beings were beyond description and just out of her sight. She felt more than saw them. What she saw resulted from their actions more than the things themselves, like how you can see the leaves blown about by the unseen wind. They raised the mountains with their words; they filled the oceans with their song. Their children became things similar to themselves: entities of power beyond understanding.

One of the creators gave birth to a child of fire. The fire consumed its mother and killed her. The father wept tears, which ripped apart the fabric of creation. Great floods came upon the earth and wiped out the creatures unfortunate enough to have been created. He killed the child of fire, dismembering it and casting the pieces across the land he had created. Each place where one of the body parts fell became a great mountain of fire inhabited by a being that formed itself out of the body part. The head became one being, the hands another, and the feet another still.

The blood of the child was special. It was collected and cast out over the land like refuse, yet it became its own great mountain of fire like its brethren, one that looked like Hinokami. Out of that blood, a red star rose and ascended into the heavens. The father hated that star, a reminder of the death of his beloved. He had a more favored child now, the sun. To the sun passed all of creation to rule as she pleased. All gods bowed before her and swore allegiance. Not so with the star.

She saw the star creating light in the sky to rival that of the sun. It refused to bow and extinguish its own beautiful light. The sun went to war against the red star. All gods gathered to her aid and bound the star within a great stone, forever to be its prison.

Time rushed by in millennia and eons. Aiko saw the rise and fall of strange creatures that once walked the valley floor. Saw the ocean that once filled it. She saw the arrival of hairy humans as they lit fires in the trees. Aiko saw the star rise out of the mountain, to outstretched arms. As long as those arms reached out, the star could rise. She saw the red star fall back into darkness as the people moved on to other gods, forever bound to its cell beneath the mountain.

Aiko came back to the world of the cave. The vision was so real; she wept out of both fear and ecstasy. No drink, no drug, no man could ever hope to replace that pure and unfiltered... what is the right word for it? Joy? No, something more than that.

Rapture.

A voice called to her from farther in the darkness. She turned and walked towards the giant stone hidden in the black pit. The voice was weak, barely a whisper, yet she could hear it calling to her. This stone was in her vision. The one the gods used to capture the star. Beneath her feet, the ground trembled. Down below, a faint light shimmered above the petrified magma. It rose and fell, intensified and dimmed; it breathed. Something was down there. She could feel it move through the rock, responding to her presence.

How cruel. Why do this to one who just wanted to make its own light?

Aiko's hatred turned toward the creator she saw in the vision. Another abusive parent.

What kind of father harms his *child out of grief?*

She spoke to the stone. At first, embarrassment flushed over her. Here she was, hungover and talking to a rock inside a dark cave. She may very well have hallucinated the entire vision. The voice she heard just then silenced those feelings. It silenced all feelings. She could see herself standing in a field under a starlit sky. No more headaches. No more tears. No more violent men puppeteering her life.

"Is this what you want to give me?" Her voice startled her as it echoed throughout the silent chamber.

She stared at the stone and nodded her head.

"What do you want?" she asked.

She saw an open night sky full of stars.

"How can I help you?"

She saw fire.

"I don't understand."

In her vision, the fire spread and covered her father. He was sleeping on his side in the tatami room, his left hand clutching a crushed beer can. As the orange wave engulfed him, he opened his eyes wide with terror. He couldn't even scream as he was consumed. Aiko held the match and the can of kerosene as she stood over her father's spasming body.

In the dark and cold cave, Aiko smiled warmly.

26

Cody opened his eyes and saw the fire from below dancing on the walls. The image of shadows writing on the rock made him think he was still in that vision. Vague puppets of black velvet performing for him their devilish play. He got up and shook himself awake. It felt like he had gotten some sleep in the cave. He felt a modicum of sanity being restored to him.

All that he had seen in his mind remained there, clear and lacking in no detail. Cody understood now: this place was a prison. This stone in front of him once held the dark god captive. But how did sacrificing Aiko's father release it? He felt this was the crux of the vision, the point. Nothing else mattered but unraveling this one element of the mystery. It stumped him. He understood one thing without reservation: Amatsu was real. Whether he was truly a god, something powerful and ancient was at work in this village, and Aiko was but an extension of it, not the orchestrator.

If this cavern was its prison, why did he see the star descending into the mountain at sunrise? Why would it go back? Maybe it had no choice; it had to return here for some reason which eluded Cody.

One thing disturbed him most of all: why was the vision shown to him? He couldn't imagine the deity doing so. It revealed too much, and it showed potential weaknesses. If not Amastu, then who?

"You really are exceptional, Cody Baker. I knew as much the first time I saw you."

He looked back, past the stone bridge, and saw Aiko standing at the entrance to the chamber. The red of her robe shone brighter than ever in the effervescent glow of the cave. Her silver eyes added their cold glow to the room. Though he couldn't see her pupils, he could feel wild intensity behind the lights.

She walked forward.

"Even before then. When you were up on the hill looking out over the valley with your friends. You almost turned back. You could have turned back. I am so glad that you chose us instead."

"I didn't choose you, you sick fuck."

Her smile inverted itself. A look of slight hurt came over her face.

"No, don't say that. What we have is special. All that shame and guilt that you carry. You couldn't save Rick, you couldn't save Mia, and that eats you up inside. The thing is, you don't need to save them. They are home now, right where they should be. And Rachel... You couldn't help her either, dear child. The Red God was watching you that night. He knows your pain."

"So that's heaven for you? To be a mindless slave of some god who demands to murder people so it can what—be free?"

She knitted her brow, and the silver of her eyes grew in intensity.

"Do not dare to stand there and presume judgment over our God. You feign understanding of that which is beyond you."

"No, I get it. Daddy hit you because you couldn't be loved. He blamed you for your mother's death, you know. I see the connection Amatsu has with you, both unwanted by your fathers."

Cody stood tall. So did the hair on his arms. He had never spoken so brazenly to anyone in his entire life. He didn't mean those words just now; he wasn't a monster, but he knew it would strike the right nerve. Now, seeing the color of Aiko's eyes change from silver to red, he felt he had made the biggest mistake of his life. While she hadn't wanted to kill him before, that may have just changed.

The red in her eyes filled the room and drowned out the firelight.

"How... dare you." She hissed each syllable out. "How did you even know?"

Cody said nothing. He looked at his feet and saw a few small stones. He grabbed the largest one nearby, about the size of his fist.

Aiko's skin quaked and rippled, barely holding back the tempest that raged inside her. Cody's eyes darted around the cave, and the hair on his arms stood up. He was dealing with an unstable nuclear bomb while standing over a lava pit.

Fuck it, if I'm going to die, anyway.

"How'd I know? Maybe your god showed me. He's tiring of you. I mean, how many decades has it been? Your daddy issues are the only reason you worship him any—"

Aiko's hand gripped his throat. When did she even close the gap? He hadn't seen her move; she was just... there. She lifted him off the ground, his feet kicking as if treading water.

She pulled Cody's face closer to her own. Her eyes grew brighter. The crimson light burned his skin and seared his eyeballs. It was like staring into the sun.

She smiled and put him down, the hand still gripping his flesh.

She spoke, and her once feminine voice of lightly falling snow changed to a storm of death. It was thunderous. It shook the walls of the cavern.

"No, I guess you are not so special, Cody Baker. At least, not in the way I had hoped for you. I wanted you to join this family and experience what He offers you, as your friend Mia now enjoys. But," the red light penetrated deep into Cody's brain, "you will make an exceptional sacrifice. All that pain to be released. It will be a sweet incense unto Him. The light of your suffering will keep us warm for generations. It will keep Him ascended for centuries."

The light burned. It sizzled. It scalded his eyes. Cody turned his head to the left and shield most of his left eye. The right eye had no chance. He heard a pop. At first, there was no pain, just disbelief and shock. Soon, the liquid heat of what was once his right eye ran down his face and scalded his cheek.

Oh God, how could something hurt so bad?

Cody screamed his soul out. The socket of his right eye was on fire. He twisted and jerked in Aiko's hand but was helpless. He kicked her in the stomach three times. His arms were free, and he swung the rock at her head. It made contact, but she did not flinch. The rock cut her cheek, but it healed just as fast. The smile that cut across her face was full of malice and enjoyment. She pressed Cody into the ground and put a sandaled foot on his head.

"You are alive when I say you are alive. You die when I say you die. You come back if I say you come back. I can smash your brains out right now, like a fucking watermelon, and not bat a fucking eye, you little piece of shit."

Cody yelled into the dirt, the red fire eating his face. Cody was aware of the details of each pebble in front of him on that floor. The things the human mind latches onto to escape terrible pain. There were green, smooth ones and craggy brown ones. Eight in total in front of his left eye. He also noticed that all pretense fled Aiko's voice. What was once so regal and under a perfect cadence descended now into unbridled fury.

Aiko snapped her fingers. The fire on Cody's face went out. As did the pain. He wanted to cry. He never felt so welcome a relief.

"See? You do not even fucking feel what I don't want you to." She snapped again, and the pain split Cody's mind apart. He flopped on the ground in primal suffering. Aiko threw her head back and laughed. The high-pitched echo bounced across the walls in a symphony of ridicule and cruelty.

"You are just a thing, a small thing. There is not a fucking thing that you can do to me."

She snapped her fingers once more, and the pain ceased. Cody could have kissed her feet in gratitude. She lifted him into the air again. A cat playing with a bug she had just caught in the garden. Too amused at its helplessness to kill it.

She dangled his body over the river of lava below.

Cody strained to look down. If she dropped him, that was it. It would all end in an instant. He was ready. To die now and escape an eternity of pain was all he wanted at that moment. She had taught him the most important lesson of his life. If he could be spared the pain that caused him to shake uncontrollably on the cavern floor, that was all he desired. He would do anything to make it stop. Words such as guilt, shame, ambition—none of that mattered now. All that did was to spare her the eternal flame of her red god.

She cocked her head like a dog listening to its master.

"No, too easy." She gently placed him back on the ground. She patted his head and ruffled the dirt-colored hair. "No, no, no, child. To the pyres of everlasting light with you."

Two men dragged Cody between them. His feet scraped through the streets. His skull ached and splintered. At least the fire had cauterized the wound and stopped all bleeding. Otherwise, he surely would be dead already. The sun was out; the dark clouds had gone. Cody figured that the sacrifice would have to wait until later that evening.

As the men carried him, he looked back towards the mountain. Golden rays of light were clearing away the last vestiges of those black clouds. He saw the red star. It descended towards the earth. It rested right above the mountain and entered it. Probably through the crevice Cody had seen in the dream. In its red glow, Cody could see a shadow moving inside. A form that looked like a man, but much, much larger.

In a moment, the light and its shadow disappeared into the mountain. As soon as the star had vanished, steam and smoke rose from the volcano. The smoke shot out into the sky and covered it, shielding the acolytes of Amatsu from that hated sun. If only Cody could see that light one last time.

He was sure he never would.

27

Cody sat there in the dark, cradling his face. The smell of rotten meat seeped in from somewhere nearby. He could see a faint, sickly yellow light just under the door. It felt like maybe an hour since those men had put him here.

It was not only his eye that was taken from him—he could feel the leathery hide of the third-degree burns across the skin on the right side of his face as well. If he could see his reflection, he knew a stranger would stare back, and not just because of his disfigurement. Did he really just stand up to that demon in the cave? That was not like him. It made him feel an inch taller, stronger than he had ever felt in his life before. And what did it give him?

Writhing pain.

He had fallen to the ground in agony and had been willing to grovel and worship and sacrifice to her just to make it go away. That was more like the old Cody he knew well. Not that it mattered. In less than —what, five or six hours?—he knew he would be carried out of this cell, chained to a stone platform, and he would see—yes, actually see — the red god for what it truly was.

Of this he was sure. What had been hidden until now would pull the covers back and show him its face. It wasn't just the threat of burning alive that terrified him; it was the knowledge that something truly unknowable and alien would open its eyes and rest them on his face. And Cody would be forced to look back into the face of a god, a demon, whatever the hell it was.

Or maybe it was hell. Pure and simple, he would go to hell. Isn't that what he had learned in Sunday school? An eternal lake of fire for the unbelievers? Only here, Cody believed, he truly believed in the god of stars. There was no need for faith when the proof gave a ninety-pound woman the strength to lift a full-grown man off the ground and ragdoll him.

Oh, he believed.

And he was scared shitless.

He started having a breathless panic attack.

Hours passed as Cody wept for himself in the dark of that cell, the phantom tears of his right side stinging his soul. Is this where they took Rick before they burned him alive? He too was maimed before his interment. Cody wondered if that was part of the ritual, severing a body part to make the suffering longer. Wet, freezing air clung to his skin. It was mostly dark in that cell, yet he could see the cloud of his breath as it puffed out of him.

He shivered, curled up on the stone floor, hugging his chest and pressing his face into his elbows. No matter the pressure he applied to his face, the pain did not subside. Rather, it throbbed and pulsated with ever-increasing intensity, splitting his skull down the middle. Never before had Cody wished so pathetically for his mother.

Darkness filled the cell. It reflected the emptiness he felt, the deadness of his heart. He had no more tears for Rick or for Mia. Of course, he felt horrible for their fates, but his own was what occupied his mind at that moment. Never again would he see the sun. Never again would he see a friendly face. Never again would he feel anything but a world of fire.

The lock clicked open. The door swung inward, filling the cell with yellow light. The sun was still up. At least he was wrong with the prediction that his time had come, yet it somehow filled him with even more profound sadness. The silver lining was that he knew that at least for now they hadn't come for his death. In the doorway stood a dark figure. Cody's one good eye winced in pain, though he was glad to see anything but the dark of the room.

The figure came forward. Dressed in a black-and-red robe, the visitor knelt, placed her hand on Cody's back, and caressed it. Mia had done this many times in the past few days, and each time she left a mark of warmth where she placed her hand. Now it was cold. Dead. Lifeless.

She looked like Mia, yet the dull robe made her seem like a different person entirely. The same hazel eyes instead of ghastly silver, at least for now. Her ponytail undone, with all her hair lifted and set in place with several large red pins. She was clean. Cody almost wouldn't have recognized her without the layers of mud, dirt, and blood that had been her mask these past few days. No, that wasn't the mask. This clean, smiling face, free of imperfection—*this* was the mask. Something else was wearing her face and passing itself off as Mia.

"You poor thing." She dabbed his disfigured face. He recoiled. She had a bowl of soup in her hand and put it on the ground.

"Mia, I'm sorry that this happened to you. I couldn't... I tried."

"Sorry? For what? I'm finally free, Cody, don't you see that?" She rose and paced the room in front of him. "My whole life I've felt afraid and alone. Now everything is different, I feel His love inside of me." She took his hand and put it over her heart. "I am alive in ways I could never have imagined before."

Cody retracted his hand and stood up with shaking knees. He held onto the sides of the wall as he did so.

"No, did you forget about Rick? Is your 'peace' worth anything if it costs this much?"

"And what does it cost? The sacrifice of a few? They led lives of no consequence. They would have died having given nothing back to others. Now, they serve a purpose greater than themselves. We have already put Rick back where he belongs. He'll do more as a sacrifice than he could ever have done otherwise."

As she spoke, Cody glimpsed the rust-colored hall outside the door. In the open cage across the way, he saw a child's bright pink backpack. Hello Kitty cartoons were emblazoned on its back. The smell of decomposed flesh was filling his cell more than when the door was closed. He gagged and pointed at the evidence of murder.

"That was a child! Nothing is worth that evil. Take your 'peace' and 'serenity' and fuck off." He kicked at the cement floor in front of her.

Mia stood there and seemed to ponder his words. She smiled.

"Those children are with him now, Cody. They do not suffer and never will again. Neither will you soon." She approached him and took his hands. "Soon, you will burn. It will hurt. But that's because He has to cleanse you of your filth. And then you will see Him, and oh, Cody, He is so beautiful. Then you will understand." Tears streamed down her face. She really believed in what she said. "Or—and this is truly your last chance, Cody—you can bow and take of the ashes, take of His flesh, and be united with Him as I am now. She was angry with you before, and that's why she sent me. One last offer of peace."

Cody's face twisted into a sour expression, and he shook her hands off his face.

"Never. I'm sorry I couldn't help you. We're done here," he said.

"Yes, it would seem that we are." She walked out of the cell. Before closing the door, she looked at him. "See you tonight."

Her mouth stretched into a smile that reminded him of the girl in the forest, the one with the stapled-on expression. This wasn't Mia; no, it was something else talking through her. How did he know? Her eyes did not dance.

She's in there somewhere. But what can I do?

The door closed, the lock clicked shut, and darkness enveloped him again. He looked over at the soup bowl and drank.

28

Why is this happening to me? I don't deserve this.

This self-indulgence was not new to Cody. He was well-versed in playing the victim. At least now that role matched his circumstances perfectly.

He remembered playing soccer with Rick when they were both eight years old. Rick, of course, was the star of the hour. He sped like a demon through the grass, scoring a goal with a precision hit right through the goalie's legs. The winning shot. Everyone ran onto the field and crowded around him, slapping his back and hooting like apes.

Cody's stick legs could barely keep up, and he collapsed onto the field, taking massive inhales of air to keep from passing out. Alone on the grass, he cried. He had felt he did just as well as everyone else; it wasn't fair that Rick got all the attention. Rick noticed him then and fought through his admirers to come over to Cody. Smiling, he lifted Cody up and smacked him softly on the cheeks. He explained that sitting there crying would do no good. If he wanted to be praised, he'd have to score the goal. He didn't, and that's fine, but get over it and come out to pizza.

Cody wiped his tears away. He was resentful of Rick's fame, always had been. But in that moment, he pulled himself together. Soon, he was laughing with all the other kids at Chuck E. Cheese, playing Skee-Ball.

Why am I *thinking about fucking pizza when I'm about to die?*

Cody thought his mind was unraveling like a spool of yarn. But Rick's words of "suck it up" and "if you want the party, then score the goal" buzzed in his mind.

It felt like several hours had passed since Mia had left his jail cell. He knew the knife was dangling over his head—the sword of Damocles—and it could come down swiftly at any moment.

If these are my last hours, get up, and *at least try to do something about it.*

He got up and began searching the cell for anything he could use. There was nothing, not even a rag, inside that hole. There were no windows. There was only one door, a thick piece of wood he would never smash through. A slight gap at the bottom allowed some dim light to come through.

But if Rick had been here earlier, then he surely tried to do it. That was his personality in a nutshell—just smashing things.

Bending down, Cody felt along the door. He could see nothing but felt a crack along the bottom. The height at which someone might kick a door. He felt along the line to the hinges.

No fucking way, one hinge is *loose!*

He felt cold metal in his palms. It shook loosely when he grasped it. He tried but failed to rip it off the door. Felt around its edges and cut his finger. Pushed through the wince: if he survived this, there'd be plenty of time to worry about things such as pain. He felt the top of the large spike that held the hinge together. It wiggled as he pulled at it.

It wouldn't come straight out, but it was loose enough to be turned. It moved slowly. He held the head of the spike with two fingers from each hand—there wasn't space enough for more. He squeezed and turned it counterclockwise. It moved faster now. After ten spins, it began turning faster and more smoothly until pop!—it was out of the hinge. A metal spike the size of his index finger. He pried at the metal casing on the wall, and it came off. There were two more hinges, but their nails didn't budge no matter how hard he squeezed them.

He stood for a moment, holding the spike and pondering his next move. The hinges wouldn't move beyond where they were now. The door was too thick to bust through.

Stab the next person who comes through with the spike? No, by then it will already be dark, *and whoever grabs me will be invulnerable. If I'm going to use force, it has to be now.*

He looked at the cut on his finger and squeezed out a drop of blood. Cuts! He drove the spike into the part of the door where the lock was located. With a dead-on strike, it did little. But when he angled it downward, it caught on the wood, and he chiseled off a shaving of it.

One down, 10,000 more to go. Get going.

Cody gouged the spike into the wood again and again. Wood shavings flew off. His cell was turning into the world's saddest woodworking shop. He struck again, and the spike slipped. A small splinter stuck in his right palm. He ripped it out and kept going. Another splinter, smaller, yet it jammed itself right under his right thumb's fingernail. Cody bared his teeth and kept going, using the pain to drive him forward.

And I used to sweat in *the dentist's chair.*

On what must have been the thirtieth strike, a piece the size of the spike itself broke off. That was the bursting of the dam. With each hit thereafter, bigger pieces split off the door. Again, again, again. His hand now held multiple splinters like a pincushion. He didn't care. Again, again, again.

He stripped the wood until a small hole had formed, and he could see into the hall. He stood back and lunged forward with a kick on the spot. A mighty crack rang out. With another kick, his foot broke through to the other side. He struggled to pull his foot back out. When he succeeded, he put his hand through the hole and felt for the lock. Thank God they didn't use a key: the lock was a simple latched one.

He flipped the pin and opened the door.

Cody was right; the clothes and other items across from his cell belonged to a child. Several children, in fact. He saw mounds of clothing, toys, and dolls randomly strewn about the cages that lined the hall. What was that under the pile of rags—a rock? He leaned closer and gasped. The petrified remains of a child no bigger than his seven-year-old niece glared back at him. The shadow of its skull chilled him more than any of the horrors he had seen until now.

Cody never knew he could so thoroughly hate anyone until that moment. He thought he hated people before: his boss, Rachel, and Rick at times. No, those were games and passing moments. What boiled inside him now was pure. Pure, undefiled hatred.

Before he left, he picked at the splinters in his right hand. He pulled out the longest of the pieces, but the smaller ones broke off and hid deeper into his skin.

Just have to bear it.

The knob of the door at the end of the hall shook. Cody rushed quietly to hide behind the door as it swung open. He could hear a single set of footprints enter. A wheezing, belabored breathing accompanied the man as he stumbled inside, his back to Cody. A reek stronger than that of the bodies and clothes filled the air. Cody almost gagged, but forced his hand over his mouth and silenced the urge. The man never looked behind the door where Cody hid. Whether out of cockiness or stupidity, Cody didn't care. Now he found the first outlet for the rage and disgust that burned inside him.

He crouched behind the man, taking care to pad on the stone floor. He rose to a standing position. The man was gawking at the open cell door, perhaps trying to process what he believed to be impossible. Surely if the big and muscular one couldn't break out, how could the scrawny one do it?

I'll show you, motherfucker.

Gripping the metal spike in his right hand, his left over its top for support, he raised it above the man's head. With no hesitation, he drove the spike down into the skull. He put his arm over the man's mouth and squeezed as the jailer slumped to the ground. Blood spurted up once, like a drinking fountain, and then stopped. Cody held the face tighter as the man squirmed. With his free hand, he pushed the spike further down until he was sure it hit something soft and squishy.

The man twitched a leg. Just the nerves. Cody let go, and the body slumped to the ground. He watched it to see if it would get back up. It didn't. He had figured the people here were only strong and monstrous once the stars were out. Whether that meant this man would rise from the dead when it got dark or not, he didn't want to linger around and find out the hard way. He was dead for now, and that was good enough.

Cody's pulse was electric. His sweat was cold. He tuned his senses to every detail of his surroundings. He felt as if he could sense every scent around him, even the smell of the flowers just outside the windows at the top of the wall. Cody could feel a slight breeze from the open door. Could hear the buzz of the yellow lights and the soft crunch of feet against gravel from outside. He felt no remorse, no guilt over what he had just done. He felt alive for the first time in years. Fuck yeah.

He listened in silence for any approaching footsteps. There were none. Aiko's neglect of Cody saved him. Had he been perceived as a greater threat, then no doubt there would have been a squad of guards posted here. But he was Cody, the one-eyed skinny kid who couldn't stand up for himself. The man-child who couldn't stop the death of one friend and the enslavement of the other.

Cody tried to pull the spike out of the skull, but it was stuck. For a moment, he tried to yank it out by putting his foot on the dead man's shoulders. He abandoned the task when it seemed the head would come off before the weapon would. He reached into the man's pockets but found nothing of use.

Cody went through the open door and came out into a large circular room. A stone staircase opened up into the room at the far end. More cages lined the sides, but there were no other cells. His was the only one. Light was pouring in from windows situated high up. He could see a street. A pair of legs walked by the window, casting lanky shadows across the basement, but soon left. He scoured the room for a weapon. He found one immediately but didn't like what he would have to do to get it.

There were dead bodies in some cages. Wading through the thick scent of rot, he came near and saw that each body was still wet. They were recently killed. Several of them had been dismembered, their innards piled up in the corner of their cells like a heap of refuse.

Limbs were detached, though not fully: they held on by their sinewy threads. Heads were broken apart like cantaloupes. These must be the bodies of rejected sacrifices. Cody had only seen three sacrifices on the surface, three chained corpses, one belonging to his best friend. There were dozens of bodies down in this basement. This god was picky.

Each body in the cells was pierced through with a metal rod. Whoever had exacted this macabre display of bloody art enjoyed themselves. They so thoroughly enjoyed doing, so that they left their instruments of death lying around. There was no fear they would be retrieved and used against them.

Now they would be.

Cody went up to one bloated corpse in an open cage. It wore faded green shorts and a Hawaiian shirt. Shattered sunglasses lay by its side. In the cage next to it, Cody saw another body, dressed in the same patterns, wearing a skirt. A couple on vacation? A honeymoon?

Rage pushed Cody past disgust. He grabbed the metal pole that was lodged in the man's chest and ripped it out. He apologized to the dead and silently promised to avenge them. The pole was equal to half of Cody's height, and someone had sharpened its end. It was a twisted spear that was in no danger of breaking.

Perfect.

Before he left, he noticed a utility closet by the stairs. He opened the door and was about to leave, not seeing much he could use. Nothing but an old rag, a box full of rusted nails, and an orange tin can full of some kind of liquid. It had an X made of duct tape that had been stretched across it. Wait a minute... He opened the cap and smelled it: gasoline. This could come in handy.

Cody climbed the staircase and came to another heavy wooden door. This one was unlocked. Gently pushing it open, he peered out from a low angle so as not to be seen. The door opened out onto a hallway.

There was no one there. He entered gently, closing the door behind him. Heard a click from the door. He tried the knob; it had locked itself automatically. Stood at the end of a hallway with bleached-white walls. He recognized the hall; he had glimpsed it only yesterday before dinner. Cody walked forward and came into the main living area. He saw a red door with a portrait of a harsh-looking older man to its side. Reading the caption, he saw it read:

1928/04/13—1967/08/23

This was Aiko's house. Which meant that behind the red door...

Cody put the gasoline down, opened the door, and saw the remains of Aiko's father, chained to the platform in the middle of a serene garden. The body was fitted atop a short stone pyramid, no higher than two feet, yet it was a replica of the one in the courtyard. Cody hadn't noticed it the last time that he was here. It may have been the shock that blinded him to the details. A butterfly soaked up sunlight while resting on the corpse's face, beauty in the macabre. His dead face had a silent scream etched onto its hollow mouth.

This was a man of pure evil: Cody had seen some of what he had done to Aiko in that vision. He deserved this fate, Cody thought. Like father, like daughter. Still, an ounce of pity tugged at his heart. She was a monster, but this was the creature that made her one. Cody looked up at the open gray sky and couldn't see where the sun could be: only thick and darkened clouds with not much daylight left to reveal them.

He knew he had little time.

He was going to leave when a thought struck him. What had Aiko said to him in the cave as she scorched out his eye? *The light of your suffering will keep us warm for generations. It will keep him ascended for centuries.*

The suffering of the sacrifices will keep them warm; it will keep him ascended. What if... what if this god *needed* the sacrifices? Why else would they burn each night? Sure, it was possible Amatsu simply took pleasure in their pain. Cody was sure that he did. But there had to be a reason his hold seemed weaker during the day and insanely strong at night. What if it's not just about the sun, but about having his sacrifices around that gives him this power? It's worth a shot.

I'm fucking freeing this thing.

Cody took the spear and struck at the point where the chains were attached to the platform. The metal skidded off the chains without leaving much of a scratch. This would take forever, even longer than the door took to break through. There was a faster, less savory approach, one he had already experimented with on Rick's body. Cody placed his right foot on the corpse's left wrist. With his left foot, he held the body back by its skull and pushed. Then he stabbed the spear into the burned arm with all his strength. It went right through it with a wet sliding sound.

It made Cody uneasy to think how a sixty-year-old dead man could still be wet on the inside. Did that mean the bodies back in the basement weren't necessarily recent? He twisted the spear and started stomping down on the arm. It broke at the wrist. One down. He did the same to the other wrist, and in moments the body was free, minus its hands.

Cody put the spear under his arm and dragged the body out of the garden, away from the gaze of any star. The moment he took the body off the pyramid, the ground shook. The portrait of Aiko's father fell off the wall, and the glass pane shattered. The shaking ended.

Somebody's not happy about this. Is this going to do anything? Maybe not by itself. But if he's still going to burst into flames tonight...

Cody went into the dining hall. He looked up at the painting of Amatsu and flipped it the middle finger. He hid the body in a closet at the end of the room. Cody stuffed a few blankets and pillows over it. It was surrounded by paper walls and dry wood—the perfect conditions for a fire.

He heard a sliding door open from the other room, accompanied by the ringing of tiny bells. He crept up to the entrance of the dining room and saw Aiko running down the hall. To his horror, he realized then that her father's body had left behind a black trail of ash and grease. She was looking down at the trail now.

Now or never.

His heart nearly went into a thermonuclear meltdown. As Aiko bent down to examine the floor, Cody rushed her from behind. She never saw his face as he plunged the metal rod into her back and out her chest with all his strength. He pinned her to the wall, right where the portrait of her father had hung. Her wide-brimmed hat fell to the floor, her head rotated around, and she looked Cody in the eye with her shocked expression.

"You... fucking..." she wheezed and gurgled as blood poured out of her mouth.

A bug pinned to the wall. A butterfly on a skull. Her body thrashed, her throat spasmed, and she fell motionless against the pole, hanging off it limply.

I can run now, but I might need my spear.

He looked into her eyes: no silver, no life, dead and staring into an endless infinity. He grabbed the spear, put his foot on her shoulder for leverage, and pulled it out. It took three heaves and even a ho, but he pulled it out. She collapsed onto the floor. Cody was about to leave, but turned back to Aiko, kicked her shoulder to roll her over on her back, and stabbed her once more in the heart. She didn't react. Already dead. Had to be sure.

Before he turned around, someone knocked him to the ground. Someone was on his back, scratching at his face with a knee on his neck. He heard a woman screaming, her nails scraping against the recently burned flesh of his forehead, and she dug others into his throat. But it was not yet night, and Cody was not having it. She removed her knee and bit his neck. Cody thrust his hand between her teeth and his flesh. She bit down and crunched his fingers. But he didn't yell. Instead, he forced his fist into her mouth and kept her teeth from biting down harder on his neck.

Cody brought his knee to his chest and put his foot on the nearby wall. He pushed and rolled over, with the woman underneath him. She bit down on his fist harder. Cody twisted his shoulders and partially faced her. He punched the woman with his other hand, and she released him from her bite. Cody got to his feet and grabbed the spear off the floor. He thrust it through her mouth and out the back of her head. Another bug pinned to a board. She looked no older than sixteen, with a grin far too wide for her small face.

He looked at his right hand and saw the bone exposed through obvious tooth marks. Cody gripped the pole tighter and forgot the pain. Picked up the canister of gasoline and looked out the front door, seeing no one. He heard the voices of a small group coming from just around the corner. Cody ran outside and hid behind the other corner. The voices came near and moved further away from the house.

The town was small, and he remembered his way to the stone gate entrance. He looked towards the town square and saw that the people were gathering there. He was sure that the town had emptied, and everyone was now gathered at the square. There were about twenty adults in all, all the kids (maybe six), Mr. Okayama with his kindly grandfather look, the gray-haired man holding the conch shell (he looked impatient for his nightly growth spurt).

He could see the pyramid with Rick's body at the top. In front of his body was a woman in a black-and-red robe. She was kneeling before him, her pink-and-black hair done up in pins.

Above the scene, there was a shimmer in the sky. It was still daylight, but the sky rippled like water in a pond, like something couldn't wait to break through it.

I'm sorry, Rick, Mia. There's nothing I can do.

He ran down the road, hit the stone archways, and escaped Inunaki.

Although he was confident he had the head start, a mournful scream from behind told him Aiko's body had been discovered.

No time to lose.

"Fuck, fuck, fuck."

He was at the foot of the pyramid amid the burnt cars. The body atop glowed as the fading light reflected off its gold necklace. He should have known—there was no leaving, not that easily. The sun was still high but was on its descent. The sky was deep red that painted the clouds a dark brownish color, like the embers of a dying fire. When the sun set, maybe two or three hours from now, the people would change, and the red star would find him out here in the open. Even if he ran with all his might, he would just end up back here again. There was truly no way to escape.

His breathing grew chaotic, a sure sign of another panic attack. He began sucking in air as if he had just been held underwater. He gripped his spear, shut his eyes, and let the feeling pass.

He remembered the shaking earth when he removed the sacrifice from Aiko's garden, and when he temporarily removed Rick as well.

It's my only shot.

He raced up the stairs and stood before the blackened body. He didn't hesitate to hack away. Foot on wrists, spear, and stomping. Soon, the body was free. It was too heavy to carry down the steps, so Cody chucked it down and watched it topple over like a twisted slinky.

"Sorry."

He ran down halfway to where the body had fallen and broken apart, lifted it, and tossed it down again. It slumped onto the brown grass. The earth shook with a great tremor. A tree fell into the clearing. The pyramid cracked down the middle as Cody was still running down the steps. Cody jumped off the third step from the end and landed on the ground that had become a roaring ocean of hateful waves. It stopped. He got up, grabbed the body, and tossed it into the woods, next to a dry-looking tree. Looking up, Cody noticed the forest had lost most of its shimmer of silver light. The same shine that had appeared every time he had tried to escape before was now mostly absent.

Did removing the body work?!

He apologized once more to the corpse, grabbed a heavy-looking stone by its feet, and crushed the skull into pieces, scattering the shards of obsidian bone. He removed each of the limbs by stabbing the spear into their joints and jumping down with all his body weight. A ravenous frenzy of murder took him over as he mutilated the corpse.

He felt sick as he did this. But you can't chain up a body if there is no body to chain up. He grabbed each body part and flung them in opposite directions, a gardener spreading his seed. He took the pieces of the skull, dug a shallow pit with his hands, and buried them. When he was finished, panting for breath, covered in ash, he wiped his greasy hands on a tree trunk.

He unscrewed the gasoline and poured it out in a line from the rib cage he had left on the ground. He kept pouring every few feet as he ran towards what he hoped would be the cliff walls that had trapped them in this damn valley to begin with.

If anyone follows me, and the body ignites at nightfall, at least I'll have something separating me from them. It could even send up some more smoke for people outside the valley to see.

The canister dripped out its last drops of fuel. Cody threw it carelessly into the trees and kept on running.

29

Cody ran along the dirt trail and through the woods. The shimmer in the trees was not entirely gone. He could detect a slight flash, yet it was nowhere near the shine it had once held.

Without his glasses, his vision blurred slightly, and he lacked the depth perception that having two eyes conveniently provides. For the first time, he could see streaks of blue through the mass of gray. But he could see it, the sky! This furthered his conviction that he was right: take away the sacrifices, take away his worship, and Amatsu's hold would wane. Aiko had said that their burning, their sacrifice, was what kept him ascended.

The vision in the cave came back to him, the vision of the red star lying dormant for centuries on end as worship of it had ceased. It needed us to praise it in order to be in our world, to escape its stone prison. But would this hold even at night, when the stars came out? The hint of the silver shine in the leaves told him no. It was still there; it still had some power in the air. No sense in testing it.

He hit a steep hill, and his run slowed to a strained hike. Midway up, he had to grab roots sticking out of the ground to help pull himself up. He scrambled up to the top of the hill on his belly, tugging at what he could. Before he could lift himself up to safety, a figure appeared on the ledge. Mr. Okayama's face twisted, his eyes were half-closed, and a smile of anticipatory satisfaction cracked his face. He kicked Cody in the face. The sole of his work boot smashed into Cody's nose, and he lost his grip on the roots.

For the second time that week, and not the last, he hurtled towards the ground from a high fall. The ground met him like an old friend. It embraced his body fully and without discrimination.

He coughed and shot up a cloud of dust with his breath. He could feel dirt mixed with blood caking on his face. His body was sore, and his nose felt smashed and was sensitive to the touch, probably broken. Rocks and debris came tumbling down the hill. Mr. Okayama was sliding and racing down it like a mad dog. It was still day, just barely, and the old man was feeble, yet despite this, he looked terrifying. Cody grasped the spear that had fallen to his side, confident he could take him. That was until he saw the dozen townsfolk who were behind the old man, also tumbling and running down the hill.

Cody fled in the opposite direction.

He flew over fallen logs and moss-covered stones. Ran past some jizo statues hidden in the grass, their red scarves standing out in the green-and-gray landscape. He remembered the last time he had seen them, well outside the town's limits. Soon, the trees parted, and he came into a clearing with a river flowing through it. The water raced towards a sudden drop before spraying out to become a waterfall. Cody looked down and saw large boulders with sharp edges. A faint rainbow arched through the mist of the water's spray. Cody ran to the edge and spun around, spear in hand. On his sides, thick and thorny bushes. There was nowhere else to run.

The crowd of crazed forest denizens emerged into the clearing. Even though they were mostly elderly, with only a few younger men in the group, plus two children, Cody knew he couldn't take them on. They would swarm and overrun him in an instant.

If this is how it's going to be, so be it.

Mr. Okayama led the pack. Geriatric though he was, murder inflamed his face. He licked his lips and almost seemed to be aroused at the thought of tearing Cody apart. The townspeople did not slow down. Rather, they sprinted full speed towards Cody like a swarm of hornets, stingers at the ready. They would crash into him with no care for their lives in a matter of seconds. The perfect drone of a chaotic hive.

He braced himself, holding out the spear with shaking arms.

A glare blinded Cody. It was coming from Mr. Okayama's glasses. A glare from the sun! The old man stopped in his tracks and covered his face with his hands in defense. It did not matter. The sun was pouring out through the clouds. Blue sky ripped through the sea of endless gray and then came the warmth, a wholesome light that warmed Cody's back. It exploded into the clearing like a missile strike.

Mr. Okayama screeched like a car slamming on its brakes. The rest of the pack followed suit. These creatures had not seen the light of day in how many years? How many decades?

Pure golden light streamed into the clearing, filling every space with its brilliance. There was no barrier of cloud between the monsters and the fire of the sun.

Mr. Okayama burst into flames.

He screamed and fell to the ground, writhing and shaking like a child throwing a tantrum. His skin boiled and fell off his face. He rose to his knees, as if trying to rush at Cody like a suicide bomber. He was mostly bone at this point, shaking intensely. Took one step towards Cody before exploding. Bits of him flew across the clearing. One by one, the same effect hit the rest of them, like a chemical reaction, human bombs popping all over the grass. The field looked and sounded like a war zone. A few people escaped into the dark woods, but the sun incinerated most of them.

Where once an angry mob had stood, now there were only steaming holes and tiny islands of burning flesh. The pieces burned up quickly until only ashes remained. Whether Aiko and the other two he had killed would rise again at sundown, he was sure those in front of him would not—so total was their destruction in the light of the setting sun.

It worked; *it fucking worked.*

Removing the corpses from their platforms must have weakened the hold of Aiko's god on the valley.

Smoke wafted through the air as the sunlight drained out of view. Cody looked out over the waterfall at the valley. Here and there, the mist was broken by the parting of the clouds. A few distant explosions rocketed into view. He saw the trees shake and smoke rise. He could also see the town itself. No light touched it. It was still an island of gray, protected by a thick mist. The tops of the buildings were hardly visible. The volcano trembled. He saw a flicker of red shoot out of the top. Whatever Cody had done had worked—at least enough for some sunlight to pour through.

How many townspeople died today? Thirteen that he knew of, and the few he saw explode in the distance. That meant that only a handful, perhaps fifteen people—were left in the town. He was sure everyone who had been pursuing him was dead, obliterated by the sun, or was lost out in the forest running for their lives. They would never catch him if he ran now unless they could fly. Cody shuddered at the realization that at least one of them could. All the more reason to book it now.

The sun was just above the hills in the distance. The stars came out, much earlier than they had the right to, and showed themselves like 1,000 watchful eyes searching the valley, searching for him. It was twilight. Mere moments before the nightmare world would take over once again.

If he ran now, he'd reach the edge of the valley by sunrise at the latest. Then he'd claw and fight his way up that rock face, no matter what, even if he had to break every bone in his body to do so.

He started down the path he thought would take him home.

He stopped.

Mia was on his mind. She could have been one of the explosions he had seen in the distance. In that case, her suffering was at an end. If not, she was fated to walk forever in an eternal night, bound to an evil that was beyond this world.

He thought of Rick. He was the only sacrifice remaining. If Cody left now, Rick too was bound to an eternal fate, one of flame and terror and pain.

The community would rebuild.

More cages full of children's clothes.

More sacrifices for the god of stars.

Cody saw the heavy door in his mind. The bathroom door. Blood lined it. Pills spilled out from the crack at the bottom. The wood heaved as if breathing; residue built up on its face, running down its length. He felt something inside him say, "Just leave it closed. Run and be safe." It was almost as if something wanted him gone. "Just leave and take your life with you." In that moment, Cody honestly thought he would do just that: leave. But he also felt dangerous, murderous even.

In his mind's eye, he pushed at that door, no matter what horrors lay on the other side of it. He opened it. Walked through it.

Cody turned around and headed back to Inunaki.

30

Mia stood over the heap that was Aiko's body. Blood had spilled out of her chest. It blended well with the red robe, while it stained what was once white. Mia wept bitterly.

"Oh, mother, we are lost without you."

She could not remember a time before the loving embrace of Aiko Koike. Could not remember the pain that had once driven her life. She could not even remember her own name. But she knew the dead woman on the floor was the reason for her newfound serenity.

Mia cried out in anguish. She held Aiko's hand. Six people, all that was left of the town, stood just outside the home.

They wailed and moaned and tore at their clothing. There was no way of knowing who had been lost in the sunlight. She had heard distant booms and concussive shakes that she prayed came not from her family. Maybe others had survived out there in the forest and had taken shelter under a dark patch of branches and leaves, though she knew in her bones that they did not make it. She had lost much in this day, and her grief knew no bounds.

The sun set. The last of the light drained itself from the room, taking away the vibrancy of the red display on the floor, and the cool light of the stars replaced it. Mia could feel the rush of His presence fill her body.

The guiding light of the stars connected her to them. Her pain lessened as the night fell. The sweet embrace of the night gave her some solace in the face of what she had lost.

Aiko opened her eyes and flew up as if from a bad dream, taking a deep, gasping breath.

Everyone clasped their hands over their mouths. Their tears flowed over their ecstatic faces. Mia's heart overflowed with so much joy she could dance.

The hole in Aiko's chest filled itself in. Bone and muscle reattached themselves until her skin was whole and untouched, unblemished, though her magnificent robe was ruined and tattered. Mia knelt and embraced Aiko as she cried tears of joy.

Aiko's hair was disheveled and her eyes were bewildered, like a deer that had just avoided being clipped by a truck. As Aiko struggled to focus on what was happening, a clanging sound came from the basement. A man emerged from the staircase with a metal spike in his head. The object pulsed and shook as if something inside his head was trying to push it out, yet it remained stuck. Blood covered his face, and he stumbled into the room. Three townsfolk ran to him and took him into their arms, removing the spike the rest of the way. His wound healed in seconds. His eyes, along with everyone else's, burned with their silver light.

Aiko stood and clasped Mia's throat.

"The sacrifices!"

Aiko lifted Mia off the ground, her feet dangling inches above it. Mia's eyes were wide, like an innocent child unaware of what she had done wrong.

Aiko released her and dropped her to the ground. Aiko flung the red door open. She shrieked a deep yet hollow cry that echoed off the walls. Her eyes flashed blood-red, and their crimson hue enveloped all that she beheld. The people cowered before her in silence. Then, a young man approached her, his eyes cast to the floor.

He bowed his head low and said, "Mother, everything will be alright; we will find the one responsible for this."

Aiko punched her fist through his throat, the viscera splattering onto the wall behind him, giving the wall a chunky paint job. She shook her hand and flung him off like a dirty rag. He struggled on the ground, grasping at the open wound, blood spurting out. His wound healed, and Aiko scoffed at him. She lifted him off the floor. Her nails grew into claws almost as long as her forearm. She slashed at his neck, ripping open the throat and exposing his spine. She grabbed his head and tore it off, dropping it to the floor.

The head landed near Mia. She could not understand the violence, the cruelty on display.

We are supposed to be a family now.

The man's headless torso groped for his head, like a child blindly looking for his favorite toy in the dark.

"The sacrifices! We must find them right now!"

The flock scattered at the bellow of their shepherd.

Mia noticed fear in the eyes of her mother. This disturbed her. All was supposed to be peace, security, and love in the valley. Aiko's eyes spoke of a different reality: one of impending terror and doom. Mia climbed to her feet, her heart gripped by a fear that was absolute and pure.

A roar erupted from the bowels of the house. Aiko's face dropped, and her knees shook. She nearly fell. The cry came from the dining area. One man ran towards the shout, and soon he was screaming as well. Fire followed him, clinging to his body and spreading to the walls.

Mia looked into the room and saw the sacrifice. He was in the closet, screaming, burning with the light of her God. Fell out and crawled across the tatami floor with no hands. He inched his way towards Aiko. The fire spread to the entire room: to the floors, the walls, the painting of her beloved God and savior on the wall. Aiko's face shook and tears formed in her eyes as she watched the sacrifice move toward her across the floor.

Though it had no eyes and no jaw muscles, it felt like it was grimacing at Aiko with an intense hatred. Mia stood there as Aiko fled outside.

"Everything was supposed to be different," Mia said.

Silver tears fell from her eyes as she beheld the light of Amatsu consume the house. Soon the fire had barred the door to her. She could run through it and be fine, of course, but she stood there in shock. She was alone, save for the thing crawling on the ground, encircled by the flame. Where had her mother gone? Why had she left her here alone?

She went to her knees and lifted her hands to the sky.

The last word on her lips before the fire took her was the name of her beloved, the name Amatsu.

Aiko ran out of that damned house. The fire clung to her blood-stained robe before she tore off the offending pieces.

Idiots, all of them. No one understands what is at stake.

She looked around her and saw the remaining faithful, three in total, running away from the house. She commanded them to return, but instead, they fled into the forest. The only one who stood beside her was Atsuki. He had already grown to his full height. His gray hair glowed in the starlight.

She looked up at the giant with gratitude. "My father is there," she pointed to the burning pit of her former home. "I will take care of him.

The other sacrifice on the outskirts is missing. I can sense it. Find him quickly."

The tall man nodded, leaped over a nearby roof and sped into the forest.

The fire had now fully engulfed her childhood home. It spread to the buildings on either side. Aiko surveyed the other side of the town. Fire was coming from there as well, from the forest itself. The entire town was being invaded by waves of flame. Embers blew across the town like a snow flurry, lighting the wooden homes as they blew past.

Eaves and roofs collapsed. Aiko stood alone, abandoned by her entire flock, save for Atsuki. Tomoto, the headless man, rolled around the street in flames. He was useless. Worse, if they did not offer unto Him what He desired, and soon...

She ran to the town square, avoiding the flaming debris as it rained down from above. At the top of the pyramid, Rick was in flames, screaming into the night.

Good. At least one is in place. If there is at least one, all is not lost. If we lose him, we incur the wrath.

She was alone in the town square. Aiko could see the smoke trails of the ones who ran into the woods while still on fire. She would discipline them when they returned, for return they must. There was no other choice for them to make.

Her world was falling apart in front of her. All that she had endeavored to build over fifty years. Her paradise was burning down. But she could rebuild. She just needed to keep Rick on that platform for one night, and the next day she would go out and find more people. She hadn't needed to leave the valley for years in search of fuel, but she had done it before, and she could fix this. Had not her God given her eternal life and power beyond limit? Her heart grieved for the destruction, but she held onto the faith that all would be well by tomorrow. Just hang on until tomorrow.

For now, let's take care of dad.

"Aiko!"

The voice rang out amid the chaos. She saw a man painted brown and red, caked with mud and blood, with only one eye, half his face blistered red and sagging. He was holding a sharp metallic object.

How dare he! This insignificant insect. I'll rip out his spine and keep him alive while I do it. Fuck the sacrifice, I'm ending this now.

Just as she ran towards him, the roof of a nearby home collapsed, causing the house to fall sideways like a top-heavy house of cards. The wreckage spilled out onto the street. It crushed her under its weight like a flaming avalanche. A beam landed across her back, pressing her face into the dirt. The flames spread over her body as she tried to lift the roof off of her.

Cody had arrived at the village ten minutes earlier. Hid in the alley just across the street from Aiko's home. Cody saw a few people gathered outside and Mia inside, crying over Aiko's body. He looked up at the pyramid. Rick. A lifeless skeleton not yet set alight. There was still time.

Cody ran up the steps and came to the platform. He looked down at his friend and apologized. He raised the spear and hacked away at the remaining (handless) arm that had been fastened to the base and a brand new chain. A chain was now attached to his right ankle. After several strikes, he broke the arm at the wrist. With a few more hacks to the ankle, Rick was free. Cody put his weapon under his left armpit and lifted the body up.

Too little, too late.

The sun had set. A howl erupted from Aiko's home as smoke ripped through the cracks of the roof. A blanket of darkness washed over the town. Soon, the burning homes of Inunaki created a sea of light, an inviting bonfire that warmed him. Out in the forest, other fires erupted from where Cody left the body parts of the gold-chain wearing skeleton scattered. Each shard became its own individual match: the valley was ablaze, and the tidal wave of the inferno came towards the town.

The stars flamed in their hollow brilliance, their light washing over Cody with an icy feeling. Rick moved, and Cody dropped him. Rick's corpse shook, twisting his head from side to side. Ash fell from him as he moved. He turned his face towards Cody. Could he see with no eyes? Immense pity welled up inside him.

"I'm sorry."

The skull nodded in assent. It understood. It went up in flames. With no chains to bind him, Rick flailed on the platform like a fish out of water.

What could Cody do now? His friend thrashed about in suffering. Cody thought about just kicking him off the platform. Cody moved closer to Rick and prepared himself. Just then, the fire consuming Rick intensified and became an inferno. The heat burned Cody's skin, and he had to move away.

Screams from Aiko's home again. A headless man stumbled out of the entrance and collapsed on the street. Several others ran past the helpless creature and fled into the woods. At least one of them was on fire.

A cracking sound from below. The tall man, standing just outside of Aiko's home, was coming into his own, his spine stretching out, his limbs growing to hideous lengths. Aiko herself soon came out of the house. Cody's face fell at the sight. She said something to the tall man, and he bounded away with incredible speed, flying over the flaming homes like stepping stones. Cody hid in plain sight.

Even when Aiko herself scanned the pyramid, she missed Cody, who was standing right there, out in the open. Too many thoughts must have infested her mind for her to notice. She was alone now on the street, spinning around with a desperate look on her face. Cody gripped his spear and descended the steps.

Cody looked across the courtyard at Aiko as she struggled to lift the burning wreckage of the home. Pure and unrestrained fury poured from her coal-red eyes. Their vermillion intensity blinded him. He shielded his one eye against the assault. The collapsed rubble of Aiko's house shifted. A flaming figure of a small woman stumbled out and crawled towards them.

It was Mia. The skin of her face had melted down to expose the tendons and bone. It gave her face the look of a perpetual smile and shocked, sleepless eyes. Her long pink hair had been reduced to nothing but tufts. But the way she walked was the same, so Cody instantly recognized her. She rose from the ground and stood, still on fire. She gazed intently at Aiko, at Cody, at Rick. "Insanity" was the only word Cody could conjure to describe her wide, lifeless eyes.

She shook and clasped her hands to her temples. Great horns sprouted from her head. They curved outwards, black and thick as a human arm, and looked far too heavy for her frame to support them. That was until her spine extended. Each spurt of growth produced a sickening pop. Muscles ballooned her flesh in a grotesque caricature of what should have been possible. When it was done, she stood over ten feet tall, broad-shouldered, skinless, and incendiary. A nightmarish Minotaur, born of hate.

"Help me," Aiko commanded her. "You must retrieve my father and place him on the altar."

The thing that was once Mia ignored the request. She even snorted at it. It lowered its head like a bull and charged at Cody.

The sweat of his grip nearly cost him the spear. Mia charged at him as he held his ground. The ground shook with the rapid advance of her rush. Cody readied the spear above his head. He lacked the depth perception and the talent to throw anything with precision. Of this, he was fully aware. His arms shook as he steadied the projectile and aimed it.

Mia was upon him.

He thrust the spear into the air, sending off a silent prayer as he threw it with all his might. It struck true. It pierced right through the horned beast's throat and lodged itself inside.

Cody nearly gasped at what happened. How could his aim have been so on target?

Mia crashed onto the ground, her horns nearly knocking into Cody. He jumped out of the way just in time.

Blood poured from the monster's open wound, dousing the flames that were still on its chest and shoulders. Steam shrouded its face from the bloody shower.

Mia rose to her knees, clasping at her neck but still very much alive. She pulled out the spear and threw it into a burning home. Mia smacked Cody with her massive taloned hand and sent him flying into the steps of the pyramid. Luckily, she had not opened her fist as she did so, or Cody would have surely been ripped in half. He hugged his ribs and gasped for air. Smoke hung low and filled his lungs, causing him to cough uncontrollably.

Mia rose fully to her feet, the wound in her neck sealed.

"Mia! Leave him and help me. We have little time. You must protect the sacrifice," Aiko screamed as she finally lifted the heavy beam that had pinned her to the ground. The flames were reducing her robes and skin to ash. Even so, she did not yell out in pain – only in fury tinged with an unmistakable tremor of panic. She walked out of the burning home limping and headed towards Mia.

Mia turned her flesh-stripped and bare face towards Aiko and pondered her for a moment. The desire to end Cody (or was it a broken heart at having been abandoned inside the house?) proved too great. She wavered between the two choices. And this was the final undoing of Inunaki.

Mia kicked Aiko in the chest, sending her to the ground. Mia stepped on her stomach like someone putting out a cigarette. She squashed Aiko into the ground until she went silent.

Then she turned and looked at Cody. He had hoped for a glint of sympathy, of her former self to be hidden in those insane eyes, but all he could see was starlight and rage.

She walked towards him. Cody tried to stand, but the pain that shot through his spine made him double over. Mia towered over him, holding him in place with both of her hands on his shoulders. What was once her touch of empathy was now the prelude to murder. Her jaw widened and unhinged itself like a great horned boa constrictor from the late Paleocene.

Cody shut his eye and waited.

While the three down below were preoccupied, Rick started to move and crawl. It took some time for him to realize what was going on. The blinding pain of the flames lit up every one of his remaining nerves, which somehow cruelly regenerated after last night. The pain went deeper, into his mind, into his soul. Everything hurt. There was no relief. All that his undead mind could comprehend was pain and the light of the fire.

That was until he looked down and sensed more than saw Cody throw a metal object into the body of some monster. He felt in his heart that it was Mia, the love of his life. He spasmed in pain and desperation, and experienced something new since his transformation into a human torch. His arm and leg were no longer bound to the platform.

He tried to stand and fell headfirst down the steps. The pain was almighty, all-encompassing. The fire held him down on those steps like a weighted blanket. He heard Mia cry out—roar out—in pain. She was wounded. He saw Cody fly across the courtyard and land on the bottom steps. Something greater than his pain took hold. Using the stub of his left arm, he steadied himself, got back up and walked. He tripped over what remained of his legs and stumbled. Soon, he got the hang of how to balance on the bone extending from his left ankle.

A flaming dead man on the move. This would have been the sort of thing he would have loved just a few days ago. "A great name for a band," he would have said. But there was no room for such thoughts now, or for any actual coherent ones. He was a thing of pure instinct at that moment. Pure emotion. Pure suffering. Pure love. He walked and stumbled down the stairs towards the ones he loved. Every step was full of pain and shot electricity through his nervous system. But he held back his screams and forced himself to walk on. Mia was standing over Cody now. Her massive jaws unhinged as she salivated.

Then she looked up, away from Cody. She turned her head towards Rick as he descended the stairs. She froze. In the depths of her silver eyes, a faint glimmer of recognition showed. Rick walked past Cody, who was barely conscious. He stood in front of the behemoth and extended his one arm to her, embracing the monster.

And there they stood, the two lovers bound at that moment, wreathed in flame.

Cody came to his senses. Rick had just walked past him. He could feel the flames as they warmed his left side. He could hardly believe it. And now Rick had come to the thing that was Mia and held her. She released her grip on Cody, and he fell to the ground. Mia and Rick stood like that for a minute. Cody hobbled to his feet.

Aiko had woken up. She felt her ribs reattach themselves and her organs shift back into place. Her body inflated with substance as she healed herself.

That bitch. When this is over, I will beseech Him and undo what was done. Then she will join her lover as a sacrifice.

Aiko rose to her knees and yelled, "You fool! Stop him now! Bring him back to the altar!"

She rose to her feet, a fiery wraith of a thing that could strike terror into the stoutest of hearts.

But she was too late.

Something snapped in Mia. She backed away from Rick and puffed smoke out of her nostrils. She grabbed him with one hand and brought him to her face. Then, as if he were a piece of trash, she hurled him across the courtyard. His body broke apart and scattered across the pavement, a comet of burning human wreckage. The fire that had been consuming him went out as he tumbled into nothing but a pile of bones.

Aiko cried out in fear, "You fool!"

The violent quake instantly leveled all the remaining homes. Everyone fell on their faces, even the hulking thing that was Mia. At that moment, all the fires went out. They were all snuffed out at once. The fire on Mia's torso, the flames that ate away at the homes—all gone. The stars disappeared. Save for one, the red star. Its crimson spotlight lit up the town.

Silence reigned in a stillness that spoke of something terrible to come.

Cody stood there, hugging his broken bones, and a sense of something approaching came over him. That feeling one has when they walk into a dark room and some animal part of their nervous system alerts them to the danger hidden in the shadows. All the hairs stand on end, the body chills, the heart quickens, and you prepare yourself to fight, flight, or play dead.

"No, no, no," Aiko cried out.

She was badly burned. Her hair was now patches of mowed grass, and most of her clothing was in blackened tatters. Cody feared that at any moment she would heal herself fully, as she had probably done countless times over the decades. But something was different now: she looked afraid.

Her burns did not heal.

Some of the townspeople who had fled earlier had returned. They approached the scene with hunched backs and cowering shoulders. Their silhouettes were barely visible in the red light. One such shadow must have belonged to the tall man: it towered over the others. He was shaking. They all looked to Aiko as a child does to its mother. She was no better in that moment, a lost child herself.

It was quiet.

It was a living silence that swallowed them, the entire town, whole.

The ground quaked once more, sending everyone to their knees. Aiko's eyes lost their light. The silver in the people's eyes went out. The tall man collapsed inwards on himself and shrieked as something forcibly compacted his body back to its original size.

Mia began reverting to her original form. The horns shrank, and her body cracked back into its tiny frame. The snapping of bone followed each stage of the transformation. Then she was Mia again, but the flames had scarred her, and she did not heal. She screamed and twitched on the ground in obvious pain. Cody felt nothing but pity for her; if he could end it for her now, that would be the greatest gift he could offer. But he held no weapon. He had no fight left in him. He felt on the edge of death himself.

The red light went out. All was darkness so thick that Cody could not see even the movement of his hands in front of him now. The shadows had deepened. Some of the townspeople wept. Aiko's pleading prayer was audible.

The air began to ripple and flex. He could feel something moving, unseen, through the very air itself.

Looking up, he could see the darkness of the sky folding back, like a curtain being tugged at from two sides. The very fabric of reality ripped open and revealed a darkness that was deeper than the blackness of space itself. Somehow, it was a pit so deep that light could not enter it.

That deep well of obsidian night broke something in Cody's mind. He could sense that this was the true nature of the universe. Behind all the smells and tastes and sights of the world and its scientific laws, behind all our human activity and politics and war and love, whatever lay in that darkness was the true foundation of reality, the true meaning of it all. In that black pit was the true god. Not a god of stars. A god of death.

They all stood there motionless, even Mia, whose cries had softened to soft whimpers.

A red light sparked to life again and pierced that infinite dark. It came from directly above, from the red star that had now shown itself from within the tear in space. Something was coming, something that the residents of Inunaki had not seen before—their terror made that much obvious.

The red haze lit up the courtyard. It gave everything a surreal feeling of being inside a fish tank under a heat lamp. The people were dark shadows, their features detailed through a hideous filter of blood. They all somehow looked horrifying and pitiable all at once. The villagers wept, and a few tried to run. They would never make it far.

Then he saw it.

He saw what emitted that red light, the same glow that had painted terror on Rick's face the night he was sacrificed. That brilliance engulfed Cody's body. He felt the heat it gave off.

Above him, in the dark abyss of the sky, a great red eye was looking back at him.

It was peering out from the rip in space. From some other world it beheld him, it knew him; it saw him. There would be no safety from this gaze, no place to hide. Cody had never felt more terrified.

The eye's size covered nearly the entire sky. It looked as if it had once been white, but now uneven stains covered it, streaks of varying shades of red painted its surface. The eye's veins pulsed like crimson lightning flashing across the heavens. Its pupil was a deep wine-purple. Cody felt the weight of eternity crash down on him. Whatever that eye was, it had always been, it would always be, and it was looking at him; it was looking directly at him!

Cody's clothes smoked. He broke free of the trance of the eye and ran. Seconds later, a fountain of fire erupted behind him, where he had just been standing. The blaze caught the few remaining townspeople, save for the tall man who was further off, and immediately reduced them to ashes.

The eye quaked and vibrated incessantly, twitching from side to side, throwing any sense of balance and orientation into disarray.

Aiko ran to the top of the pyramid. Mia followed her, having gotten the pain under control.

"Please, Amatsu, Lord of the stars, God of fire and blood, spare me! I have always done what you asked of me. I gave you this village. I have given you sacrifice after sacrifice over decades of service. Am I not worthy of you?"

Mia clung to the rags that were once her robes and asked, "Mother, me too. Spare me too."

Aiko punched her in the face and knocked her off the platform. Mia fell down the steps and tumbled down.

Cody ran and did not look back.

This can't be right. This can't be happening. I'm the reason he is free; *I'm the reason he has been given life anew. He* must *see this. It's not my fault that the sacrifices were corrupted.*

Aiko descended into hysterical gasps for breath and a hyena-like laugh. "Please, Lord, please."

Then she saw it. She had seen the great eye many times before as Amatsu consumed the incense of the sacrifices. She alone was granted that privilege. But she had never seen *Him* before. Never seen Him unveiled. She had seen the shadow that walked inside the red light, but never had she, even as the high priestess to the star, never had she seen *Him.*

For the short remainder of her life, she wished she had never seen it. In her last moments, she wished she had never come home and gone into that cave all those years ago. Life in Tokyo wasn't that bad, despite the abuse and the drugs. None of those horrors could live up to what she saw now. She tried to remember her mother, the spring sun warming the riverbanks, butterflies coasting along the blue-green water. Her mother's sweet laugh.

The last comprehensible thought that Aiko Koike ever had before her mind snapped was one word, one image: *Mommy.*

Something fell from the great eye. A massive drop of red hung down from the opening in the sky and came towards the ground. Like a bloody tear. There was no light in the sky. Just an endless sea of darkness. The only light visible was the red lava glow from down in the courtyard, where the tear had fallen. The liquid, a combination of blood and fire, rose and took shape. Its light burned to ash all that was near it.

The blast zone immediately leveled Atsuki, the last remaining towns person, to nothingness upon arrival. The blast knocked back and cleared away all the rubble of the homes, as if from a bomb blast. The ground became a pool of fiery destruction that swept everything away.

Mia climbed up from the bottom step, trying to escape the destruction below.

The thing held the shape of a man, but stood far taller than Atsuki ever had. Amatsu's flesh was blood, fire, shadow, and light. He transformed every moment Aiko beheld Him, an ever-changing illusion. He held the appearance of magma flowing from a live volcano. In another moment, He was a set of stars burning in the depths of space. Her eyes could not rest on what He looked like long enough to comprehend His appearance.

Amatsu bent down towards the earth, where Mia was still alive on the bottom steps, on her knees with arms outstretched before the God of stars.

At that moment, His face was a mask of bone. Skeletal limbs radiated out from it like a headdress of feathers. Their bony hands covered the mouth of the God. Fire poured out from the holes of the mask where His eyes were.

The God grabbed Mia and lifted her into the sky. Aiko couldn't see what Mia saw up close, but she saw the skeletal hands move away from His face, uncovering what lay beneath that mask of death. Mia screamed in terror. He crushed her in His hands. Her head popped off and fell to the flaming hellscape of the ground. He opened His hand and there was no more trace of Mia: she was gone. The God inhaled the smoke of the destruction He had wrought, the incense of sacrifice.

"No, please, Lord!"

Aiko was on her knees, arms lifted in reverence, head bowed down.

The God looked down and regarded her indifferently. Soon, Aiko felt great fingers wrap around her body and burn her flesh. She was lifted up into the sky, before the face of Amatsu. The hands covering His face quaked and slithered away. No more bone—that was a mirage, a momentary mask to cover what He truly was. Whatever Aiko saw at that moment, it turned every bit of remaining black in her hair to a silvery white. She screamed and screamed until there was no voice left in her throat.

But the God did not crush her as He had done Mia, as He had granted unto that small one a measure of mercy. He lifted Aiko higher into the sky and opened His palm. She looked out over the dark valley.

Aiko felt hot. She felt her bones and her blood boiled. Steam emitted from her flesh and blinded her. Aiko's body erupted in red flames as she cried out in anguish.

All thoughts left her. Her world had become a singular reality, the reality of pain.

She floated up into the sky from the hand. Higher and higher she went as the God beheld her, her God, her beloved Master. She soared higher into the sky, burning and screaming as she went, until the earth below showed her as nothing more than a shining red star, forever fixed in the sky.

Amatsu looked at what he had created, almost as if he were transfixed by the beauty of His own making.

"Shit, did you see that?" Taro said.

"See what?" Ms. Tanaka asked, straining to see what he was pointing at through the dust-filmed windshield.

They had gotten the car through the rock pile thanks to Ryu, her brother-in-law, and his set of destructive tools such as the jackhammer he always kept ready at hand. (Whether he actually owned them or had pilfered them, she didn't know and didn't care.) Ryu was in the back seat, his frame so large Tanaka couldn't see out the back window. He said nothing, as usual, as they rocketed down the bumpy road in the dark. Only the purple lights of Taro's headlights lit up the path: it was unnaturally dark out.

"There it is," Taro pointed up and to the left at a red light in the sky. "The first was coming down; this one is going up."

Ms. Tanaka and her brother-in-law nodded in assent. Whatever it was, it was strange—a glowing red light levitating into the sky. Its path was too straight off the ground to be a plane. Maybe a helicopter or drone? But why would that be out here, out in the middle of nowhere?

The car hit a hole in the road that probably had not seen fresh cement in decades. It bottomed out and refused to move, the tires spinning uselessly.

They all got out of the car to survey the situation.

Ryu, without a word (unless you count the familial grunt he shared with his brother as language), brought his bag out of the backseat. He produced a small shovel and two cutout squares of carpet. Ms. Tanaka had learned long ago not to question Ryu when it came to physical solutions to physical problems. Emotional ones, like he had with all three of his ex-wives, were clearly out of his depth. But give the man something concrete and in the here and now, and he could take care of anything.

He tossed the shovel to Taro and grunted towards the tire.

"What am I supposed to–"

"Dig the tire out, you idiot," said Ms. Tanaka to the man with exquisitely manicured hands and nails painted black.

"I've never done this before."

"Never used a shovel?" Her disdain colored her face. But in a way, it was also endearing that this man-boy was so sheltered. "Fine, I'll do it." She grabbed the shovel and went to work on the mound of dirt and mud the tire was stuck in. Ryu dug out the left tire with his hands. He grabbed Taro down to his level and forced him to do the same.

In five minutes, they broke down the dirt wall enough for Ryu to grunt in a lighter octave, this one meaning it met with his approval. He laid out the carpet squares in front of the two tires and motioned to Ms. Tanaka to get behind the wheel and hit the gas. The two men pushed the car from behind as Ms. Tanaka floored the gas pedal.

The car rocked back and forth a few times before finally climbing out of the hole and coming back out onto the smoother pavement. The men got back into the car.

"You take the wheel, Taro," Ms. Tanaka said as she scooted back into the passenger seat.

"I'll just hit another hole. Ryu, how about you?"

He stared blankly at the young man with no discernible movement on his brick face. Taro stuttered out, "Yeah, no, got it, I'll do it."

They started driving again; the cement resembled ocean waves more than a drivable road.

Then they all saw it: another red glow, not too far away.

"Holy shit," Ryu said.

Good reason broke his monk-ish silence. They all saw something walking through the forest. It was taller than the trees. It radiated an immense light and burned everything it touched. The giant creature shook the ground and the car with it.

Taro started whimpering that they should go back.

"No, this is exactly why we're here," said Ms. Tanaka. "Taro, floor it."

Cody was on the ground in a daze. Something had struck his face hard. He could taste iron on his tongue. The darkness prevented him from seeing anything as he ran. Behind him, the remnants of the town were aglow in red, and he heard shouts of panic that were cut ruthlessly short. He felt the ground shake from a great blast. Some more light came from the sides, from where the forest was burning. The path ahead was obscured from his sight.

He got up and ran. He heard screams in the distance. Mia. Then her screams stopped, as did his heart. Soon after, he heard another woman scream—Aiko. Her screams did not end. He stopped and turned, seeing a red light emerge from the town. He could hear desperate pleas emanating from the star that rose until it had risen so high that no sounds reached him. It stopped far above the earth and remained in one place.

A new star.

It was so bright that it gave off just enough light to see the way in front of him. Another red light appeared in the sky. Then another. One after the other, red torches lit. He could hear an orchestra of screams from the sky, as if each individual star were once a person, forever trapped in the depths of space, forever bound to burn. The entire valley was lit up red.

Cody walked for what seemed like hours. He stumbled through the woods, unsure whether he wasn't walking in circles. His stomach tore at itself, and his muscles shook in their exhaustion. Off in the distance, the horizon turned a barely perceptible pale blue— the first signs of dawn, though it was still far off.

The ground shook again. The dirt beneath his feet moved once, then stopped. It shook again and settled down. In succession, these minor quakes came, like far-off bombs being dropped.

Like footsteps coming his way.

The red stars fell from the sky.

He could see them grow larger until they fell to the ground. As they came into focus, he could almost swear he saw a person's shadow in each one. They crashed into the forest, setting the impact area ablaze. Each strike shook the ground. It was as if the sky were falling apart, the seams of the physical universe coming undone in a thrash. One fell near him. The tree that it hit combusted and sent shards of bark into his side. A sliver the size of a knife embedded itself just above his hip.

The pain seared his body, shooting up from his side to his fingertips. He remembered from some movie, probably a cheap action movie, that the absolute worst thing to do was to remove something that had stabbed you. Something about losing more blood.

He lay there on the ground in pain, wishing a star would fall on him and end it. He was tired, near death, and broken.

Yes, just one star, have it land right here.

He pointed to his chest.

He saw Rachel in his mind. It was years before she took her own life. They were walking through Golden Gate Park, holding hands. It was foggy out and the air was chilled, but they kept one another warm with the coffee in their hands and the laughter on their faces. They sat down on a bench opposite some old men playing chess on a stone table under a weeping willow.

"Do you think we'll get to that age? Not like old dudes playing chess, but you know, grow old together and still want to be around each other?"

Cody brushed her raven-black hair from her face and smiled.

"Of course, I promise."

He came back to the present moment and wept. The tears and snot bubbled out of his nose and poured off his face.

I couldn't give her that. I couldn't help anyone.

Despite the blinding pain, he stopped crying and stood up. Cody remembered the smile on Rachel's face that day. He couldn't give her the help she needed and couldn't give her peace at the end, but that smile he gave that day, maybe that was enough. A new feeling filled him: the urge to live.

The ground rolled in waves. It wasn't only the falling stars that shook the earth—there was another source, one that was closer to where Cody stood. It was the sound of footsteps, one after the other, left foot, right foot.

He turned around, but the trees were too tall to see what was coming. Only a line of pulsating red above the leaves, like a blood-red sunrise coming to meet him. The trees shook and splintered to the side. Something pushed through them and toppled them. A great, thriving red thing, a living fire cloaked in shadows, emerged from the trees.

Everything it touched ignited into flames and quickly became nothing but ash. The process was so fast that the fire did not spread to the forest, only to what the thing touched with its truck-sized hands. The red eyes blazed across the distance between it and Cody. It was wide until it narrowed to a single focus. It locked onto Cody's face.

He felt the heat blistering his face.

What the fuck is that?

He knew it had come from the great red eye. He felt the familiar chill of being watched. That same feeling he had every time he looked up into the night sky in this valley. The same feeling he had that night in San Francisco, sitting on the curb outside Rachel's apartment. This is what had watched him for so long, and all Cody wanted in that moment was to be anywhere else.

It spoke to him, not in words, not in feeling, but somehow spoke to his very core, down to his genes and his blood. He knew it was calling him to it, calling him to stop running, to come and bow.

Cody bolted forward into the darkness. Even running off a cliff or right into a sharp branch would be better than ever having to see that face of death again. He was bleeding all over. The wounds on his face and in his eye socket throbbed and split his head.

Every movement sent intense pain throughout his body. But the adrenaline that fueled him pushed his body past all limits of comfort and pain. He ran until it felt like he was nothing but the rush, nothing but the pumping of his blood, nothing but the wind. He was one with the moment, one with the action of running; nothing else existed. He could go on like that for days, it felt like. He had never shown prowess in gym class or sports when he was in school.

Becoming an adult with a full-time job meant he exercised even less than he thought possible. But when life was on the line, and he was being chased by an ancient demon from space, he found that anybody could run through the pain.

He heard the crashing of the trees behind him. And the thunder of the footsteps. And the heat of its gaze. Until he didn't. Everything went quiet and cool. He didn't stop running to see why. Why the thing had ended its pursuit, he could scarcely care to know, nor did he allow himself to relax.

He came to the crest of a bare hill. With no trees or brush nearby, nothing but knee-high grass in the clearing. More pale light was pouring out into the valley. The sunrise was near. Just beyond the opposing tree line, he could see a mountain range. And on that mountain, a paved road that snaked through its crevices and out of the valley. Halfway down the road, he saw a pair of purple lights swerving down into the valley. The lights were not stars; they were not the townsfolk, nor did they belong to the demon that pursued him. They were headlights from a car.

Elation filled his body. It almost lifted him into the sky. Then he felt it: the heat that was at his back was now above him. As was the red glow. He looked up, and his heart nearly stopped then and there.

The thing was above him, in the sky. It looked like it was walking—crawling—through the air more than it appeared to be flying. It moved through the sky as if it were solid ground. Walking above him at incredible speed and overtaking him. It was now in front of him. It fell out of the sky and landed in the clearing, knocking Cody on his ass with the force of its impact.

Cody pulled himself up and stood on his trembling feet. The thing bent down from its massive height and brought its face near Cody.

Cody hyperventilated. His chest heaved violently and threatened to crack open. He almost fainted. That would be easier—just give up and let yourself die.

Maybe it would just crush me, kill me instantly. A quick and merciful death.

He knew better. This thing desired pain. It wanted suffering; it needed the suffering of others to exist in our world.

A star fell behind him with a scream. He cowered before the shower of flame that came raining down. The fire from the explosion closed off any route of escape behind him. The monster stood between him and the mountain pass. Fire had now formed a ring around the clearing; there was nowhere to go.

The god bent down further so that its face was level with Cody.

He couldn't understand what he was looking at. Fire, light, darkness, blood, all at once—and yet, if he were asked, he could not describe it at all. The glow of the thing died down until its body merged completely with the darkness of the night. Cody could see nothing. There was a black hole where something should have been. Deep in that darkness, Cody lost himself. He saw the universe, the stars dancing in the orbital ballet around the dead nothingness of space.

A single red star went nova in that space. He was at the beginning when the universe was born. In that primordial light, Cody saw himself. He saw a long life, an endless life ahead of him, one without pain, fear, or guilt. In this new world, his eyes flashed silver and red. He had power; he had respect; he had eternal life.

He saw his fate if he refused. Beyond the light of the stars was the abyss. Deep wells of darkness that had no end. He would be cast out into that dark, forever burning as a star.

To escape, all he had to do was bow and offer a sacrifice. He knew this in his gut.

If he did not, the demon would take Cody as a burnt offering.

Either way, it would win.

The fire from the forest was crawling towards him as the smoke enshrouded him. He choked on the fumes. The thing offered a hand to him. Cody understood it could save him. It could take him from this place of certain death. It could give him all he had ever wanted.

But Cody remembered. Remembered his friend's look of terror as he gazed into that red-eye and burned. He remembered his pain and suffering. He remembered how, even in death, Rick had saved him. He also saw Mia, the joyful girl who distrusted him at first. Then a friendship grew between them in this hell. Her exuberant zest for life had carried him for days in the valley when he would have certainly given up. He remembered the cages full of dead bodies. Of children's clothes.

The thing in front of him caused it all.

It was not worthy of his worship.

Cody pulled away from the hand and broke the trance that the dark vision had placed upon him. He backed up towards the wall of flame.

"Fuck... you." He gasped these words as the fire licked at his feet.

Before he collapsed, he flipped his middle finger at the god.

The deity took hold of Cody and lifted him into the sky. His skin burned against the touch of that great hand. The wind rushed past his face. Cody looked down and saw he was above the trees. A fall from this height would surely kill or paralyze him. The purple headlights from the road had vanished.

Cody let go. In that moment, he prepared himself to die. There was no more guilt, no more fear. Rick and Mia were annihilated back there in the courtyard. Permanent death was better than the fate that had been forced on them. At least Cody could smile at that. And smile he did. Right in the face of the god of stars, he smiled and made peace with the idea of death.

His clothes, and then his skin heated up. The god's eyes were upon him. Cody could feel his blood about to boil and his flesh about to burst into flames. Steam came off his body, and he clenched his teeth, preparing for the end.

The sound of crashing metal erupted below. The god rocked forward because of the thing that had crashed into it.

It dropped Cody to the ground—his old friend. It rushed up and greeted him with a deafening crunch. The saving grace was that the god had lowered its hands before dropping him; otherwise, he most certainly would have died. His body rolled over to the base of the last standing tree in the clearing. Shouts in Japanese erupted from behind the god. Cody glanced and saw a burning car at the deity's feet and three people running away from the wreck.

Amatsu's body flashed in brilliant vermillion. It lifted one hand, and the sky opened back up to that dark void. Trees ripped from the ground and flew into that abyss, igniting as they went. The wrecked car levitated piece by piece into the dark. Cody clung to the roots of the tree, his lower body lifted into the air.

It was taking them all. Taking them... somewhere.

The first rays of sunlight streaked across the valley.

This time there was no cloud cover to dampen the rays.

It showed clean and bright across the hills. The mist of the valley quickly dissipated before the light. The golden beams hit the deity squarely in the face.

Cody could see the light eroding the body of the creature. The light was washing its form away, like a fresh painting that was hit with water. The void above closed up. The gate to that black hell shut. Cody's body fell back to the ground, followed by the descent of trees and rocks and the car that showered back down.

Amatsu reached into the sky and pulled itself upwards into the retreating dark. Its flight left a red streak across the sky like a madman's brushstroke, leading back towards Mount Hinokami. Cody saw it enter the mountain.

Cody coughed up blood. He couldn't even roll over to let it drip away from his open mouth; it pooled and suffocated him. He couldn't move at all. Aside from being able to shake his head slightly, his body responded to nothing. He could feel nothing.

Before he passed out, all Cody could see was blue sky.

"Koitsu daijoubu kana?"

"Shinisou."

The voices fluttered about somewhere in the dark of Cody's mind like passing ghosts. The words were unintelligible to him, but he detected concern in their whispers. His eye opened.

Above him, an angel appeared in the form of a middle-aged woman wearing purple glasses. Two men were beside her: a young man with creamy white skin and electric blond hair and a brick-faced older man with hands the size of a baseball mitt. They bent down and put their hands on him, though he couldn't feel their touch. They lifted him up, the strong-looking man draping Cody over his shoulder like a scarf.

Cody saw the world pass in a heaving motion as his rescuer marched him through the forest. That forest, once cold, shrouded, and smothering, was now bright in the golden sunlight.

He heard birds singing.

Ms. Tanaka took a long drag of her cigarette. She had the carton of Mevius strapped to her side like a utility belt. She savored every moment of that sweet nicotine as it coursed through her lungs. Knew one day it might claim her life, but after what she had seen, it was time to focus on the here and now. The karaoke program was on the TV, but she did not know what song was being played. She was lost in thought. She stared at the wall just above the TV, at a stain that had soaked into the wallpaper from some unknown grease.

Tomorrow, cleaning this entire apartment. Maybe I'll go for a walk or check out that new hot yoga studio down the street as well. The past few days nearly gave me a heart attack.

Her husband was somewhere in the kitchen: she could hear the *cha-ching* of the online casino game.

She was thinking about yesterday, when she, Taro-kun, and her brother-in-law found one of the tourists she had set out to find. Just one. Where were the other two? The man rambled on about their being dead. About staying away from the town because of some kind of monster.

She bent her head to the side, an arduous task because of the cast around her neck. Thank Buddha that Ryu was a workhorse of a man. He, with minimal assistance from Taro-kun, carried her and the foreigner out of there.

She laughed and coughed as she blew smoke out of her nostrils.

Of course, she couldn't believe that. But then again, she saw... *it*. Taro-kun destroyed his precious car as they all jumped out at the last moment before it ran into that thing's legs. She saw it only three times. Once as she pushed Taro-kun to speed up the car, twice as they rolled across the grass and came to a stop, and the third time as she saw it disappear back into the night.

Ryu never said a word about it, while Taro-kun descended into near-hysteria afterward. She would have to think of some way to bring the boy back to his wistful self, if that was even possible now. And that foreigner Cody... She closed her eyes and shook her head at the thought of what life would be like for him from now on.

None of the police wanted to go into the valley to investigate. Even after she had told them that somebody had obviously tortured the young man and likely murdered his two friends. Richard Davis and Mia Silvano were missing, and the one she had found alive may never walk again.

Something had happened, and nobody was going to do anything about it.

Well, at least I did something about it. That boy would have died if we hadn't come down that road. If we hadn't chiseled down that boulder with Ryu's jackhammer. And then Taro-kun, of all people, noticed the meteor shower in the distance and convinced us to drive towards it. He was the one to notice the tall red thing with something in its hands, some person. And wouldn't you believe it, that's where we found him. But not the other two, not the handsome one with a cute smile or the tiny bubbly girl. Life is short and unpredictable.

She took another drag of the smoke.

Yeah, this shit will kill me one day.

She smothered it in the ashtray and walked into the kitchen.

Her husband hunched over his phone, chain-smoked and gambled away. At least he wasn't whoring as well.

"Hey, idiot."

"Eh," he replied without looking up.

"I love you."

He looked up. They both laughed with rare affection. He went back to the game. She went back to watch karaoke with a fresh beer in her hand.

31

Five years later

The sun was setting over the bay. Streaks of red and purple splashed over the calm waters and reflected that great orb in the sky. Several sailboats and fishing trawlers were sluggishly returning home before nightfall. Seagulls trailed after them in hopes of an easy snack. In those last minutes of the day, the air was cool, and the sunset was divine. Cody loved the sun. He did not pass up any chance to feel the warmth of its rays. He sat there on the verandah of his home and just watched nature's art on display.

Bailey rested her head on his knee. She held a dirty tennis ball in her mouth. Cody ruffled her fur and patted her side. He took the ball from her and tossed it into his apartment. She chased after it, came back to his side, and fell asleep.

Stroking her head, he gazed out over the bay and smiled as he saw a school of dolphins, almost beyond his sight, out past all the commercial ships. They frolicked and played and danced in the water. He thought they could be as close as only two miles away. He wasn't good at judging things by their distance these past few years.

The sun was setting. As always, this caused Cody to hurry and gather his things. People—especially his mother—didn't understand this habit, the near-panic he displayed daily.

"Cody, I know you went through some terrible loss out there in China (she never could get those Asian countries right), but you have to get over this tick of yours. Nothing is going to hurt you. It's not normal."

She said this to him two years after he came back from Japan while sipping her chamomile tea and watching her afternoon stories, barely making any eye contact with him as she spoke. No, she could never understand what he had seen, so he didn't bother telling her. He also couldn't stand being in that house anymore. Although once it was all he had wanted to escape to, now it was a prison of unwanted memories.

The sun disappeared behind the horizon line between sky and sea. The last of the day's hope sank under the weight of the coming night. He got up, grabbed his cane, and went inside.

Funny sight, at thirty-nine years old and I already walk like an old man.

The sweet smell of veggies and steak on the stove lured him to the kitchen. Jazz was playing on the Alexa. The smooth, lo-fi kind that he could fall asleep to easily. He wrapped his arms around the woman who was salting the frying pan.

"Hey, you need to wait, Mister" She smiled and swatted at his head.

"I don't think I want to." He kissed her cheek and tickled her with his stubble.

"Too bad, you're going to have to."

In moments like this, he realized how much he loved Jess. The way her auburn hair fell to one side when she cocked her head to laugh. The way she didn't care about all the scars on his face. This was all he wanted out of life now. To stay home, to be with her, to watch the sun over the water with his golden retriever, Bailey. This was all he needed now. This was all he wanted.

Of course, he never told her about what happened in Japan. All she knew was that he had lost two friends in a hiking accident. That was all he had told anyone when he got home. Most people didn't ask for details beyond that. They feigned concern and empathy, but nobody actually wanted the details, unless they thought they could find a juicy story in them. The hardest conversation had been with Rick's parents. Rick's mom could barely hold back her sobs when he sat them down in their seaside time-share.

She never really got over the news. Rick's father never showed emotion during that painful hour. But Cody could tell that somewhere deep in that stoic face, the old man's heart broke and would never recover.

"Hey, can you pick up some oranges from Whole Foods tomorrow?"

Cody snapped back to attention.

"Yeah, sure, no problem."

Stop reminiscing; *the past is* past, *and now is now. Don't miss what's happening right in front of you.*

Jess eyed him with a furrowed brow. "Hey, you okay?"

Cody kissed her on the cheek again. "Absolutely."

She spun back around to finish dinner, twirling her skirt like Marilyn Monroe. Bailey lay at her feet now, chewing the remains of the tennis ball into oblivion. Cody stood there for a moment and soaked in the scene. He didn't know it at the time, there in that hell on earth, but this is what he had survived for. He lived for this woman and this dog in his kitchen, in his apartment, overlooking his view of the bay. Cody smiled at the thought of what he had gained. Then he left the room.

The joy of what he had soon became tainted with what he had lost. He passed by a picture of Rick and Mia on the wall of the hallway. It was taken on their first day in Japan in front of some noodle shop in Tokyo, days before their hike. Rick held Mia up in the air and against his hip, while his left arm hung around Cody, pushing his head down. His own face looked horribly uncomfortable. At the time, he wanted to tell Rick off for always making him do stupid shit like that.

He had gained a heart of steel since those days. He spoke his mind and took action. Most of his old friends and family didn't like the new him: they yearned for him to be the nice, quiet boy they had once known. That boy was dead. Incinerated by red starlight. Still, Cody's heart broke for the simple days when Rick dominated his life. And in the end, Rick saved him when the monster that was Mia had him in her jaws.

Mia. They had only grown to tolerate each other and even formed some bond of affection in the last few days of her life. She was the rock that carried him after Rick's passing. He wouldn't be here today if it were not for her courage.

Cody touched the side of the picture frame and smiled a heavy smile.

He went to the bathroom and lowered himself onto the toilet via the handicap bar mounted on the wall, did his business, and hoisted himself back up to a standing position. He couldn't stand without help since the day that a god dropped him.

He hobbled over to the mirror and washed his hands. He splashed water onto his face with both hands and let the cold freshness soak in. Drying his face off with a towel, he looked into the mirror.

He had gotten used to the patch over his right eye. When he met Jess for the first time, standing in line at Starbucks, he introduced himself as an actual bona fide pirate. She laughed, his face grew beet red, and the rest was, as they say, history.

The scars were harder to get used to. The entire right side of his face drooped down as if he had suffered a stroke. Facial hair no longer grew on that side, including his eyebrow. Most of the skin was baby-smooth, devoid of any lines or creases. But there were a few deep rivets where the fire had burned away the muscle underneath. Months of corrective surgery saved him, but he could feel nothing on that side of his face again.

But he was alive.

He saved his friends from eternal pain.

He did not bow to that fucking thing.

And the pride that he now felt, along with the love of his new life—this was enough. His was the body of an elderly man, broken and bent by multiple blunt-force traumas. Every movement beyond that of a few inches caused him to wince. Still, this was enough.

It had to be.

Cody returned to the kitchen. He and Jess ate dinner, watched some TV, and then she went to sleep. Recently, she's been waking up at 4:00 am to get ready for her shift at the hospital. Cody admired her ability to grind day after day without so much as a single complaint. He was wide awake on the couch, watching TV with the sound off.

Some infomercial about a soap dispenser that was guaranteed to kill COVID-19 on the spot. The man yelling into the camera with his bleach-perfect smile and wavy, greasy, black hair unnerved Cody. The fakery of that smile was evident in his eyes. It reminded him of a sixteen-year-old girl in the woods with a smile too large for her face. He shook those thoughts away and changed the channel for any amusement to distract him from the darkness of the night that lay just outside his apartment's walls.

The curtains were drawn as always. Jess never really understood why he never went out at night. In the beginning, all their dates had been lunch. No matter how hard she tried to go out for drinks or a late dinner, he had always refused. Only if necessary did Cody venture outside after the sun had set, and the stars had come out. Even then, he dared not look up. Deep inside, something told him that if he did so, something from beyond this world would see him and know him.

The sheer horror at the thought of what lay beyond the darker-than-dark hole ripped in space chilled him to this very day. He believed that the creature he had seen was not the god of the stars in the flesh. It was an avatar, a mask of the real thing. The reality of the creature existed in the dark. If the sight of its masked face unraveled his mind as it had done that day, what eternity of madness awaited those who entered that darkness like Aiko had done? She entered the void and was there to this day.

Cody was sure that he could find her star if he tried hard enough, if he had dared to look up. There had been some news reports immediately after the incident about just that. Some science nerd in Hawaii spotted a new star through his telescope near the Big Dipper. Scientists worldwide expressed shock and disbelief at the discovery until it was corroborated several times over. "A miracle find," the newspapers had said. Cody knew what it was, and due to that fact, never looked up into the night sky.

He caressed the charm on his neck. Now, the yellow sun had faded from the shell's painting. Most people thought it was a banana. Cody knew better; it was the sun, the thing that saved him that day. As there was a deeper world beyond the night sky, Cody now believed there was also one behind the sun. Gods and monsters around every corner.

There was something there, something good in the sun, and it saved him. If Cody had been told five years ago that spirits and gods lived inside the ordinary things of our world, he would have laughed. But he had seen it face to face, that beneath our world, there were things that existed beyond our comprehension. What man had labeled as divine, as gods—these were just words that simple apes gave to the terrifying things that were real and that inhabited the world, that preceded the world.

If there were something in the stars, what else was out there?

Cody had no interest in going out anymore. No interest in coming face to face with the natural world, where monstrous creatures dwelt. Unless under the light of day, he would not go. In this apartment, things were safe.

The curtain fluttered.

Another infomercial had ended, and the TV had turned to static. The buzzing white glow danced across his face in staccato waves.

Cody woke and thought it was the wind, but the windows were closed. He looked at Bailey. She was in a full comatose sleep on the floor, snoring herself into hours of dreams.

The curtain moved again.

Cody's blood ran cold.

No, it's been five years, *and I've seen nothing. Things are better* now; *things are safe.*

The curtain moved a third time, twice more than necessary to convince one it wasn't a damn fan or the wind, especially when neither of those things were present.

Cody grabbed his cane and stood up. He could use the cane as a weapon if need be. He held onto his sun talisman and prayed. Drew near to the curtain, resting on his cane, held onto the wall with his free hand, and smacked it with his cane. Nothing. He stuck the cane into the curtain and, with his breath held, flung it open.

There was nothing. He laughed.

But... a magnetic feeling tugged at his heart. It drew him near the glass door behind the curtain. It was dark out, and the only thing visible was the moonlit water of the ocean. Cody did not want to see the sky or the stars—especially the stars. But in that moment, he had to. Something compelled him; an unseen puppet master led him by invisible strings.

He opened the door and went out onto the veranda.

The ocean air chilled him. A fragile wind blew across the waves. He could hear their gentle crashing on the rocks below. Every few seconds, the chime of the bell buoys as they rode the soft waves.

All in all, a peaceful night.

He was about to go back inside without lifting his head. He didn't want to look up. The ground was fine; the ground was safe. On the floor of the verandah, he saw a light. A faint red light illuminated the chairs and the flowerpots. The back of his neck warmed up as if there were a heat lamp overhead. What should have been a welcome warmth to escape from the cold air into, instead froze and twisted his intestines.

Shaking, he looked up into the sky.

There, high above him in the vacuum of space, a single red star was shining.

He felt watched.

He felt known.

He did not feel alone.

Get a Free Book In My Newsletter.

Sign up for my newsletter below and get my Japanese cannibal ghost novella, "Devoured."

For ebook readers, click this link: https://dl.bookfunnel.com/hlaez dpu8g

For print readers, go to my website here, and the sign-up form is the first thing you'll see: https://www.shawnbrookswrites.com/

Get Book Two in the Black Sun series: Under the Amber Wave

Find it at shawnbrookswrites.com

About This Horror

Thank you all for reading my debut book! This is the first in the "Black Sun" series; a set of five books connected thematically within the same universe. Characters from one book may or may not make other appearances, as I would like each story to stand on its own.

However, I have a plan to tie everything together in the end. All five novels will take place in Japan and be based on actual folklore and myth. Of course, with my twist on things. One element that will prominently feature in each story is the horror that comes from the wild places of the world, the unknown and secret haunts of nature.

The idea for "Endless is the Night" was born after I watched a documentary about the urban legend of Inunaki. The verified aspects of the legend stem from 1988 and involve the murder of a man by would-be car thieves. They burned the victim's body with gasoline in the Inunaki tunnel. In the late '90s, rumors began spreading about Inunaki: that the constitution of Japan did not apply there, that people were going missing, and that the residents of the hidden town worshipped some kind of demon. Today, the location of Inunaki (in Fukuoka Prefecture) is under water. Buried under the weight of a nearby dam.

I spent a few days hiking the mountains in Wakayama, where I placed Inunaki, and what struck me beyond the beauty of those trails was the isolation, being wrapped in thick mist, and the potential for some hidden terror to be lurking around every bend.

Some notes about Japanese authenticity in this story. First and foremost, this is a work of fiction, so I bend things to fit the story. That said, there are two things I would like to point out. One: When Cody reads the dates on the portrait of Aiko's father, they are in the Western calendar year (think 2024, etc.). In Japan, especially Japan in the 60s, you would never see this. The years are always based on the Japanese Imperial calendar (Showa 59, etc.). I kept the Western convention since most readers in the English-speaking world are not aware of this. Two: the dark god Amatsu-Mikaboshi. In some documents on Japan's ancient religion of Shinto, he is spoken of as the only evil god in the pantheon. Hence his inclusion in this book. However, people worship him today as a peaceful god. If you visit Japan, you can visit his shrines (not the lonely one on Mt. Hinokami). And no, he does not require human sacrifice, thankfully. There is no disrespect meant here to those who may pray to him. I hope it came across in this story that the "gods" are neither Japanese nor Western. They are simply what humans have labeled the dark and unknown things of the world. Therefore, in this story, we can be mistaken about what we pray to.

I thank you sincerely for your support in reading my work. Hope to see you at the next one.

Leave a Review for Endless is the Night

If you enjoyed this book, please leave a review! Thank you.

UNDER THE AMBER WAVE: BLACK SUN BOOK 2

Chapter One

The sea was an open grave. Welcoming to all, discriminating of none. Beneath the violent waves, below the churning waters, how many souls had lost their way?

Upon the gray horizon, stretching past Mako's sight, there was no past and there was no future. There was only one moment, only a hideous and persistent now. What the present held for her, she didn't know. Yet she couldn't shake the ice that had filled her stomach, weighing her to the deck, paralyzed by fear.

She looked out into the endless expanse of water as the boat sped across it. Mist sprayed over the gunwale each time the vessel slammed into the sea. She could feel the salt clinging to her cheeks and her hair curling in the humidity. Her clothes were wet, but her throat was dry. She sat on a bench with a back support in front of the captain's chair. Strapped in a seatbelt.

Mako looked down at her enlarged stomach and gently placed her hands over the life inside.

The child, boy or girl, was also buried in the depths of her body. Just like the earth beneath the sea. Just like her future, in the horrible now.

Her heart told her to protect the child, to give it the future she could never have. She would have done it. Would've given everything for the baby. Yet, looking out at the infinite sea in front of her, she doubted that she'd see anything else ever again. Nothing would exist past this, not for her, anyway.

"Ryotaro," she said, her voice barely above a whisper, barely above a whimper.

He stared straight ahead from his position in the captain's seat under the canopy, hands gripping the wheel tightly. A smoldering nub of a cigarette hung loosely from his lips. His eyes were red. He hadn't shaved in days. His very aura gave off the air of a madman.

Mako cleared her throat. "Ryotaro."

His eyes met hers, and she winced at the intensity of the gaze.

"What?" he shouted over the chainsaw roar of the motor.

"Where are we going? You told me it would only be a few minutes, and it's been at least an hour, hasn't it?"

She remembered him telling her he had a special surprise for her. Some beach strip he wanted to take her to. Mako was never one for the outdoors but couldn't say no to Ryotaro. He was smiling when he pleaded with her to get on the boat, and when he smiled, no one could resist. The sun was shining. A warm wind blew through her shoulder-length hair. She was undeniably happy.

For the briefest moment, she thought he was going to finally leave his wife for her.

That was then; this is now. Here, in the middle of an uncaring sea, things like the past didn't matter. Clouds filled the sky, and the wind lashed her face with its intensity. Happiness was not to be found here. All she could feel was despair.

Ryotaro hadn't said a word since they boarded the boat. Didn't look at her. Didn't even pretend to smile.

Mako glanced around. Five fishing poles were tied to the side. Sliding across the deck were a bucket for gutting fish and a steel rod for killing them. It hadn't been cleaned out in a while, by the looks of it. She gazed behind Ryotaro at the shoreline. The mountains surrounding the harbor were quickly shrinking to foothills. Soon, they would be mere smudges staining the canvas of the sky.

"Don't worry about it," Ryotaro said. He took his mad eyes off hers and gazed back at the sea. She felt some relief in this.

"My mother is going to worry about me."

He didn't reply.

The wind picked up and scattered her hair. Ryotaro piloted the vessel faster. The boat bounced off the water, and with each crash against the surface; she swallowed her breath.

"If this is about the baby, I won't tell anyone it's yours!" she cried into the wind, though she doubted her voice reached his ears due to the increased roar of the boat. Even if they had, they couldn't reach *him*. "I swear, your wife will never know. I'll keep it a secret."

Nothing. No movement on his face. No attempt to hear her words. His knuckles were white against the steering wheel. He bit through the remainder of the cigarette, and it fell to the deck.

Mako knew that sleeping with a married man could have its consequences. But she never imagined this. This boat ride into infinity.

Ryotaro killed the engine. The sudden stop pushed Mako's body forward. The ragged seatbelt snapped. She covered her stomach with her arms. She smacked her head against the railing in front of her. Lightning crackled through her brain. She didn't feel pain—not yet—but she felt something thick and wet trickle down her face.

The boat rocked from side to side in the still water. The wind had also vanished. There was hardly a sound to be heard. The sudden change from speed and rest was unsettling.

She stood on shaking legs and wiped the blood off her face with the sleeve of her light blue blouse. Something she chose specifically for what she thought would be a fun day at the beach with the man she once, if not loved, had at least hoped would be her way out of the small town she was trapped in.

Her eyes scanned the environment. Mostly open water. The shoreline was too distant for comfort.

To her left, there was a small island. There was hardly a beach to speak of: rock walls shot straight out of the sea on all sides of it. Atop the ridge, a few dead trees curled up towards the sky, their branches beckoning would-be travelers to crash upon the rocks like a siren. The island was the color of ash, with a few tar-black rocks spread throughout. No sandy beaches here. Only the hard and uncaring surface of some scorched alien piece of land that looked like it didn't belong on Earth.

"Take me home now!"

She stepped forward and kicked something. Looked down and saw the steel rod, coated in a dull red by the blood of countless fish. She picked it up.

With the weapon raised above her head, she repeated her demand.

Ryotaro got up. Mako's head only came up to his neck. His arms were twice the size of hers. Years of wrestling tuna out of the ocean chiseled him into an imposing man. He walked over to her.

"No!" Mako brought the rod down. Ryotaro stepped back. She flew forward and fell on the deck.

"It didn't have to be like this," he finally said as he took the rod out of her hand. "Sit down."

She got off the deck and sat back by the bow of the boat. "Please don't hurt my baby. *Our* baby!" She was choking back the sobs. Trying to sound firm. She didn't even convince herself.

Ryotaro struck the side of the boat with the rod. The sharp clang resonated in Mako's bones. Her hands shook as she pressed them over her stomach, tighter now. Anything, any act, to protect what was inside.

As long as he doesn't touch the baby.

Her mind raced through her options. Fighting back was meaningless. But she could always target his ego.

"You're nothing, know that?" Mako let out in a voice that did not feel like her own. It felt loud and firm. Almost strong. "Couldn't make it as a fisherman, couldn't make it as a husband, father, or even as a fucking man."

He looked down at his hands. Mako saw his lips quiver. Was he crying? Did he feel something akin to remorse?

"You don't understand; I have to do this," he said. Refusing to look her in the eyes.

Ryotaro lifted the metal rod and took a step forward. A flash of light reflected off the metal. They both covered their eyes against the intense glare.

Ryotaro dropped the rod and backed up, looking stunned.

Mako felt something warm coming from behind her. Despite not wanting to take her eyes off the man who meant her harm, she turned around. Dark clouds still covered the sun. But something glowed in the water.

A pink and golden light radiated from the water between the boat and the island. A reflection? Of what, the sun somehow? It warmed her skin, but something inside her chilled. No, it wasn't either of those colors. It was softer and brighter than they were. It was beautiful. It was terrifying. "Amber" was the word that came to her mind.

Mako's eyes widened, and her pupils dilated as she stared into the light. Her hands clutched her belly—her child— tightly. All warmth left her veins.

A shadow formed in the light.

"The ocean is an open grave," she said.

A sound of shoes scraping quickly against the wooden deck.

A tight grip around her neck.

Closing in tighter.

She couldn't breathe.

Then all was dark.

AUTHOR BIO

Shawn Brooks is a horror and fantasy author living in Japan with his wife and Siberian husky. He teaches history for his day job, enjoys hiking and paddle boarding, and loves winter storms while lying comatose next to a fire with a good sake and a better book.

Other books by Shawn Brooks

Endless is the Night (Black Sun Book 1)

Under the Amber Wave (Black Sun Book 2)

Iomante (Black Sun Book 3)

Dead Roots of the Earth (Black Sun Book 4)

Above the Ashen Sky (Black Sun Book 5)

What Dances in the Dark (Short Stories)

Pine Haven (Short Stories)

www.ingramcontent.com/pod-product-compliance
Lightning Source LLC
LaVergne TN
LVHW011002200726
843509LV00011B/952